Stealing with Style

STEALING
with STYLE

A NOVEL

Emyl Jenkins

[signature] 9.17.08

ALGONQUIN BOOKS OF CHAPEL HILL

2005

Published by
ALGONQUIN BOOKS OF CHAPEL HILL
Post Office Box 2225
Chapel Hill, North Carolina 27515-2225

a division of
WORKMAN PUBLISHING
708 Broadway
New York, New York 10003

This is a work of fiction. While, as in all fiction, the literary perceptions and insights are based on experience, all names, characters, places, and incidents are either products of the author's imagination or are used fictitiously. No reference to any real person is intended or should be inferred.

Library of Congress Cataloging-in-Publication Data
Jenkins, Emyl.
    Stealing with style / Emyl Jenkins.—1st ed.
      p. cm.
    ISBN-13: 976-1-56512-445-5
    ISBN-10: 1-56512-445-6
    1. Women detectives—Virginia—Fiction.   2. Appraisers—
Fiction.   3. Virginia—Fiction.   4. Antiques—Fiction.
5. Auctions—Fiction.   I. Title.
PS3610.E544S74 2005
813'.6—dc22   2004066035

10 9 8 7 6 5 4 3 2 1
First Edition

For Chuck Adams,
friend, mentor, and all-around great guy

In memory of my mother,
Louise Brockwell Joslin,
1905–1999,
and
my grandfather
Sherwood Brockwell,
1885–1953

We risk all in being too greedy.

—JEAN DE LA FONTAINE, "LE HERON"

Stealing with Style

Chapter 1

I'VE MADE A LOT of mistakes along the way because I've spoken first and thought second. Like when I agreed to write a column on antiques for a newspaper syndicate. Deadlines, questions almost impossible to answer in just a few words, plus all those letters about things that are no more than a few years old. Seems most people think anything that belonged to their granny is an antique. Not so. Any lawyer will tell you an object must be at least a hundred years old to be an "antique," and connoisseurs insist that true antiques predate the 1820s or 1840s when new machines and tools eliminated a lot of hand work. Yes, I should have thought first and spoken second.

But probably my biggest mistake was the time I said, purely matter-of-factly, "Invite me over to see your things one day and after about thirty seconds I'll know all about you."

I wasn't bragging or trying to be smart. Honest. I was just making casual cocktail-party conversation. But from the horrified look I got from the well-heeled couple I had hoped would be my clients, I knew that not only had I said the wrong thing, I'd scared them half to death. Every family has more than its share of skeletons, if not in their closets, then in their grand-mother's trunks—skeletons they want to stay put. But, you see, I'm an appraiser. People not only invite me into their homes to look around, they *pay* me to tell them all about their things. Along the way, I can't help but uncover their deepest secrets.

I don't need to dig around in musty old trunks to learn about my clients, and I certainly don't need tarot cards. Just a glance around the room tells me everything—whether they're educated or self-made, if they've traveled or stuck close to home, if they're rich or poor. Where there's money (and there usually is in the houses I'm paid to visit), it's easy to tell if it's old money or new. The evidence is all right there. It's in the books people put out on their coffee tables, the pictures they hang on their walls, the lampshades they buy, the figurines they display in their corner cupboards. It's in their choice of the corner cupboard itself—antique or new, plain or fancy, traditional or modern. Yes, people lay their lives out in their homes, just the way Granny used to do when she hung her laundry out in her backyard for all to see.

In my profession I'm surrounded by lust, greed, envy, some-times even malice—the latter usually when I'm not looking. But what do you expect when antiques bring such big bucks? Oh, those treasures from the past may exude an air of gentil-ity and sophistication, but the truth is the antiques market is a lot like the stock market. Glamorous on the surface. Sizzling and seething just one layer down.

Think of it this way. Crime, they say, follows money. If crime can happen on Wall Street, and we know it does, then anything can happen just down the street from you in antiques malls and shops and auction houses. Money breeds greed, and greed lurks behind every door on every street in every town. I've seen it almost daily when doing appraisals for the rich, the very, very rich, the wannabe rich, and sometimes just nice, simple people who have watched *Antiques Roadshow* one time too many. What they all have in common is the hope that their things will be valuable.

Even my friends working at the auction houses and museums find it's hard to be around fabulous objects when they can't afford them. The waters get murky, malice sets in, and sometimes they take what they can't afford. I say they're just "stealing with style."

I'm no goody-goody myself. I have expensive taste in clothes, jewelry, and, of course, choice antiques. Occasionally I, too, lust after something I've seen and can't afford, or can't have. But a little lusting is as far as I go. I have a perfectly good life as an appraiser tucked away in Leemont, Virginia. Anyway, I don't think I'd be a very good thief.

I've learned, too, that if I wanted to stay in business, I had to keep the deepest, darkest secrets to myself, especially since I ran in the same social circles as my clients, thanks to my former husband. Which also explains how I got my name, Sterling Glass. I know the chance of an antiques appraiser having such a name is a stretch, but I came by it honestly. I was born to older parents who figured there wouldn't be any others, and they stuck as many names on me as they could, including my father's. I was christened Clara Elizabeth Sterling Smith. Then I married Hank Glass, listed in the *First Families of Virginia* as Henry Ketchington Glass V. Twenty years later, when the marriage shattered (no pun intended), I kept the Glass name, partly for my son's and daughter's sake and partly for my own. In Virginia, giving up the Glass name would be like giving back Kennedy in exchange for O'Malley. And I rather like my name. Those who get it, never forget it.

But there have been times when I've wished my name wasn't so memorable. Just as I've wished that people weren't quite so greedy. Maybe that's why I feel compelled to tell this story—a story that began on a late January day that started full of promise but turned into one of *those* days. A day that began unraveling my trust in human nature right in my own hometown and in the very heart of the antiques world, New York. A day that turned my nice quiet life into a mess that I've never quite recovered from.

Chapter 2

Dear Antiques Expert: My grandmother has an old quilt from the 19th century. It doesn't look like the ones I usually see with various patterns all mixed together. Some of its squares have birds and one even has a house on it. Does this make it more or less valuable than those patchwork quilts?

You have an album quilt. While the majority of Victorian quilts were "crazy" quilts, made of fabric scraps randomly pieced together, album quilts were carefully designed and skillfully executed. Their squares often depicted objects and scenes native to the particular region—flowers, birds, and log cabins, for example. Whereas a crazy quilt usually sells for a few hundred dollars, much rarer album quilts often bring tens of thousands of dollars.

I'D JUST E-MAILED my column off to my editor and was three-quarters out the door to do an appraisal when the phone rang. Any sensible person would have let it ring, but since my next job usually comes from the voice on the other end of the phone, when Ma Bell beckons, I hop-to. I had bought one of those little black boxes that flashed the caller's name and number across the screen. Trouble was, some of my best clients lurked under the pseudonyms "Unavailable" or, my favorite of all, "Personal Adviser." This time the caller ID said simply "Private."

"Sterling Glass," I said impatiently.

"Ms. Glass, you don't know me," the man on the other end of the line began, his thick Brooklyn accent unmistakable. If I hadn't been in such a rush to get to my morning appointment, I might have been tempted to tell him that lots of people I've never met call me for professional reasons.

"I'm not looking for the usual sort of appraisal, the kind where you've got an antique and you want to know what you can sell it for," he said. "I've got these old molds that can be used over and over to make new stuff." He stopped and took a rattling smoker's breath. "I need to know what they're worth —commercially. In commerce," he repeated.

"As much as I'd like to help you, I'm not sure if I can or not, Mr. . . ." I paused, thinking, in my rush, that I'd missed his name.

"Hobstein. Solomon Hobstein," he said, wheezing.

"Mr. Hobstein. It'll depend on what kind of molds you have."

"They're wonderful molds. Beautiful molds."

"I'm sure they are. But what were they used for? Or are they still being used?"

"I'd rather not discuss that over the phone," Hobstein half-coughed, his voice now little louder than a whisper.

I glanced at my watch. Mrs. Markus was known for her promptness and I had no intention of being late. And I wasn't sure that I really wanted to hear any more from someone who sounded as if he might expire at any minute.

"Mr. Hobstein, I'm really sorry, but you caught me on my

way out the door. Could I call you back later in the day? Or . . . you could call me."

"When?"

"I should be back around one, maybe one thirty."

"Okay," he said, and without as much as a good-bye hung up.

For the second time that morning, I started out the door.

TRUE TO HER WORD, Mrs. Markus wanted only three items appraised.

Most people would tell me they just had a handful of pieces and that it wouldn't take me more than an hour. Then once I was in their homes they began pulling out things that hadn't seen the light of day for a decade or more. I called these the "mightaswells," as in "While you're here, you might as well look at . . ." Add a few mightsaswells to the mix and the hour-long job quickly became a full day's work. Chipped china, faded samplers, torn maps, broken furniture—there's no end to what people have. And there is no end to where they hide the things they think are valuable—in empty egg cartons, behind TV sets, underneath radiator covers, stuffed down in the toes of old shoe bags, even taped inside the bathroom commode tank.

Then again, there was the time I found the family cat eating her Meow Mix out of a Steuben bowl worth upward of a thousand dollars. And the day that I found an exquisitely beautiful 1708 Queen Anne sterling silver teapot being used by the five-year-old at her dolls' tea party. It later sold at auction for something around eighteen thousand dollars, dents and dings and all. No, people have no idea what they have.

But Mrs. Marcus belonged to that rare breed of woman who threw the morning paper away the minute she finished reading it, whose hair was always in place, and who meant what she said. Of the three pieces she wanted me to look at, her four-poster mahogany bed and drop-leaf dining-room table were fine-quality old reproductions, the kind lots of people would already call antiques even though they were made in the 1920s. The walnut corner cupboard was a good mid-nineteenth century antique. All were simple, straightforward pieces that only needed measuring, describing, and valuing for insurance purposes before being shipped off to a niece out in Oregon.

I was in and out in an hour and five. That left plenty of time to make a quick run to the Salvation Army's Ye Olde Thrifte Shoppe and still get home before the one or one thirty time I'd mentioned to Mr. Hobstein. Very best of all, I'd been paid on the spot. I had unreportable cash in hand.

FRIDAY MORNING WAS the best time to drop by Ye Olde Thrifte Shoppe. By then the good things that had come in during the week had been tagged and put out for the weekend shoppers. Since most folks didn't start wandering in the store until at least noon, there was plenty of good picking. But it was also the best time to catch Peter Donaldson at work. He was seldom to be found after one or two on Friday afternoons, and he rarely showed up on Saturdays—especially if he'd been to an estate sale early Saturday morning. I had a feeling that many Friday nights Peter never got to bed. Crowds started gathering as early as 2 or 3 A.M. for the very best Saturday morning house sales, and Peter was usually the first in line.

He had been my dearest friend since he moved to town about three years ago—just about the time my divorce came through. I called him my salvation, and with good reason.

Peter's deliberate ways and calm nature slowed me down. And he was terribly attractive.

Peter Donaldson was not your usual store clerk. He'd inherited money and land from his grandfather and married a socialite, Emily Butler, finished Yale Divinity School, and had become an assistant rector at an old Episcopal church down in Charleston by the time he was twenty-seven. The congregation was so fond of him that when the church's pastor retired, Peter took his place. Then one day Peter Donaldson showed up in Leemont. Gossip had it that he'd left the church when his wife's untimely death shattered his faith. He was, they lamented, only in his early fifties.

Others, less kind, said that the Virginia aristocrat who was accustomed to getting everything he wanted, became disillusioned when he learned, secondhand, that he was not going to be nominated for bishop coadjutor of the diocese.

I came to know Peter about six months after he moved to town. We had met earlier. Every meddling matchmaker in town had tried to pair me with this pleasantly attractive man with no children and courtly manners who was five years my senior. Sounded perfect. But it went nowhere—until the day I was going into Cotswold Antiques and Peter was coming out. Left to our own devices we struck up a conversation and continued it at Rumors, famous for its delectable bread pudding doused in strong whiskey and topped off with rum raisin ice cream. Soon we were chatting like lifelong friends. Looking back, I can say that. At the time his forthrightness caught me by surprise.

"I had to leave Charleston after Emily died," Peter said in his unhurried Virginia drawl. "I was already questioning how much longer I could remain in the church. Emily's death threw me over the edge."

"Charleston's so beautiful, though," I said, trying to make the conversation a little less personal.

"True. And at times I miss it. But even before the flowers on Emily's grave had withered up, it seemed that every available, or soon-to-be-available, woman in town was inviting me to dinner or a concert or an art exhibit. Under the circumstances it was pretty unnerving, especially since it was my money, not me, they were after," he said with a quick shrug.

"I doubt that," I said, forcing myself to take my eyes off his melancholy brown eyes and sandy blond hair thinking how many a woman would've jumped at the chance to support him.

"No," he said. "I was pretty dark back then."

"But why move here?" I asked.

At the mention of Leemont, Peter brightened. "I've always loved Virginia, but I didn't want to go back to Lexington. This is a beautiful area, and without any family or close friends here I figured if things didn't work out I could leave. Anyway, Leemont's large enough to get lost in—but it isn't Atlanta or Houston."

Leaning across the table and flashing a wry smile, Peter said, "Bet you don't know what my day job is." He dropped his voice. "I don't tell many people."

I thought for a minute. "Haven't a clue," I said.

"Come on. Guess. You're an appraiser." He waved his forefinger to make his point. "Sometimes antiques need rescuing the same way people do."

Peter settled back in his chair and waited patiently while I tried to imagine what he might do.

I tried to think of a witty answer, but still nothing came.

"Okay. I give up."

"Not even a try?"

I shook my head no.

"Then come over to the Salvation Army shop. You'll find me in the back room sorting through things."

"You're kidding." I was too surprised to make a more intelligent comment. "Ye Olde Thrifte Shoppe? *Why?* I mean, why *there?*" No sooner were the words out of my mouth, though, than I could have crawled under the table.

Peter chuckled, obviously amused at my reaction.

"Let's get something straight first. The name, or actually, the pretentious way it's spelled," he said. "I didn't add those unnecessary *e*s and that extra *p*. Somebody else did that long before I arrived." He stopped and smiled. "But you know what? That silly spelling draws folks in. I've gotten so I kind of like it. Now back to your question of why there. Not too long after Emily died, I was on my way to my office at church as usual, but I was so distracted." Peter paused. "More than distracted. Consumed, really. Consumed by my own thoughts. Anyway, I stumbled, actually, fell is closer to the truth. I *fell* over an old black gentleman huddled in the doorway of the Sunday school building. I don't know which one of us was more startled. We must have made quite a sight as we struggled to our feet. That's when I realized the poor fellow was wrapped up in an antique quilt. At first I thought it was just a typical Victorian crazy quilt, though even that would have been quite a surprise. But on second glance I realized that I was staring at the most beautiful album quilt I'd ever seen."

Peter put down the piece of bread he had begun buttering while talking. His hands freed up, he drew the quilt in the air.

"In one square was a tobacco leaf outlined in gold thread. In another was a log cabin that was so carefully stitched that the strips of brown cloth looked more like half-timbered wood than scraps of homespun cotton. I was speechless."

"What did you do?" I asked, secretly impressed by his knowledge of quilts.

"First I did the Christian thing," he said straightforwardly. "I found Miss Fanny, the church's housekeeper, and we fixed Charlie, Charles Dunlap was his name, some coffee and toast and eggs. Then I asked him about the quilt. 'That old thing?' Charlie said. 'Got it over the river at the army building. Didn't half keep the wind off.' "

Peter smiled. "Seems a worker at the Salvation Army had told Charlie to pick out a blanket from a pile and he'd chosen that one because it was pretty. The whole time we talked, Charlie kept complaining that it hadn't kept him warm. Needless to say, we arranged a better place for him to sleep that night at Safe Shelter and found him a warmer blanket."

"And the quilt?"

"Aha." He nodded. "There was one more design. A horseshoe with yellow daisies embroidered all around it. I figured that was a talisman, a good-luck sign. I took the quilt straight back to the Salvation Army, hoping to track down where it might have come from so it could be returned," Peter said. "Unfortunately, though, it had been in a bundle of stuff dumped into one of the collection boxes located around town. There was no way to know when it had been dropped off, or by whom."

"Oh dear," I said. "So many treasures have been lost through such carelessness."

"That's when the army captain told me that since I had

found the quilt, and because I'd looked after Uncle Charlie, I should keep it. I took the quilt to a reputable antiques dealer who instantly sold it for something close to twenty thousand dollars. After his expenses and commission, we presented a check for almost sixteen thousand dollars to the army's after-school program." Peter was beaming like a kid. "Can't say that I ever touched that many people from the pulpit.

"The very next week I started scouting around house sales. In a month's time I had sold enough goods that I'd bought at those sales—at a profit, mind you—to some of the fancy shops along King Street that I added another three thousand dollars to the program. Some people serve God's flock better outside the pulpit than they do inside. I'm one of those," he said. "Of course, others didn't see it that way," he added.

"I'll bet they didn't," I said, stifling a smile. "I can hear them now, bemoaning how you were wasting your life and throwing your education away. What are those Wordsworth lines my mother used to quote? 'Late . . . and . . .' Ah! 'Late and soon / Getting and spending, we lay waste our powers.' Bet your parishioners thought you were next best thing to a bum—out hunting for antiques rather than working on Sunday's sermon. Wasting your powers."

"Yep. That's the way they figured it." Peter said. "I figured that like lost souls, lost things need looking after, too. And if the lost things can help some of the lost souls, all the better. But that was too worldly a view—even for some Episcopalians."

From that day on, Peter and I became dear friends. Over time we'd grown to become soul mates—in the platonic sense of the word. Sometimes I've thought our relationship might've amounted to more, if Peter hadn't still been in mourning for

Emily and if I hadn't been so newly divorced that I couldn't distinguish between desperation and affection. But time wasn't on our side. Anyway, we were perfectly content with things the way they were.

Well, I wasn't . . . exactly.

Especially when I looked at Peter's broad shoulders and that shock of hair that fell in his face when he laughed, or those moments when I caught him while he was busy moving furniture and books around and he was as sexy as hell. But what could I do? Peter Donaldson was my twenty-first-century Ashley Wilkes. Problem was, I didn't know if I was his Melanie or Scarlett.

It was like Mother once said: *That's the thing about the South, Sterling. It's all so damn tragic.*

Anyway, Peter and I enjoyed talking about antiques, and he was happy to have me as a faithful customer. He knew the value of antiques and he marked things fairly, and he always gave me first refusal on the good stuff.

But the real fun came when Peter and I decided the best way to get the most money for some newly uncovered treasure. I didn't go to church very often, and when I was able to help I felt like I was making a contribution to Peter's good cause. *There but for the grace of God go you,* Mother had told me whenever we'd see a needy family or someone down on his luck.

Mother was full of quotations. Memorization had been part of her schooling and I don't think she ever forgot a single verse or line. When I was a child, I hated the way she always had some profound quote. But since her death, and my divorce, I'd had only myself to talk to. I guess that was why I no longer minded it when her sayings popped into my head.

On that particular Friday, I found Peter, his shirt sleeves rolled up to his elbows, his face smudged with newspaper print, behind a stack of books precariously balanced on somebody's twenty-five-year-old Maytag dryer. He looked as happy as a kid rooting around a comic-book stand. Peter was pulling a cardboard box from beneath his desk, which was nothing more than a wooden door propped up on cinder blocks on one side and supported by a rusting filing cabinet on the other. He pawed through the box, flinging layers of old newspaper about like a backyard dog digging for a bone.

"Look at this," he said, holding up a china box no bigger than a stack of three-by-five-inch index cards, a crudely painted spray of orange and yellow flowers its only decoration. I didn't have to turn the box over to know that it would be marked MADE IN OCCUPIED JAPAN. I'd seen hundreds of similar boxes in flea markets and malls and my clients' homes. My frown said it all.

Catching my look, Peter shook the box once, smiled at me, then shook it twice, then twice again. The dull sound of metal against china was unmistakable.

"Gold? Diamonds? No? Okay, priceless Burmese rubies set in platinum," I said flippantly.

Peter rolled his eyes.

"Have to admit, the chances you'd guess this one are pretty slim. Nothing to do with you," he added quickly, "it's just unlikely that these little goodies would show up in Leemont. But you'll know what they are once you see them." He handed the box to me. "I can't get more than fifteen or twenty dollars for the box here, and it's not going to bring much more than that in an antiques mall—"

"Obviously," I butted in, opening the box.

"But I do think you'll like what's inside," he said, ignoring my interruption.

"You're right, I do like them. But where'd they come from? Wonder who . . ."

My thoughts and words tripped over one another as I sprinkled the array of small pins, charms, and badges—some gold, some bronze, some silver—stored away in the simple box for so long, onto Peter's make-do desk. I picked out some of the better nineteenth-century Mardi Gras favors—a silver bow and quiver, a gold lyre outlined in tiny garnets, an enameled yellow pansy set with one center cabochon amethyst.

"At first I thought this would be another unsolved mystery," Peter said while I sifted through his find. "But I knew exactly where the box came from. Ibby Wilson's estate. Her grandson brought it in with a half truckload of furniture, clothes, kitchen stuff. You name it. Those books were hers," he said, gesturing in the direction of the Maytag. "When I found these in with the costume jewelry, I called the boy and told him what they were."

I stopped sorting and listened.

"I might as well have told him that I'd found a bunch of dirty socks or, better yet, a barrel of empty whiskey bottles. The kid said that these had been his great-grandmother's from Louisiana. He made it clear that the family didn't want them. Something about his mother being born again and Mardi Gras being the work of the devil. You know, sometimes I think those born-again types get head-to-toe blood transfusions that drain every drop of life out of their very souls." Peter raised his hands in exasperation. "I told him his items were worth a thousand dollars, maybe more. But he said they had enough to see about and didn't want any tainted money."

"Well, look at it this way," I said. "The family voluntarily gave these things up. Did you happen to see in this morning's paper about the rash of robberies down in North Carolina? The real tragedy would be if your family's things were *stolen* from you."

I looked carefully at the tiny treasures spread out on the table. "But tell me, Peter, how did you know that these were Mardi Gras mementos?" I asked. "Most people would have thought they were just little charms and trinkets without any historical association."

"Emily and I had friends in New Orleans who'd invite us down for Mardi Gras parties," Peter said. "We always had a great time, but we'd have to leave before the glorious Fat Tuesday celebration so we'd get back to Charleston for Ash Wednesday services."

I thought back to how I had first learned about Mardi Gras memorabilia. I'd had a couple of clients with New Orleans ties who had some beautiful, and valuable, Mardi Gras items. I *had* to learn about them. I never knew when some little tidbit I'd picked up in one house would come in handy later on. "Remember back last April when I went down to New Orleans to appraise a family estate for some clients in Norfolk?" I said. "Guess what they had. Drawers full of Mardi Gras memorabilia."

"Most Virginians find Mardi Gras too raucous and rambunctious for their blood," Peter said. "A little too French for their reserved English tastes. Like the Wilsons. No room for any *bon temps* in that household. So what would you recommend we do with these precious gems, Madam Appraiser?"

"Send them back home to New Orleans. That's where they belong."

"You're right. Any of the French Quarter dealers would be delighted to have them."

"At a pittance of their worth, of course. That's why it's probably wisest to send them to auction. Neal Auction Company would be my choice."

I picked up a gold and white enameled pin in the form of a Persian saber with a single freshwater pearl dangling from the handle, turned it over, and pointed to the engraved inscription.

"Look, Peter, 1902. And—" I turned the pin first this way, then that, to get a better look at the faint script. "Aha. Rex. Knowing this was a favor for the 1902 Rex Ball, somebody will bid, oh, two, three hundred for it. That's just one piece. Get some competition going and all together these are going to be worth much more than a thousand dollars."

"Which is why I waited for you to see them before making any decisions. I was even going to bring them to the museum tonight to show to you. Wanted to catch you before you leave for New York."

"Oh, I don't leave until Thursday," I said. "Look, there's no rush on getting rid of these." I placed them back carefully in the china box. "It's too late to get them into the February sale. Put them away for now and when I get back I'll make a list of them and send it off to Neal's. You know, now I think about it, Neal's recently sold a sterling and enamel pin with a colorful parrot and a monkey from 1914 or 1915 for about $375, if I remember correctly. Even favors as recent as from the 1950s can sell in the $200–250 range. Yes," I said, feeling more certain, "when we add them all up, these will be worth closer to $2,000, maybe even $3,000."

I LEFT THE SALVATION ARMY, happy to have been with Peter, and that I'd been of some help. And I hadn't spent a penny on something that I didn't need for my already cluttered house.

I felt so good about everything, in fact, that I turned off Leemont's tree-lined boulevard that ran along the river onto the cloverleaf leading to the business section where all the fast-food joints were clustered. I headed straight into the drive-through lane at Taco Bell and ordered a Mexican Pizza and a large Diet Pepsi. Pizza in one hand and steering the car with the other, I planned the rest of the day.

I vowed not to work right up to the last minute but to leave plenty of time to get dressed for the museum party that night. After all, most of Leemont's elite ladies had begun preparing for it as soon as their husbands had left for work that morning.

Chapter 3

*Dear Antiques Expert: I recently read an article about the
English silversmith Paul Storr in an antiques publication. The
pieces they illustrated were absolutely magnificent. I'd love
to own one. Is it possible to find silver pieces made by him
in antiques shops today—and are they affordable, or would
I have to mortgage the house?*

Paul Storr is known for his extravagant and magnificent
pieces commissioned by his royal and noble patrons in the
early 18th century. Those pieces are now mostly in museums
or belong to wealthy collectors. Even though Storr made
smaller pieces—teapots, wine labels, even flatware—his
reputation and fine craftsmanship have pushed all his prices
steadily up. Pricewise, a pair of Storr's sauce ladles or serving
spoons can still be purchased for under $2,500, and a cream
jug or sugar bowl will probably cost around $5,000, but his
monumental pieces easily run $50,000–100,000 and higher.

I GLANCED AT MY WATCH. Just in time. Sometime between
four and four fifteen, Roy Madison would call from Leemont
Savings and Loan to check on the appraisal I owed him. I didn't
blame Roy for wanting the appraisal, especially since it was

Friday afternoon, that traditional "clear the desk" time. Well, he was about to get the answer he was calling for. And I knew he was going to be thrilled with the results. I'd found a similar urn in an auction catalog.

Lot 338. Important silver tea urn, circa 1807, made by Paul Storr. Raised on ball feet, the pear-shaped body beautifully gadrooned and engraved with a period armorial. The hot box still intact. Fully hallmarked. From the estate of John and Mary deCamp. Estimate $35,000–50,000.

I hadn't figured out how Sarah Rose Wilkins had come to own such a valuable piece of silver. No one had known that she owned the urn. True, she was not the sort of person who would have shown it off or bragged about it, unlike most folks. Still, there should have been some knowledge or record of the piece. The only reason the tea urn had surfaced at all was because Roy, the overconscientious junior S&L trust officer in charge of Mrs. Wilkins's modest estate, had called me the afternoon of her death.

"It's something of an emergency," he said. I heard the urgency in his voice. "The police are there and we need you to go over the apartment contents ASAP."

"Tomorrow morning?"

"More like today. Say, in thirty minutes," he said. "See, there are some unusual circumstances, which means the locks are going to be changed, and honestly, Sterling, we'd really appreciate it."

He'd caught me at home that day, and I couldn't come up with an excuse for why I couldn't. After all, the bank had been a major client some twelve years now. Hank's granddad had been on the bank's board, but even after the divorce they had continued to use my services on a regular basis. What could I do?

Looking back, I should have said I had a bad cold. Said the dishwasher just overflowed. Said my car battery was dead. Any excuse, as long as I could have stayed put at home.

It was closer to an hour than thirty minutes before I arrived at the apartment. Roy met me downstairs in the building and filled me in: Sarah Rose Wilkins, that crusty old gal, had gone to the doctor early Monday morning with a long list of complaints. After a couple of days in the hospital, when nothing major showed up, she demanded that she be allowed to return home. She was driving everyone in the hospital crazy, and no one objected. Within a few hours of arriving home, though, she called 911. Her message became garbled. She began gasping for breath, like she was having a heart attack. But not before she was heard demanding that somebody get out.

At the door, an officer nodded us in, admonished us not to touch anything, then gave us free run of the small apartment. This was, after all, Leemont.

Chalk marks, just like the ones you see on those crime shows, marked the spot near the bedroom where her body had been found. I shuddered and turned back into the living room.

What seemed strange, even to me, was the way a small side table and chair were toppled over. A china teapot and cup and saucer lay broken into pieces. Near the front door, pieces of a once delicate porcelain figurine, a ballerina with a lacy, flower-decorated skirt, were scattered about.

Based on the 911 recording, plus this disarray, Roy said the police first suspected a break-in, but Mrs. Wilkins's front door had been locked when they arrived. And there were no signs that anyone else had been there in broad daylight. The back door was undisturbed. No window screens were cut. In the soggy winter ground around the building, there were no footprints or ladder marks. Inside, absolutely nothing suggested a burglary. There were no fingerprints about other than Sarah Rose's. Her body bore no bruises. There was no blood or cuts like you might expect from the jagged shards of broken porcelain.

By the time the police captain got around to acknowledging that Roy and I were there, he had pretty much concluded that Sarah Rose Wilkins was taken sick in the living room and had started back to her bedroom, knocking things over as she went. She must have been trying to make the phone call when the fatal heart attack struck, he said. It made sense. Certainly there wasn't any reason to perform an autopsy.

What it didn't explain was the part where Sarah Rose was heard telling somebody to get out—which, it would appear, is why she had called 911 in the first place.

Then one of the young cops suggested that she might have been hallucinating, maybe Sarah Rose Wilkins only *thought* someone was there. His grandmother had seen her dead husband as clear as day while she lay dying, he said. "My grandma even talked to my grandpa and told him she'd be there real soon."

I believed him. Some people called them ghosts; others said they are angels. Still others, trying to be correct in these PC times, called them spirits. Whatever you called them, visitors who were unseen but nonetheless vividly visible to the dying, were well documented. A nurse once told me that she believed these spirits were helpful apparitions who came to escort the dying on their journey that lay ahead. Then again, that made me wonder: if Sarah Rose had been visited by friendly angels, just why would she be telling them to get out, and so angrily?

Do not go gentle into that good night, Mother reminded me before I could pose my question out loud. Knowing Sarah Rose's uncompromising nature, Mother's explanation made some sense.

All I knew was that I wasn't used to making house calls where the body was still warm and the police were on the scene and people were talking about ghosts and apparitions. Perhaps that was why I had kept procrastinating and hadn't finished the job for Roy Madison. I didn't like the eerie feeling I'd had in Sarah Rose's apartment, and I didn't like the way it kept creeping back every time I worked on the appraisal.

Leemont Savings and Loan's trust department had been named the trustee of Mrs. Wilkins's estate when Mr. Wilkins had died some twelve years earlier. Bob Wilkins hadn't made a great deal of money as a pharmacist, but he had inherited some land that had become fairly valuable when Leemont began growing in the 1960s. He'd sold the land, and being a conservative man, he had put the money in a trust for his Sarah Rose, which explained why I was standing there with the bank officer in the middle of a crime scene.

With all that going on, no one had seemed very excited when I discovered the tea urn in a brown bag inside a moth-eaten blanket in the closet. But then that was the thing about antiques. Not many people had a clue what made one piece a giveaway and another a million-dollar treasure. Oh, *Antiques Roadshow* had tried to educate the public about quality and rarity and craftsmanship, but most people turned a deaf ear to everything until the appraiser asked, "Tell me, do you have any idea what the value of this piece is?"

That was always the tagline that sucked them in, just the way it had that afternoon when, after unwrapping the urn and recovering from the surprise myself, I turned to Roy Madison and said, "Do you have any idea what the value of this piece is?"

"No," he had said, quickly adding, "but a coffeepot can't be *that* valuable."

"Tea urn," I corrected him. "Some 175-plus years ago, long before Mr. Coffee and Mrs. Tea, the finest, most expensive silver coffee and tea urns came equipped with hot boxes to do the trick, like this one. See?" While I talked, I pulled out a cylinder-shaped metal piece that fit inside the urn. "Either a heated iron rod or red-hot coals were placed in this box to keep the brew warm. Over the years, most urns have lost this clever device, which means that the ones that have the box still intact are all the more valuable."

From the outset Roy seemed dead set on making sure that the tea urn wouldn't be anything of substance. After I'd put off giving him a concrete monetary value for the urn for the third time he became more insistent about the urn's value or, rather, its *lack* of value.

"Just give it your best guess, Sterling. What? Three hundred? Four? Let's be done with it," he had pleaded. "Look, nobody would have known about the coffeepot—tea urn—if you hadn't found—"

"And what are you going to do with it now that I *have* found it?" I said. "Sell it after the fact and *then* try to explain to the IRS how that old three-hundred-dollar coffeepot, as you call it, sold for twenty-five thousand or more?"

That's how I had bought a little more time.

I looked at the picture in the catalog of the tea urn estimated to sell for thirty-five thousand to fifty thousand dollars.

Mrs. Wilkins's urn was even finer. It had been made in 1810, two years later than the one in the catalog. Paul Storr, its maker, undoubtedly had refined the design in the interim. The urn in the catalog had nice, but simple, ball feet. Sarah Rose Wilkins's urn had a much more elaborate base, and the feet were exquisite classical dolphins, in addition to a fancier lid. And it bore an exquisitely etched coat of arms and two crests. Identify the duke, earl, or lord who had commissioned this piece and its value would take a giant leap. But there was no reason for me to try to hunt down the identity of some dead British royal. That was the work of a specialist. I was just a generalist appraiser, sort of the GP of the antiques world. I did know fine objects, though, and of the two urns Sarah Rose's blew the other one out of the water.

I flipped to the back cover of the auction catalog where I had stapled in the sales results for the auction.

Lot 338. $55,000.

That much simpler urn had sold for five thousand above its highest estimate some four years ago. What would Mrs. Wilkins's urn be worth? It could only be more valuable than that one, no matter whether the stock market was up or down. Sixty-five thousand dollars? More? Seventy-five thousand? Maybe on an extraordinarily good day. But probably more like sixty-eight or seventy thousand.

The bank would want a conservative estimate, I reminded myself. Either way, those mid-five-figure prices were a "fur

piece," as we say down here, from three or four hundred
dollars.

Personally, I'd had a love affair with silver since I was a little girl. My parents' home was filled with all sorts of useless,
enchanting Victorian silver—napkin rings decorated with
sparrows perched two abreast on a tree branch; a pickle jar
having on its lid a boxer dog raised on his back haunches; a
butter dish with a cow, udders and all, on top of its domed
cover. But most captivating were the seals and sea otters
swimming around the base of our 1870s tilting water pitcher.
I'd look at those totally frivolous pieces and they became a
pathway to another place, another time.

Now my tastes were a tad more sophisticated. Instead of
frolicsome nineteenth-century dogs, cows, and sea otters, I'd
become fond of refined eighteenth-century shells and dolphins,
scrolls, and acanthus leaves on my silver. Still, I used any excuse I could find to leisurely wander, page by page, through a
silver auction catalog, rather than surfing the Net or logging on
to ArtFact, gazing at masterpieces that I could only see, never
possess. That, to me, was as thrilling as riding in a Ferrari.

I marked the page in the catalog that told me what I had
known all along but needed to have as substantial evidence. I
laid the catalog on the desk just as the phone rang. Right on
cue.

"About that coffeepot," Roy started in without so much as
a hello.

"Well! Good afternoon, Roy. And, by the way, it's a *tea
urn*," I corrected him for the umpteenth time.

"Have it your way. Tea urn."

"I think you're going to be, well," I paused for effect, "*amazed* by its value. You can close Sarah Rose Wilkins's file now. I've figured the value of the property in the estate at about"—I glanced at my notes—"twenty-three or twenty-four thousand dollars. That includes the good china and crystal, the one small nineteenth-century sampler that I put in at four hundred dollars, and the furniture. There just wasn't much of substantial value in Sarah Rose Wilkins's apartment, and the pots and pans and that nice pottery, as well as the everyday kitchen things, even including the appliances, don't amount to more than about"—I took a long pause—"another six or seven hundred."

I heard papers shuffling on the other end of the line. I could see Roy, as fresh at the end of the day as after his morning shower, impatiently shifting the days' files to their appropriate slot in his in/out shelves while I rattled on.

"Twenty-four thousand dollars total for all the property, let's say. No car. Add in the seventy thousand for the urn and that brings the total to—"

"Seventy thousand? Are you out of your mind? Sterling, there's no way. Where did you come up with that figure? Did you actually say seventy thousand dollars?"

I waited for Roy to calm down and absently shook my plastic Magic 8 Ball left over from my childhood. Its message wavered beneath the ball's cloudy liquid. "Yep. Seventy thousand. *It is decidedly so.*

"Look, Roy," I said. "I know it's none of my business why on earth you are so upset that this is such a valuable piece. I'd think you'd be delighted. You're going to come out of this looking like a champ. Doesn't the trust department get a percentage of the total estate? Ninety-four thousand dollars sure sounds better than twenty-four thousand. At least to my ears. Add on the money in the trust . . . Am I missing something?"

Somehow, Roy's silence, followed by a throat clearing, a sigh, and finally a long "Well" on the other end of the line came as no surprise.

"This is in strictest confidence, of course," he said eventually.

"Of course. I was doing appraisals for Leemont Savings and Loan while you were still in high school," I reminded him.

"Now I'm gonna be honest with you, Sterling."

Roy's condescending tone didn't set well with me. I rolled my Magic 8 Ball, glad that video-telephone conferencing was still unheard of in Leemont. *Don't count on it,* the message read.

"You know the Wilkinses had no children, and their closest relatives, who weren't very close, lived far away," Roy said. "Both the Wilkins were so active in the community that it's only logical they left their money to local charities."

"So their money is going to stay in Leemont. Doesn't that make it all the better?"

"Not really. Or at least not as far as the *bank* goes," he replied.

I wasn't sure if I heard Roy's door close or if I imagined it.

"By the will, the library gets the cash in the trust, which is just fine. But the money from the sale of the property goes to Hope House."

"So?" I said.

"Don't you read the papers, Sterling?"

"Yes. But? So?"

"Hope House is trying to buy the old sock factory to renovate for a halfway house," he said as if that explained everything.

"This is a big infusion of cash. Just what they need to make the project possible."

"What's wrong with that?"

"The *bank* owns that building, Sterling."

"*So?* I'd think the bank would be chomping at the bit to get rid of what's left of that building before it falls down. Lots of people think it's pretty irresponsible of you all to let it just sit there being an eyesore with the windows boarded up and bricks crumbling underneath the kudzu—especially since it can be seen from the highway. Not exactly the kind of first impression Leemont wants to give to visitors and passersby. There's no telling who's living in the building, Roy. I've seen fire trucks out there more than once." I didn't say anything about the Confederate flag that had hung there for several days before it disappeared as mysteriously as it had appeared.

"Wasn't there an editorial or a letter in the paper saying that the bank ought to just give the property to Hope House as a goodwill gesture?" I asked. "If this urn makes it possible for Hope House to put the building to good use, it's a win-win situation."

"On the surface maybe," Roy said pompously, as if eager to show me how dense I was. "But Sparks Burns has won the state senate race. Once he's in Richmond, well, who knows what business might become interested in moving into that spot? And if the right tenant comes to Leemont, the state might even get serious about doing that roadwork the city's been trying to get the highway department to approve for the past ten years."

Sparks Burns had made millions in land deals and the construction business during Leemont's recent growth spurt. Though a local boy, rumor had it that he had been handpicked and financially backed in his run for office by some Washington businessmen with Virginia connections. He'd easily won. Sparks Burns was also on the bank's board of directors, just like Hank's grandfather had been. I mulled the situation over.

"Oh," was the best I could muster.

In politics there is no honor, my mother often said, quoting Disraeli.

It was late in the day and the week, and Roy had taken most of the wind out of my sails, but still I wasn't about to see that magnificent urn swept under some bank's boardroom table.

"Well, Roy, I'm just the appraiser," I said. "I can't make the urn go away. What you do with it is up to you. But I will say this. That urn isn't just about money. It's about craftsmanship and connoisseurship. Did I mention culture? It may not be as valuable as an old master painting or a piece of Fabergé, but that's just because silver hasn't gotten a lot of publicity, aside from the Hunt brothers' silver scam back in the seventies." I took a deep breath. "Look. It's your responsibility to do the right thing by the *urn*—if not by Sarah Rose Wilkins's will."

The words were out of my mouth. I couldn't take them back. So much for any future work from those guys—former in-law family connection or not.

"I'll get the report to you by Monday," I said more calmly. "I can either fax it to you or run it by on my way out of town. You still go in at eight thirty don't you?" I asked.

"Better bring it in." Roy's tone was decidedly cool. "Bring it in a sealed envelope and put your bill in as usual. I'll see that your check is cut right away. This is one estate I'll be happy to see the end of. And Sterling," Roy added a shade more cordially, "thanks for your, ah, diligence. I would have done the same thing."

I hung up, pondering his parting statement and my wisdom, or lack of it.

Chapter 4

Dear Antiques Expert: My great aunt left me a diamond ring that I believe dates from the 1870s. The cut of the diamond is different from the ones I see now—almost rounded—and it seems to sparkle less. The jeweler said it was "mine cut." Does that make the diamond any less valuable?

Before modern gem-cutting tools and techniques were developed, diamonds were cut with a high rounded top, a flat bottom, and not as many facets as today's diamonds. In contrast, today's diamonds are cut with a flat top, rounded bottom, and high number of facets. An older mine-cut diamond may not have as "brilliant" a sparkle, but many people prefer that antique look, especially when the diamond is in a lovely antique setting. Generally speaking though, mine-cut diamonds are less costly than comparable brilliant-cut diamonds.

SO MUCH FOR THE lovely evening I'd looked forward to.

Without a husband and with the kids gone, I often found my self-worth in my work, and Roy Madison had just slapped me down. I generally tried to be tough and let the little bleeps fade off the screen, but the truth was, without someone to talk things over with and reassure me, well, I could get pretty down. Which was where I was right now.

All I wanted to do was to slip into my flannel jammies, curl up in the bed with a glass of wine, and watch an old Chevy Chase movie. But I had said I'd be at the museum party. I had to put the recent conversation behind me and change my mood. I put on a Marvin Gaye CD and drew a hot bath. I resolved to put the exchange with Roy out of my head. "Guess the old adage is right," I said half-aloud. "You just can't fight City Hall."

"Or the biggest bank in town," I thought as Marvin and Tammy Terrell sang "Ain't No Mountain High Enough."

Only after I was out of the tub and half dressed did I notice the light blinking on my caller ID box. The number had a 718 area code. A message was waiting.

"This is Sol. Solomon Hobstein again. I couldn't get back with you earlier." I recognized the Brooklyn voice touched with a slight European accent. "Look, this is what it is. I have these old molds."

"Yes, yes," I said impatiently to the absentee messenger.

"I got your name from a newspaper article. Something about appraisers. You know the one I mean? Anyway I liked your face. You look honest. See, I don't want anybody from around here knowing what I've got." He coughed. "These New Yorkers only care about the money. They don't give a damn about the things. I've checked up on you. Called around. What I need to know is when you're coming this way. I want to make an appointment. I'll pay for the trip if I have to. Give me a call."

I put the call out of my mind for the moment and returned

to the business at hand. I brushed a nice "natural" blush across my cheeks and carefully applied my requisite brown eyeliner and mascara. We blondes may have more fun, but it sure takes us a long time to make our eyes come alive. I misted my short locks with a quick fog of superhold hair spray I'd bought on the promise that it would give a professional hold with added shine and still leave my hair loose and touchable. I dabbed a little Trésor behind my ears, on both wrists. Then I fastened the sapphire and diamond clasp of my predivorce pearls.

Makeup first, then the pearls, Mother had drilled into me. It was so unusual for her to comment on such a minute detail, I had listened. *And always after the hair spray. And never, ever put perfume on your neck. Hair spray and perfume—they both eat away the pearls' lustrous nectar.*

JAGS, MERCEDES, TOWN CARS, and BMWs were filling up the parking lot by the time I arrived. I slipped my eight-year-old Mercedes into a tight space, threw my coat around my shoulders, and made a beeline for the front door.

"Sterling, dear!" said a man's voice.

I turned to see the Creightons huffing to catch up with me. Petite people by birth, they had shriveled up little by little with each passing decade.

"Who is that, Howard?" Martha Creighton asked, sounding frightened. When they were parallel with me, out of the blue she said, "I've lost my silver casserole dish. Sarah Rose Wilkins stole it."

"No, no, dear. Now don't say that. Nobody has stolen anything. It isn't *your* silver that people are talking about. It's a silver *urn* everyone is talking about, one that belonged to Sarah

Rose," her husband said. He turned his head and whispered to me, "We played duplicate bridge in the same club as Sarah Rose Wilkins before she died."

News traveled fast. Then again I should have known that it would have been asking too much for word not to have gotten around Leemont.

"What are you talking about, Howard?" Mrs. Creighton was saying. "A silver urn? I sent Sarah Rose a silver urn?" She peered at me with cataract-marred eyes. "I'm having trouble remembering things these days," she said.

Then in a moment of perfect lucidity she turned back to me. "Mr. Creighton wants you to come and see our things, don't we? Why don't you just drop in for tea and we'll show them to you. There's one chair that belonged to Mr. Creighton's greatuncle. He was quite an opera lover and I'm sure that Caruso sat in it. He knew all the greats, didn't he, dear?"

"Oh, yes," Mr. Creighton agreed, cheered by his wife's clear moment. "And I've got a whole book full of stamps you'd like to see, too. Collected them as a boy. We'd love to know how much they're worth now. And then there's your grandmother's Haviland china. Don't forget that, Martha. If she were alive she'd be, now let's see, I'm eighty-seven. That would make your grandmother . . ."

Here we go again, I thought to myself.

"I'll try to do that," I said, working hard not to show my annoyance. "Give me a call in a few weeks. I'm off to New York on Thursday."

"New York! Mr. Creighton and I spent many lovely times there. Didn't we, dear. Isn't that where your great-uncle knew

—now who was that singer? The opera one?" Mrs. Creighton tugged at her husband's sleeve.

I glanced at my watch and spoke quickly. "I seem to have forgotten the time, Mrs. Creighton. I didn't realize it was so close to seven thirty. Do give me a call when you can. Right now I'm afraid I might be needed inside."

"Yes, you run on now," Howard Creighton said to me, his eyes sad. "Come along now, Martha. You know his name. Just try to remember. Just try."

I sighed as I picked up my pace. I didn't mean to be rude, but mentioning the urn only reminded me of the afternoon's telephone conversation, and now Mrs. Creighton had conjured up memories of Mother's long battle with Alzheimer's. Couldn't I have just one night of fun? And people think *doctors* hate cocktail parties because they have to dole out free medical advice. Add appraisers to the list.

INSIDE THE MUSEUM the liquor was flowing and the atmosphere was much cheerier.

The occasion was a Starvation Party to raise money so the museum could purchase a recently discovered letter from Robert E. Lee written to one Armistead Hanley, the great-great-grandfather of one of Leemont's town leaders. One of Armistead Hanley's sons had married a New York belle during the Gay Nineties, and the letter had passed along that Yankee line, rather than the Southern strand that had remained in Virginia.

The letter, a brief but moving explanation of why young men were needed for the great Confederate cause, had been offered on eBay. It had sold for a pittance to a shrewd rare-book dealer. Probably for no more than seven or eight thousand dollars, I'd learned from a Civil War buff. Now the dealer was offering the letter to the Leemont Museum—to the tune of twenty-five thousand. Outrageous markup maybe, but no worse than that charged by jewelers and car dealers. The museum was dying to have the letter, but funds were scant. So they were holding a Starvation Party, that revered Virginia tradition suggested by Moe Taylor, the board president, last October.

"That's what our brave Confederate ancestors did to raise money for the Great Cause," she had proclaimed at the joint meeting of the entertainment and fund-raising committees. "Why, they barely had enough to eat, but they kept their high spirits. That's what we should do. Make sacrifices but still have fun. The food's the greatest expense for any party. I say we *all* will need to lose a few pounds after Christmas."

Moe drew herself up to her imposing five-foot nine-and-a-half-inch height, pulled in her ample stomach, and sucked in her puffy cheeks to accent her once prominent cheekbones. She pursed her red lips, demurely dabbed at her eyes, and took a deep, swelling breath. She lowered her booming voice in volume and pitch. "Remember, this is for another Great Cause—the memory of our very own brave departed. Everyone will *love* it."

A dramatic woman anyway, Moe Taylor had pulled out all the stops that day.

John Ross Weatherspoon, looking rather like a Confederate officer reincarnated in the twenty-first century, leaned back in his chair, rubbed his beard, and added his practical two cents' worth. "What about the liquor?"

"Now, John Ross!" Cora Mae Brown, the wife of Pastor Brown, chastised him. Then she added, "He's right, though, Moe. No one will come if we don't have . . . spirits."

And so, after some discussion, it was unanimously voted that the Christmas party would be canceled and a January Starvation Party would be held in its place—with ample spirits and a few bowls of peanuts thrown in for good measure. True to Moe's promise, the novel idea had brought out the town's illustrious luminaries in their diamonds and their Diamoniques. Outside, spotlights shone on the bronze statue of Jefferson Davis, president of the fallen Confederacy. Awash in the bright lights that heightened his lean, tragically heroic demeanor, Davis cut a magnificent figure.

Inside, candles, carefully guarded by museum docents, cast a soft glow of flickering light and shadow, reminiscent of bygone days.

"Surely they didn't mean a *real* Starvation Party," a male voice said behind me, breaking my trance.

"Shhhh. *Please* don't make a scene. We can go out to the club afterward. Or call in a pizza if you want," a woman's voice pleaded.

"Damn right we will. Whose cockamamie idea was this, anyway? The *hysterical* society's?" He laughed as if he were the first to think up the overused cliché.

I moved into the parlor. Whoever they were, I didn't want to get caught by them. Had I known I would run right into Roy Madison, I might have taken my chances and stayed put.

"Sterling!"

Putting his arm around my shoulder, Roy gave me that

long-lost fraternity brother hug, like he hadn't seen me since
the last party. Amazing how a scotch on the rocks can warm
a body up.

"You aren't going to talk business, are you, Roy?"

Cassie Madison, looking cheery in a Christmas-red dinner
suit, leaned into her husband. She reached up and straightened
Roy's black tie, which didn't need straightening at all. I threw
a sympathetic smile her way. Roy dropped his arm from my
shoulder.

"Just for a minute, Cassie. Look, Sterling, after we talked I
went in to see El Presidente. We decided the only thing to do is go
ahead and sell the coffee—tea urn." He grinned in satisfaction.

"See? I'm learning." He took a short swig of his long drink.
"We've got it locked up in the safe, but we don't want to mess
with it. What would the bank do with it?"

"Are you serious about this?" I looked Roy straight in the
eye, trying to forget everything about Hope House.

"Dead serious. What do we need to do to get rid of it? Nobody around here's gonna drop that kind of money for a piece
of silver. Can you take care of it? For a fee, of course." He
smiled his most persuasive cocktail-party smile.

"It'll have to go to New York to one of the major auction
houses."

"And you with it, I presume."

I shrugged.

The antiques market was still going strong, even in New
York. Most everyone had expected the bottom to fall out of the
antiques market after September 11, 2001, when everyone's
lives had fallen apart. Who would have thought they could still
think about antiques? But I knew the power that things held

over people and even in hard times they would buy antiques
—saying it was for sentimental reasons. In truth, though, there
was more to it than that. In times good and bad, antiques were
the collector's comfort food.

I'd seen how objects from the past provided people with a
much needed sense of security. Every time a picture was stolen
from a museum or objects were looted during wartime, it was
a reminder to the modern world that old things could be just
as fragile as people. Buying something that had managed to
survive hundreds, sometimes thousands, of years of war and
turmoil was a way that we humans could entertain immortal-
ity, grasp at a little bit of hope, possess something that we believed would outlive us. Owning antiques—touching them,
feeling them, gazing upon them—was a subtle, unspoken way
of assuring ourselves that everything would be all right.

That was why serious antiquers flocked to New York the
last week in January, myself included. It was the Super Bowl
week of the antiques world. Three major events were held in
Manhattan that week—two major auction sales and the famed
Winter Antiques Show, where the most elite American and a
handful of British and Continental dealers showed off their
finest wares. The auctions and the show were a great place for
collectors—if their pockets were deep enough. And I intended
to be there right beside them.

Cassie impatiently shifted her weight from one dainty foot
to the other.

"Look, banks ship millions of dollars' worth of bonds and
securities all by their dear little selves—every day," Roy said.

"It was worth a try."

"Hey." He threw his hands up in protest. "I didn't say no.

We owe you one for all that research. You've never overcharged us. Yet. Make a deal with you. We'll pay your airfare and your hourly fee while you're setting up the deal. No per diem and no pay for your travel time. Just go ahead and do it."

That was Roy's subtle way of cutting whatever bill I would present to the bank for the work I'd already done. Even though I felt I had the bank's business sewn up, there was always the chance another appraiser would offer them lower rates. Offering me this trip ensured that I'd keep my rates down.

"Really, Roy. Can't you all discuss this during office hours?" Cassie said, growing more agitated.

"Deal," I said.

What sweeter way to get my already purchased ticket to New York paid for? I didn't steal from the rich or the poor, but when I had the chance to pick up a few extra bucks by working a couple of jobs at once, I jumped at it, especially when big business was paying. I told Roy I'd go to New York on Thursday. We would both come out ahead. First thing Monday morning, he'd prepare papers giving me permission to dispose of the urn in the most expedient and profitable way.

"Now you two kids run on off and enjoy the, uh . . ." I couldn't say food. "Peanuts. Virginia peanuts, of course."

I watched the Madisons walk arm in arm toward the drink table.

There was no real reason for me to take the urn to New York; all the auction house dealings could be handled over the phone. I'd done it umpteen times before. Was this Roy's way of keeping me quiet about the bank's involvement with the old factory building, or had some "higher-up" suggested it, I wondered.

Cassie was talking to her husband a mile a minute. Despite my uncomfortable feelings about Roy and his professional honesty, I hated to see him henpecked. It was like he was getting it from both sides, at work and at home. On the other hand, maybe if I'd pecked at Hank a little more, I wouldn't have been another single woman at the party. High-maintenance wives had a way of holding on to their husbands.

I looked around. I certainly didn't want to follow the Madisons to the bar. The room was filling up. It looked like the museum would raise the needed cash, or close to it.

"Excuse me. Aren't you Sterling Glass? The antiques lady?"

I turned to face a tall, heavyset, but pleasant-enough-looking man. But unlike the majority of the men there who wore the traditional dark suit with silk tie, this fellow was sporting a string tie held in place by a Confederate flag slip. These museum events with a connection to what some Southerners called the Recent Unpleasantness, brought in all sorts of folks intent on living in the glorified antebellum days. But as long as they paid their pledges in Federal Reserve greenbacks, they were welcomed.

I groaned to myself. I nodded.

His close-set eyes gave me the once-over. Another bad sign.

"This museum's got some pretty nice stuff," he said, tipping his head in the direction of the silver and china display. "I bet you know whar there's all sorts of valuable things. They tell me you know *all* about antiques." He smiled a confident, toothy smile. Obviously he was settling in for a long conversation. I started looking for an escape route. A whiff of aftershave lotion wafted my way.

"I wouldn't go that far. There's lots I don't know," I said, looking over his left shoulder in hopes of finding some way out, all the while wondering why guys like this always had such full heads of hair. And they always combed it straight back in a sleazy way.

"You need to come see my collection. Appraise it. I've got lots of valuable things. If the damn Yankees hadn't come along I'd a had more. I live out in the Dixon Springs area now, but my family came from the Petersburg area. You know what happened there."

Every Virginian worth his salt knew about the strangling nine-month-long Siege of Petersburg that devastated the town, starved the civilians, slaughtered the forces, South and North, and struck a major blow that eventually led to the downfall of the Confederacy. But I wasn't thinking about that tragic event. I was thinking that if Southerners like this guy who were still bemoaning their families' lost treasures (if they ever had them) would just hang it up, they'd fare a lot better. His things? At that moment I was much more concerned about the very mysterious silver urn than I was about any trinkets this fellow's family *might* have had.

"Excuse me," I said. "I haven't gotten a drink yet."

GLASS IN HAND, I was starting toward the gallery rooms in the back of the museum when Peter caught up with me.

"Been looking all over for you."

"I wish you'd found me earlier," I said.

Peter led me over to the side of the room. "You had no more than left the store when look what showed up." He pulled an antique diamond brooch from the inside breast pocket of his tuxedo. "Shhh. Don't make a big show," he warned me, quickly closing his fingers as someone passed by.

I swallowed my shock. "Where did *that* come from?" I whispered.

"You aren't going to believe it. If I were a swearing man, I'd swear this is the most unbelievable find yet. LaTisha was pricing the kitchen items that the bank sent over from Sarah Rose Wilkins's place. Mixed in with the old things there were some brand-new towels and pot holders. Not one of those pot holders you double up. One that you put your whole hand in. Like—" Peter held out his free hand, fingers closed and thumb wiggling, to demonstrate.

I nodded. "Yes."

"Anyway, LaTisha said her mamma needed a new pot holder, so she was trying one on for size when she felt something sharp. When she looked to see what it was, this is what she found."

Peter unclasped his fingers. A floral spray of three large blossoms, each blossom set with a single pearl encircled by old mine-cut diamonds and accented by small, diamond-set leaves, glistened in Peter's palm. Silvered prongs held the stones in place. The mounting itself was gold.

"Peter!" I said.

"Here, give me your wine before you spill it. And stop frowning so." He nudged me with his elbow at the same time he swept his hair away off his brow. "People will think I'm the bearer of some horrible news."

"For all I know, you are. It doesn't make sense. I went through Sarah Rose Wilkins's things. I never saw this."

"Of course you didn't. Who'd look inside a pot holder for a diamond brooch?"

I put my hands on my cheeks, stuck my little fingers in my

mouth and bit them, hoping that would help me think more clearly.

"If anyone were to look at you right now, they'd think you'd seen a ghost," Peter said, laughing.

I put my hands down and managed a fake smile. "That better? But I think I have . . . seen a ghost, or a ghost's lost pin. Look, it just doesn't make any sense for two such valuable objects to show up like that. The police said there wasn't any foul play. But what if . . ."

The wheels in my head were frantically spinning. But my thoughts were stuck in a quagmire.

"What if what? Don't be silly." Peter dismissed my suspicions with such finality that I felt like an idiot. Good old unflappable Peter, I was thinking. Then he held the pin out to me.

"Want to wear it?" he asked. "It would go well with your pearls. Liven up your dress a little."

"You're not kidding it would. That baby would make a dirty apron look like a Chanel creation. You think I'd wear it and have to tell everybody where it came from? Me? A divorced woman? Not in this town."

Peter threw his head back in laughter. "Hadn't thought about it like that."

"So? What are you going to do?" I asked as he slipped the brooch back into his pocket.

"Reward LaTisha. Give her the pot holder and a raise. And maybe let her pick out a piece of costume jewelry from the case," he said as an afterthought.

"With *that*, I mean." I stared straight at his pocket, stopping short of calling him stupid. Or worse.

He shrugged.

"Peter," I whispered, "remember that story in the newspaper a while back about the pearl necklace some woman found in the Goodwill Store? Think it was down the road, in Danville. She bought it for sixty-nine cents. Took it home to Colorado or Arizona or Wyoming or somewhere, and it was appraised at fifty thousand dollars. Truth really is stranger than fiction. *You* know that!"

Peter rolled his brown eyes.

"You do, and you know it!"

If we'd been in private, I would have stamped my foot. "Haven't you ever watched *Fact or Fiction* on the Sci-Fi channel?" I said. "The stories you think couldn't have happened are the real-life ones. There's a problem here. It just doesn't make sense. First the Paul Storr tea urn worth over fifty grand. Now a wonderful mid-nineteenth-century diamond brooch worth—" I threw my hands in the air. "Seven thousand? Eight? Add it up. Both things mysteriously turn up among Sarah Rose Wilkins's things, and with no explanation? Something's not right."

"You've seen too many reruns of *Murder, She Wrote,* Sterling," Peter said calmly, putting his hand on my arm. Had I not been so distracted, his touch might have sent me into orbit. "You know as well as I do that people have all sorts of things hidden away that never surface until they're dead."

"Not people like Sarah Rose," I declared. "Well," I sighed, calming down, "at least the urn and the pin are both in safe hands now. I'll tell Roy about the pin on Monday morning. Now's not the time."

Peter gave me a look that suggested otherwise. But I knew that Cassie would have probably scratched my eyes out if I'd tried to start another business conversation. I shook my head. "Let's wait, Peter," I said.

"Wait till what, Sterling?"

Till what? I didn't have a clue.

MOE TAYLOR AND her helpers had carefully orchestrated the evening, and at the stroke of eight we all gathered in the auditorium.

Moe was appropriately dressed in a violet antebellum satin gown gathered in the back by a pleated and ruffled bustle (the sort preferred by pigeon-breasted women) and matching purple eye shadow. Draped around her shoulders was a heavily embroidered black silk antique shawl and, on her hand, a diamond ring the size of a kumquat, the kind worn by Southern women with old money, or those in the rest of the country with new money.

No one could miss the garish bauble with the way Moe gestured this way, then that, all the while reminding the guests about the importance of the museum, its place in history, and applauding the great support Leemont had lent to make it possible to purchase the sacred R. E. Lee letter. Amid enthusiastic applause, everyone agreed the event had been a grand success. Soon, Peter wandered off to see someone else.

Another glass and a half of chardonnay and casual conversation with first one person, then another, helped to put the urn and the brooch out of my thoughts. I almost forgot about Peter. I was having a grand time, but the string-tie guy with slicked-back hair was still lurking around looking at the Civil War displays. He wasn't following me, exactly, but he conveniently managed to keep cropping up wherever I was.

At the first opportunity I told Moe good-bye and slipped out.

LATER THAT NIGHT, curled up in the four-poster bed I'd slept in as a child and returned to after my divorce, I reflected on the day. It certainly had held more than its share of surprises. What I missed now was someone to talk it all over with.

Glancing around the room at what some would have termed "clutter," I thought about the urn and the brooch. Had Sarah Rose Wilkins bought them or inherited them? Either way, where had they come from, and why on earth would she have hidden them away?

If only things could talk.

My eyes moved around the room. There was my grandmother's hand mirror on the dressing table I'd had since I was fourteen. On the wall, an antique sampler hung beside a poor attempt at a needlepoint picture my daughter, Lily, had struggled to complete when she was nine. She was much better competing in soccer with her younger brother, Ketch, than she was with a needle.

I closed my eyes. The shrill ring of the phone broke my reverie and scared me half out of my skin. Who on earth was calling this time of night? I didn't even reach for the light. I grabbed the receiver.

"Hello?"

A faint click answered my greeting.

I turned on the light and flew downstairs to my office to see the number registered on the black box.

It was blank.

It took two rings for the caller ID to register.

I'd picked the phone up on the first ring.

Chapter 5

Dear Antiques Expert: My husband and I set up a booth in our town's antiques mall after we retired. A woman from out of town asked us to buy out the contents of her mother's home just a few blocks from our shop. But when I went to the house, I realized it was a job for our local auction house. Because the lady had to get back home, she asked me to contact the auctioneer. When I did, he offered me a finder's fee. Is it right for me to accept this?

Absolutely. The lady needed you to make the contact and the auctioneer appreciated your referral. This is a business transaction. Auction houses happily pay a "finder's fee" to dealers and appraisers who refer clients to them, and the money comes out of the auction company's money rather than the seller's proceeds. A finder's fee is just a token thank you—usually 3–5 percent of the final selling price. But for a large estate or expensive item, that small percentage can be significant.

I LEFT FOR NEW YORK that Thursday on a trip that was beginning to feel more like business and less like pleasure.

As soon as I was settled in my hotel room, I called Nigel

Rhodes in the English decorative arts department at Layton's, the auction house that would bring the best price for the urn. Nigel was with a client, but he told me to come right over.

The rich, the famous, the museum elite, and literally everyone aspiring to be someone someday in the rarefied world of antiques was also gathering at Layton's for their last chance to glimpse the array of antiques before the exhibit hall doors closed at 5 P.M. Like clockwork, at 5:01 Layton's moving crew would begin frantically gathering up the objects and organizing them for the upcoming sale.

Blue-blooded blue hairs would be mingling with blue-haired tattooed hipsters. Filthy rich matrons and academic types alike would be crawling around on their hands and knees to get a better view of some long-dead craftsman's saw marks and woodblocks. Sometimes the only way I could tell the socialites from the museum curators—with just their buttocks in clear view—was by the cell-phone wire running up to their ears. Those were the socialites, talking to their antiques investment advisers the same way entertainment people talked to their personal psychics. But the color of everyone's money was green. It was a real democratic process.

I wanted to see the things and the people, but my first obligation was to the silver urn. I'd sent it to New York ahead of me; it had taken hours to pack and deliver to FedEx on Tuesday. I arrived at Layton's just as Nigel was escorting his appointment to the front door. Seeing me, he waved us past the front desk and ushered me into his office where the urn was already on display.

"As always, you're right on, I'd say," Nigel said.

Nigel was a rather plain, fair-complexioned man with thinning blond hair, and he used his clothes to distinguish himself. This morning he had on a navy blue cashmere blazer and yellow polka-dotted bow tie. Nigel's eyebrows tended to move up and down as he talked, and it was becoming much more pronounced with age, especially when he became excited, as he was now.

"With the armorial, eighty-five thousand dollars at the least. You say you don't know whose arms those are?"

I shook my head.

"No matter. We'll put Rosalind on it. Her specialty, you know. Now. Let's make the estimate—Hmmmm. No. Let's don't."

Nigel paused to do the math in his head. "Sixty-five to seventy thousand. Yes. There. That's better. Estimate, sixty-five to seventy thousand," he repeated to himself. "That will entice the bidders. Make them think they can get a bargain. They'll fall all over themselves to get in on the bottom floor. But when the lift goes up, it will be too late." He laughed with unabashed glee.

Like most upper-class Englishmen, Nigel's teeth never showed when he talked. I'd often wondered if the Brits practiced curling their upper lip over their teeth so they can speak that way or if their teeth were just shorter.

Nigel leaned far across the desk. "Sterling, you have no idea how hard it has been to get in really good pieces of late. When stocks slump, the rich want to buy. Trouble is, collectors don't want to sell. They hold on to what they have like it's their last bottle of wine," he said. "Just last week, I spent a full day out on Long Island trying to convince a family to sell some of the pieces their great-grandfather had bought during the Great Depression. They laughed at me. Makes it rather difficult to do business."

Nigel inched to the front of his chair. "They said his antiques investments had been better than their stock investments. One of them went so far as to buy another period Georgian side chair instead of a thousand shares of IBM." He straightened up. "So I greatly appreciate your bringing this to me. You can be sure Charlie Buckingham and Erik Freedman will be bidding against one another." His eyebrows danced in anticipation of the auction.

Buckingham, a self-made American millionaire many times over, owned a fleet of houses strung out across the world. Either *Town and Country* or *Architectural Digest* did a feature on one of his homes every couple of years and he was always looking for a new silver piece for the next dining-room shot. The urn was the sort of piece Charlie Buckingham loved. Put it between beautiful candelabra made by Matthew Boulton on a mahogany Regency sideboard, and it was a made-in-heaven center spread, maybe even the cover.

Erik Freedman was the personal buyer for some of Hollywood's biggest stars. No one ever knew who he was buying for. Recently, he'd picked up several major English silver pieces, and he'd told Nigel to be on the lookout for more.

"Hmmm. Yes. Well. Then there's Sinclair and Sinclair," Nigel added, referring to the famed Manhattan silver gallery owned by British tradesmen whose great-great-great-grandfather and uncles had been purveyors for Queen Victoria's court.

"The other day the younger Sinclair was asking if any Storr pieces were surfacing. Said their inventory was getting low." Nigel ran his fingers around the gadrooning on the tea urn.

"Funny about him," Rhodes said, caressing the body of the urn while he spoke. "That youngster has a sixth sense. He must be able to smell the silver coming out of hiding. Guess it's in his genes."

Nigel abruptly jerked his head up and turned his attention back to me.

"Hmmm. Yes. Well," he repeated in his British way. "Now tell me how you came on this. There hasn't been an urn this fine offered at auction on either side of the ocean in more than a decade. Why, we haven't even talked about the U.K. collectors. Hmmm. Yes. Well. Depending on whose armorial that is, Sterling, it's conceivable it could break the hundred-thousand-dollar mark." He smiled broadly.

I looked for Nigel's teeth but still couldn't see them.

"That would be nice. And it would make a nice finder's fee for you," he said, raising one eyebrow as he spoke. I let the comment pass.

"So. We'll wait to see what Rosalind finds out about the *original* owner." Nigel drummed his fingers on his desk. "Are you sure there wasn't anything else? Any more silver," he baited, looking over his half glasses as he filled out the transaction papers.

I paused, debating whether to mention the brooch. Nigel dropped his eyes, shifted the papers again. "Wouldn't want you taking something else over to my good buddy Pennell Evans."

Pennell Evans was head of the silver department at Layton's competitor, Rosenberg Galleries.

Nigel pushed the paperwork across the desk toward me.

"No other silver," I said, still thinking about the diamond pin.

Rhodes hesitated for half a moment as if about to speak, then pointed to the agreement. "Just sign there, Sterling, and we're off to the races. This treasure is headed straight to the storeroom for safekeeping. Don't worry, I'll keep my eye on her."

But my mind was on the brooch that I hadn't told the bank about either. At least not yet. I had thought about mentioning it to Roy when I had called him on Monday. But his secretary said that Roy had been unexpectedly called away and would be out of the office until sometime Wednesday afternoon. On Wednesday, I learned his plane had been delayed because of winter weather in Chicago. His secretary didn't know when he'd get back. I was flying out on the 7:05 Thursday morning flight and wouldn't return to Leemont until the next Monday night. In truth, I was relieved to have extra time to think things over.

"Yes. Well. Well, that about does it," Nigel was saying as he filed the signed documents away. "Say, do you have a little time? If so, why don't you come with me while I put this beauty in her new home? Have you ever seen our back room?"

"No."

"Come along then."

I followed him.

It was a glorious sight. From floor to ceiling, in bin after bin, were rare and valuable objects—some from time immemorial, some from more recent times, each a silent reminder of a bygone day. Now they sat, waiting to be taken to a new home. We moved past row after row of china, crystal, ivory and jade, brass, and silver fashioned into every item you could imagine, or so it seemed to me. "Ah. Here we are."

Nigel placed the urn in the bin between a very simple, very fine circa 1770 Sheffield silver cake basket and an elaborately

pierced sterling silver epergne made some twenty years later.
Together, the three looked very much at home.

"I could spend hours in here," I said.

"Better than a museum."

"Especially without any DO NOT TOUCH signs. But I know
you have better things to do, Nigel. Thank you for the tour."

"Anytime. Just bring me another piece like that one. And if
you need anything at all, call me." Nigel extended his hand in
a courtly way that seemed perfectly natural, especially in this
rarefied setting.

We stepped out into the hall and straight into the path of
Dana Henchloe, one of my least favorite people in the antiques
world. He worked for Layton's as a regional associate. The
privileged few who held those highly coveted positions were
well connected blue bloods who spent their time traveling from
state to state, giving lectures at minor museums and attending
gallery galas, to scout out material for their New York auctions. Dana Henchloe was based over in Nashville, which was
how I'd come to know him. Every month or so he'd call, asking if I knew of any good estates coming up, or if I'd seen any
great steals in Leemont. I'd hinted that if I did know of such, I
was perfectly capable of handling the job. But Dana was one of
those sneaky sorts who would look you straight in the eye
while he so deftly stabbed you in the back that you didn't even
feel the wound. Until two weeks later, when you heard about
the damage from somebody else.

Years ago he'd cajoled me into telling him where a fabulous
Chippendale mirror was going to be sold once the old and
dying owner went to her reward. Which was imminent. Dana
wormed his way into her house under false pretenses and

worked a deal with the matriarch's companion. The mirror left the premises before her body did.

The next time we met was at a cocktail party. Fortified by a couple of drinks, I told Dana what I thought of his underhanded ways. Since then there's been no love lost between the two of us.

"Well, if it isn't Sterling Glass," Dana said in his best country-club voice. "Haven't seen you for a while," he added condescendingly, insinuating that I hadn't been invited to the same exclusive events he'd been to. "Oh, yes. That reminds me. Nigel, by the way, I've got a few more goodies coming out of that *Virginia* estate I've been sending to you. Wish they'd let the whole thing go, but it's just coming out piecemeal." He smiled my way.

I wanted to throw up.

"Yes. Well. I'm seeing Sterling out right now. We'll talk about it later," Nigel said.

At least *he* was a gentleman.

TIME HAD FLOWN. Before I knew it, I realized I needed to get a cab if I was going to make it to Brooklyn to see Sol Hobstein. He and I had finally made contact late Monday. When I mentioned that I was on my way to New York, he persuaded me it would be worth my time, financially and professionally, to see his mysterious molds. I still wasn't exactly sure just what it was that he had.

Chapter 6

Dear Antiques Expert: Up in the attic of my 97-year-old father's home we found a box of pink tumblers and salad plates and a green water pitcher wrapped up in old newspaper from the 1950s. Though they are different colors, the pieces appear to be the same pattern. My sister-in-law says these are Depression glass. Do they have any value?

In ancient times glass was as valuable as gold, but since 19th-century glassmakers learned how to pour molten glass into molds, "pressed glass" has been inexpensive. Your sister-in-law is right; yours is "Depression glass" from the late 1920s or 1930s. In the 1970s and 1980s Depression glass became so popular it was reproduced, which killed the market. Yet some patterns remain valuable. Consult a Depression-glass price guide to identify your specific pattern and gauge its value. The glasses may only be worth a few dollars, but the pitcher might be worth considerably more.

I'D PLANNED TO catch a cab on Madison Avenue, but when snow flurries began to fall I hiked over to Lexington. With the snow came an early dusk. As if they were synchronized, as the streetlights came on the snowflakes quickened, shimmering like tiny silver sequins. Between the threat of more snow to come and the approaching late-afternoon rush hour, every uptown cab was whizzing toward midtown to catch a fare. I stepped off the curb and waved my arm at the sea of yellow lemmings streaming south. Two drivers spied me at the same time. One cut across the path of the other and pulled up beside me.

"One Winston Place," I said, adding, "in Brooklyn."

Around Seventieth Street, Lexington Avenue changed from high-end art and antiques galleries to clothing boutiques, shoe stores, and delis. In the brightly lighted boutique windows, ski bunnies competed with snowbirds. The left-hand side of the street favored Moosejaw alpine parkas. On the right, $250 yellow bikinis splashed with strategically placed hibiscus blossoms beckoned. *Filho dental,* dental floss, they called those thong bikinis in Brazil. Vermont or Ipanema? And I was on my way to Brooklyn.

The cab swerved suddenly, cut across traffic, and turned onto East Sixty-first Street over to FDR Drive to make better time. We wove from one lane to the next across the Brooklyn Bridge, leaving the glamour of the city behind. In silence we drove past neighborhood stores along Columbia Street. A few turns later we slowed to a crawl and then a stop.

Nine- and ten-story factory buildings were slammed up against one another. Even on a bright sunny day this would be a dark street. There was just room enough between the buildings for the fire escapes jutting out along their sides. Memories of the 1911 Triangle Shirtwaist Factory fire in lower Manhattan flashed across my mind. Now considered eyesores, those fire escapes had been mandated after scores of young immigrants, mostly Jewish girls, locked into crowded sewing rooms filled with highly combustible cotton fabric, had leapt to their deaths. There had been no TV cameras to bring the tragedy into America's bedrooms back then. Did that make the tragedy greater or less, I wondered.

The dark of the night, the white of the snow, and the quiet of the street gave me an eerie feeling.

"One Winston Place." The cabbie pointed to the ticking meter. "Twenty-two eighty-five."

My instincts told me to stay put in the cab with this man I'd never seen before and head straight back to Manhattan. Instead I asked for a receipt and began counting out the money I owed him.

"How do I get back?" I asked.

"Cab, I guess. How long you be?"

"Too long for you to wait. Thanks."

I got out and stood on the corner in this silent, cold place. The cab's red taillights were the only sign of life on the block and they were fading into the darkness. It was the snowflakes and me. So much for the romance of the moment. I felt like the poor little match girl, without the matches. God, how I hated it when Mother read that story to me, especially around Christmastime. I looked heavenward. A sudden snow burst spewed down, stinging my cheeks. I gathered my Virginia-winter tweed coat about me as tightly as possible. Damn, it was cold. Not only was the temperature rapidly dropping, the sidewalk was becoming slippery as the snowflakes melted, then refroze. Black ice they called it, and rightfully so. I inched close to the building to have something to catch myself against in case my feet skidded out from under me, then made my way to the concrete-framed doorway only a few feet away. The steps were even more slippery than the sidewalk. I reached out for the iron railing, and my gloved hand slid right off. I grabbed it with a firmer grip.

I leaned long on the doorbell once, then twice. I waited. I raised my hand to knock, and then I realized that if Sol Hobstein couldn't hear the doorbell, he surely wouldn't hear me knock. I thought about taking a shoe off to bang on the door, but my feet were already freezing. As I pressed the bell again, bright lights flooded the doorway, disorienting me all the more. Bolts and chains clanked on the other side, and I squinted in an attempt to better see the man standing opposite me.

"About to give up on you."

I heard the wheezing and knew it had to be Sol Hobstein. Obviously he was out of breath from his walk to the door. He stuck his head out into the newly fallen night. "Hmmm . . . snow. Sticking? Come in."

Only then did he move to one side, making room for me to slip past him and into the narrow corridor. Even lighted, the grungy interior was dark and gloomy.

Solomon Hobstein had once been of medium height, but his shoulders were bent with age. He looked to be in his late seventies, maybe early eighties. Despite the many folds around his deep gray eyes and the loose jowls, his high forehead was wrinkle-free. His face retained traces of that lean, finely chiseled bone structure common to so many northern European Jewish men. He surely had been extraordinarily handsome when he was young.

Methodically Sol Hobstein began redoing the bolts and chains.

"Come on back."

He led, and I followed his shuffle. Sol Hobstein's gray hair spilled over his frayed collar onto his sweater that hiked up high in the back, partly from its age and partly from the slope of his shoulders. He was dressed in the old, gentleman-like style, a white shirt and tie beneath his sweater—the appropriate attire for an overseer or supervisor in the factories of a long-ago time. Other than my grandfather who had died years before, I hadn't seen anyone wearing plaid polyester pants since I was a little girl. An unexpected tinge of nostalgia swept over me.

Slowly, my anxiety about being in this place with a stranger faded, only to be replaced with curiosity. Crates and boxes were stacked three and four deep along the walls and in the middle of the vast space. Some were covered with plastic. Others appeared unsealed—empty perhaps? Waiting to be packed? As we walked past, I tried to make out the black printing on the side, but it was impossible in the faint light. Rolls of brown and white wrapping paper lay scattered about on the floor. The whole place had a rank and musty smell.

Hobstein ushered me into his office, a small space, considering the size of the building that obviously now was being used as a warehouse. A single lamp on his desk lighted the room. He pointed it in my direction. Clearly, it was so he could see me better.

"Yes. You have an honest face," he said, his deep-set eyes squinting at me. Satisfied, he motioned to a gray metal chair across from his desk. "Sit."

He remained standing until I was seated. A gentlemanly thing to do, I thought.

"What do you know about Kidders?" Sol Hobstein asked me once he'd seated himself.

"The repro company?"

He nodded.

"They're a pretty big operation," I said. "I see their stuff all around. Export-type bowls, fake Sevres vases . . . a few Capo di Monte figurines. Mostly porcelain, at least what I've seen. I've heard they've started to bring out some Depression-glass patterns using old molds they bought. Some construction workers found the originals in a building being razed to build a parking deck."

"You saw the story, too." Hobstein grinned. He took a Camel out of a pack from among the piles of papers. "Trying to break the habit," he said.

He put the unlighted cigarette in his mouth and coughed long and hard, his stooped shoulders shaking.

"If I recall correctly," I said, "the new pieces are a slightly different color from the original glass," I said. "A serious collector or dealer would know the difference, but Joe Blow wouldn't. But even the real pieces aren't *that* expensive. The fakes sell for as much as the real pieces, and it's not that much. Twenty-five, thirty-five dollars. Maybe up to a couple of hundred for a rare piece. It's not like it was a big scandal—like a fake Picasso selling for a million, or a nineteenth-century Chippendale-style chair being sold as an eighteenth-century period piece for fifty thousand. There are so many expensive fakes being sold out there, I don't think anything ever came of the glass pieces being made from the old molds. The way I remember it, the story was more about the construction workers finding the molds and a historic marker going up on the site of the old factory than it was about another fake coming on the market."

"Well, young lady. It's okay for *you* to think the pieces aren't worth that much. But I'll tell you, those thirty-fives and fifties add up. Sometimes to a fortune. Especially when you have the original molds." Above the dark circles, Sol Hobstein's deep-set eyes twinkled. "And that's what I have."

"Glass molds?"

"Something much better. Much finer."

He rose from his desk, pulled out a Bic from his pocket, flicked it aimlessly, then put the cigarette and lighter down. "Come with me," he said.

We retraced our steps through the storeroom, but this time we turned to the right.

"Mr. Hobstein, did you ever hear of the Triangle Shirtwaist Factory fire?"

"Yes. Some people still talk of it. The old ones. They had friends or sisters, or knew of someone who died in the fire. Why do you ask?"

"My great-grandfather was visiting in New York when it happened. He never stopped talking about how he'd heard the sirens wailing in the sunset hour and on into the cold night that March day. His whole life long he told stories of how the trapped girls jumped to their deaths. The useless loss of all those innocent young women's lives must have touched him very deeply. I just wondered if that story still lives on, especially now, after the Twin Towers tragedy."

"Yes, the story lives, but not much longer. When the last ones who heard the story, like you did, are gone, it will die. It is in the past," he said, dismissing the event that I would have thought would be meaningful to him.

We came to the end of the long corridor. Standing before double doors, Solomon Hobstein removed a watch chain from his pants pocket. At the end hung a Star of David and three keys. He took one in hand.

"It will be dark and cold in there. Your eyes will adjust. Mine do. One day I'm going to get Joey to help me get the ladder and replace the bulbs."

He turned the key and pushed firmly against the door.

"I'll go first. Wait for me to call you."

As the door creaked open, I saw that the floor sloped down, like a ramp, into a vast darkness. Sol Hobstein proceeded more sure-footedly and quickly than when he had walked across the flat floor. I stopped myself from calling out words of caution.

"Almost there. Let me make a light."

Fluorescent bulbs flicked on and off until they caught.

"Wait. There's another one," he said. In the silence I heard another light switch click on. "There."

A row of bare lightbulbs hanging down from the rafters added a few more dim watts to the room.

"You can come down now."

There was no hand railing and I teetered along the slope the same way I had on the icy sidewalk. Sol Hobstein was waiting for me at the bottom, his wrinkled hand extended. I don't know whose palm was colder or quivering more, his or mine. I grasped his hand and stepped onto flat ground.

"Careful now," Hobstein warned, his voice suddenly youthful in excitement.

Heeding his words, I looked down to see where to step next. When I did, I let out a gasp.

By my feet, pieces of bodies lay twisted and tangled around one another. White arms and legs were scattered on the concrete floor. Delicately molded heads separated from their torsos peered out at me from a cardboard box placed off to one side. Another box held more arms and legs jumbled around one another. A few feet away, on a card table, like Rockettes waiting for their cue, stood a half-dozen or so fully assembled female figures. Around their feet lay miniature tambourines, umbrellas, spheres, balls. On yet another table stood male figures, mostly classical sporting types, surrounded by spears and disks and javelins.

I turned. Behind me, on a slab of sheet metal supported by sawed-off four-by-fours were parts and pieces of full, lifelike figurines laid out with spaces in between—like pieces of so many puzzles, waiting for someone to match them up. Scattered about were threaded bolts and squared-off nuts.

The surreal scene was reminiscent of the horrific pictures I had mulled over in the old World War II *Life* magazines that I'd found in my grandparents' basement so many long years ago. I was just five or six. I was supposed to be napping, the way all Southern children did in the hot summertime. But I had crept off the pallet Mother had made in my grandparents' home and slipped down into the basement. It was there, in a far corner, that I had discovered the stacks of magazines carefully piled in orderly fashion, week by week, year by year. Pictures of the victims of the gas chambers had made an indelible impression.

Mr. Hobstein's soft chuckle brought me back to the present.

I looked around me. The monetary worth of the treasures all around me was staggering. No wonder he was so gleeful.

I leaned over and carefully picked up first one, then another, of the heads from the box. Aesthetically each tiny face was exquisitely formed—the demure smiles, the pouting lips, the playful looks, the impish eyes, the victorious countenances. All were little masterpieces. Each face depicted human emotions frozen in time. Each was crafted by some long-forgotten hand.

"Aren't they beautiful?" the old gentleman asked, his voice full of reverence and awe.

Mother's voice rang in my head as her favorite lines from Keats's "Ode on a Grecian Urn" drifted into my consciousness.

For ever warm and still to be enjoy'd,
For ever panting, and for ever young; . . .
When old age shall this generation waste,
Thou shalt remain . . .
. . . a friend to man, to whom thou say'st,
"Beauty is truth, truth beauty" . . .

"Beautiful? Truly. And wonderful. They're wonderful," I whispered.

"And there are *hundreds* of them!" Mr. Hobstein raised his arms as gracefully as a ballet dancer. "I've been working for days, weeks, months, trying to put a few together," he said, picking up one of the bolts and slipping it up through a slim female torso. "It's not easy."

I wanted to linger, to take in the wonder of all that was around me. I had to savor this rare and important discovery.

Chapter 7

Dear Antiques Expert: I've just started getting interested in antiques but I really love the Art Deco style. On a recent TV show about antiques, the appraiser identified a European piece as Art Nouveau. Is that the same thing as Art Deco?

Art Deco's straight, angular lines are much more familiar than the loose, curvy lines of the Art Nouveau style, particularly in America. Art Nouveau furniture, jewelry, and metalwork became popular in Europe at the end of the 19th century but never caught on in the United States. The exception was the Art Nouveau "woman," as depicted by the American illustrator Charles Dana Gibson. His drawings of beautiful women with long flowing hair became the American "ideal" and were called "Gibson girls." Otherwise, the Art Nouveau style must have been too sensuous for America's turn-of-the-century Puritan-rooted mind-set.

"IT ALL STARTED BACK in the old country," Sol Hobstein began. "My grandfather Karl was just a young man when he showed great artistic talent. He was sent from our little village in Alsace-Lorraine to Berlin. There he studied sculpture with the greats of the time. He advanced very quickly and soon his works were being exhibited in the great Salon shows in Paris."

"When was this?" I asked.

"Ah." He rubbed his chin. "The first time, I believe, was probably in the early 1890s. He showed there often. And won medals of honor. Never the Grand Prix, but many other awards. It was in Paris that he met my grandmother, Aimée. She was as talented as he. More. They married and together they made these figurines for the finest homes in Europe. They were smart people, businesspeople as well as artists. Not only were they creative designers and carvers, they had a foundry where the figures were made. Together, Karl and Aimée took such care and pride in their work that other artists brought them their creations to produce. My family's molds were considered the best. That's how I came to have this treasure."

Sol Hobstein beamed with pride. He walked, danced almost, to a far table and returned with a small sculpture of a woman no more than eight or nine inches high. Her long hair enveloped her, accenting every feminine curve. The details of her body were covered by provocative, beautifully sculpted folds resembling sheer fabric.

"Aimée was also a jeweler. She loved to adorn the little figures she made with silver and gold when a commission from a duke or even a king would come in. See the tiny amethysts?" His index finger bent crooked with arthritis, Hobstein pointed to the deep blue-purple stones set for her eyes.

"Oh!" I leaned over for a closer look and marveled at the craftsmanship it had taken to create this Art Nouveau figure of bronze and ivory, made more fetching and feminine by the perfection of every detail.

Sol Hobstein smiled at my reaction. Then he frowned.

"Yes. All was fine until Archduke Franz Ferdinand was assassinated. Everything changed. The war was all around. My family feared for their business and for themselves, but,"—he smiled again, and handed the little figurine to me, squeezing my hand affectionately as he did so—"ah, Aimée was very, very good. Her talents were so great that she and my grandfather, and by then my father and uncle, were given shelter by politically powerful patrons. That, my dear, is where the story begins. At least the story of what you see here." His aged eyes lovingly swept the room.

I smiled back at him, trying to convey that his trust in me was well placed.

"Night after night, they went out into the dark, Karl and Aimée. There, together, they dug a deep pit," he continued, his voice hushed. "Before they left for *their* safe place, they made a safe place for these little treasures. When the war was over they returned home. Soon business returned, but life had changed. Fashions had changed. But you know all that," he said, speeding his life's story forward in a simple sentence. "So Aimée and Karl set to work making figures in the new style— Art Deco."

Again Hobstein crossed the room. This time he returned with a larger figure, one of a dancer perched on an onyx base, balanced on the ball of one foot, her other leg drawn high beneath her. Her arms were outstretched, reaching far into the air. She was scantily dressed in a halter and shorts, her hair covered by a tight-fitting cap, a chorus girl from the twenties.

I laughed in amusement at the coquettish brazenness of the figure.

"You like this style better," he said, handing her to me.

"Not really. I'm an appraiser, remember. Appraisers can't have personal tastes, or if we do, we can't let them get in the way of our professional judgment. We're only allowed to pass unbiased judgment on quality. That's what determines a fair value for each piece, Mr. Hobstein. Quality," I said, all the while turning the figure over and over. "I'm simply enthralled, seeing all this, so many wonderful figures all at one time. The contrast in the styles. The beauty of the figures. It's, it's—"

"Amazing. *Wunderbar!*" He finished my sentence, paused, and then said, "Ah. You're right, you know. What you just said there about the contrast in the styles." He rubbed his chin, nodded his head, and said, "It really *is* interesting to see the Art Nouveau and the Art Deco together, isn't it?" as if he were seeing his own treasures through new eyes.

"Remember, what I told you," Hobstein said, "Aimée and Karl enjoyed such a fine reputation that other sculptors came to them. Not all these pieces were made by just my family. Why the piece you're holding looks much like ones made by Fritz Preiss and Professor Poertzel. Who made which figure? Who made this one, that one?" He shrugged. "So many records have been lost or destroyed over the years."

"I'm sure." I felt helpless to comfort him. "And so many of the figures lost, too. But you have a treasure trove. I'm close to speechless, Mr. Hobstein. You wouldn't know it, but that's saying a lot for me."

"These, too, were almost among the lost," the old gentleman said, eagerly motioning toward the Art Deco figures grouped together across the room, "had it not been for my grandparents' earlier experience. Once again when the war came too close, the family hid those, too. The tunnel already was there. They fitted what they could into the space."

"And your family?" I asked hesitantly.

"Aimée was French, remember. She was old when the second war came but still revered. It was the French who helped them, and other Jews, this time," he said. "Not everyone in our family made it, but that is past now. This"—he swept the room with a wide gesture—"*this* is my heritage."

His remark didn't surprise me. I'd found time and time again that people who cherished their material possessions as part of their cultural past were more apt to live in the present than those who claimed their family's genealogy as proof that they were somebody.

"This is my legacy. These figures," he said. "And the molds. They are very precious. Some are made of porcelain. They are packed away very carefully and safely. Now, Ms. Glass, you will help me?"

"How?"

"To know what the molds are worth, so I can tell Kidders how much money I want for them," he said impatiently.

"That's not a figure I can give you right off the top of my head, Mr. Hobstein. There are questions that must be answered first. How many molds do you have?"

"Sol. Call me Sol. You've seen my life, my soul." He gestured around the room, then clasped his hands over his heart. "I should be Sol to you. How many molds? How do I know?" He shrugged.

"And I need to find out if other old molds have been sold. If they have been, for how much. It's not a simple matter. And then, we can't forget the value of the figures as well."

I shivered, partly from the cold and partly from the mixed excitement and strangeness of the situation that I did not clearly grasp yet, other than to know it was remarkable.

"Let us go back to my office," he said, seemingly content that he had shown me what he needed to. It was then that I remembered what I had forgotten in the thrill of the moment.

"Oh! Mr. Hobstein. Sol. The snow."

"Yes. I forgot. The snow. And you, a Southerner. Yes. Hurry. We'd better move on."

WE GATHERED OUR things from Sol's office and made our way through the dim coldness to the front door. Somewhat miraculously, as nightfall had descended, the snow clouds had moved off to the east and a full moon shone brightly.

"So. The snow has stopped. But it is late. We must leave now that you have seen my treasure. It is great. Yes? You will find answers for me. Yes?" Sol asked as he locked and double locked the heavy gray door.

"Yes?" he repeated.

I nodded in agreement. I was too cold to talk. My jaw was beginning to shiver from the piercing wind.

"Remember now, I have figures and I have molds to make more," Sol said like a child, eager to impress me with his toys. "Some of both have been broken over the years. But enough remain." His smile showed his satisfaction.

Arm in arm, Sol and I walked slowly into the dark. The thin layer of icy snow crackled under our feet. We moved toward the corner three blocks away where he said I would find a cab. Eventually.

"If I sell all the surviving molds to Kidders, many will be lost in no time. Ones they do not like," Sol continued, thinking ahead. "My little figures' molds have made it through two wars and the ocean crossing, in . . . when was that now? Nineteen fifty. Yes. So many years ago. For what? Only to be lost now."

The little man stopped to cough and catch his breath in the cold night air. He was still wheezing when his eyes met mine. "Look, I know they can't reproduce all the figures. And I'll have no say over which ones they use. I know which ones are the best ones, but they wouldn't be interested in quality. Only quantity. What the public likes." The more agitated and upset he became, the harder he coughed. "What the public will buy. But these are my *family*. Then again," he said hesitatingly, stopping his own tirade, "I should be glad that any are saved. Times have changed. Yes. 'The old order changeth.' "

"Yielding place to new," I said, finishing the Tennyson line.

Calmer now, Sol smiled at me. "I see the lady is as learned in literature as she is in antiques."

"Thanks to my mother. She loved literature." I thought twice, but then spoke my thoughts anyway. "But I'm surprised *you* know English literature," I said shyly.

"Like my little treasures, great words are universal, my dear."

Sol began trudging along again but more slowly now.

"Music, art, literature . . . Antiques. My father, Julius, Karl and Aimée's son, once told me, when you know antiques, you know everything—history, technology, culture. Ah, Sterling, people who think objects are only things have missed a beautiful part of life. Antiques are a reflection, a mirror, of our lives and the lives of those who have gone before us. I know."

Sol's words caught me totally off guard. "That's lovely, Mr. Hobstein," I said, fighting back tears brought on by the stinging cold, but more so by what he'd said.

"Look, now," Sol said brightly, beginning to pick up his pace. "I walked this way to show you something. We cross here."

We held gloved hands as we crossed the deserted street. The snow was perhaps no more than a half-inch deep but treacherous nonetheless. My feet had not warmed or dried from their earlier soaking, plus I was scared that at any moment my companion would slip. I knew I wouldn't be able to break his fall. A broken bone was all we needed under the circumstances. Thankfully, I heard traffic rolling by a block or so away. Unaware of my fears, Sol forged ahead, leading me along until we came to a dimly lighted building.

"Arnold's. You see?" He pointed to the name arched across the window. "Joe Arnold is my friend. He, too, came from Europe. With a different name." He laughed, which started another cough. "We all did in this neighborhood," he said once he had regained his breath. "Young Joey runs his father's business now. So we just call it Joey's. Used to be just antiques. These days he sells what comes in and what people will buy. Look. See?"

The front window was dimly lighted by a bay of ceiling lights inside the shop. Quite a contrast to the gleaming store windows of Manhattan so nearby.

Pressing my forehead against the cold glass, I made out a mismatched collected edition of Mark Twain's works held up between a pair of old bookends shaped like violins. Next to them were a couple of old Avon bottles, a Nippon teapot, and what had to be a fake Tiffany lamp. I'd seen that Tiffany-imitation pattern in an antiques shop back in Leemont. Someone—Joey, I presumed—had tried to give the display a little artistic flair, but he didn't have much to work with.

Behind the front window, the floor was cluttered with used furniture. Just what I expected.

"See it?" Sol asked.

I squinted, partly so I could see better, partly against the cold. "See? Ah." I scanned the display shelf, wondering what I was supposed to see. Then, in the far dark right hand corner I made out a bronze sculpture of a woman lying on its side.

"Isn't she beautiful," Sol said. " 'Scheherazade.' "

My mother had taken me to New York to see a lavish production of Rimsky-Korsakov's ballet *Scheherazade* when I was a child. I had later learned how the Art Deco sculptors were inspired by the ballet to create figures inspired by the dancers' exotic Persian costumes. These days those very figurines could fetch tens of thousands of dollars—and more—at the large international auction houses.

"She's the best of all," Sol was saying. "We just put her in the window yesterday, there with the other ones. They're nice, but they're not 'Scheherazade.' She's the best."

"I'm sure she is. Perhaps she fell over?" I only saw the one figure. Maybe the others he mentioned had been sold, but I didn't get a chance to mention that.

"What?"

"Perhaps she fell. She's not standing up. She's, well, see? She's on her side." I stepped back to make room for him to stand where I was.

"I don't understand. Joey would never let something happen to her. Not *her*."

"Oh, I don't think anything's wrong," I said reassuringly. "I don't think she's damaged. Perhaps she just toppled over."

Sol cupped his hands around his eyes and peered through the window. "Something is *wrong*. The others. Where are the other figures?" He turned to me. "What time is it?"

"A little past seven."

"I thought it was later." The fear in Sol's voice matched the look in his eyes. He clasped my arm. "Joey. Where's Joey? Do you have one of those . . . those phones?" Sol put his hand to his ear as if talking on a cell phone. "He never closes up till eight."

He turned and went to the door. He punched the doorbell, then frantically yanked at the knob on the iron bars.

"Joey. Something's happened to him."

A sick feeling started in my throat and crept down through my body. My legs went numb, except it felt like a million sharp needles were exploding inside of them.

"Do you want me to call someone?" I managed to whisper.

By now Sol was breathing so hard that once again I was frightened for him. "The back. Go to the back." He pointed into the dark. "No. Wait. I'll come."

My own heart was racing. "Should I call 911?"

"No. Come."

Sol started around to the side of the building. I had no choice but to follow him.

Chapter 8

Dear Antiques Expert: After my brothers and sisters and I selected what we wanted from our parents' home, a lot of items were left over. When the antiques dealer came to purchase these things we were surprised to learn that some things we thought were really valuable weren't and conversely, the value of some things we thought were giveaways astounded us. What really makes one piece more valuable than another?

Yours is a common experience. To accurately value an antique, remember this tip: age + condition + quality + rarity = value. Truly valuable antiques must meet all four criteria. For example, a poor-quality, commonly found piece in bad condition will not be valuable, regardless of its age. And even a fine antique in excellent condition won't be extremely valuable unless it is rare. Also remember that antiques have fashions, like hemline lengths and hairstyles. That's why, to learn the real value of an antique, it's wise to consult someone who is knowledgeable about current values as well as a particular object.

BACK HOME I would have said I was scared shitless. But I wasn't back home. I was in Brooklyn. I didn't even know how scared I was.

In the pitch-black darkness I groped along behind Sol, his heavy wheezing my compass. I stumbled about, navigating around pieces of broken pavement that jutted up beneath my frozen feet at my every step. We rounded the corner into the cobblestone alleyway behind Joey's shop. Thanks to the light-bulb burning above the back door, at least I could see. But considering that it was just this old man and me, or so I hoped, in this menacing place, the light was little consolation.

Sol went first, motioning to me to hurry along.

Fighting the urge to hang back, or run away, I reluctantly followed. At the back door, Sol fumbled beneath his heavy overcoat to get to his key chain.

"I have Joey's key," Sol was hissing between wheezes when the screen door flew open, hurling him back against the building.

Sol gasped and I shrieked as a thick black shape swept past us and darted into the alley.

"Sol. Sol. Are you all right? Sol?"

Bracing himself flat against the building, the old man looked pitiful and helpless. I expected him to slump forward at any moment.

"Joey." He struggled to catch his breath. "We have to find Joey."

He moved forward unsteadily, pushing back the screen door. It made a hollow sound against the cold bricks. Acting on instinct, I reached out to catch him, but he thrust my hand aside.

"I'm okay. Come." He stumbled across the threshold into the dingy shop. Inside, he wove his way along aisles of furniture piled high.

"Joey. Where are you? Are you all right? Joey. Joey?"

Each time Sol called Joey's name, his voice faltered, until he was almost crying out.

"Shouldn't I call someone?" I said.

Sol shook his head vehemently. "No."

I hung back while Sol forged ahead, groping his way in the dim light. Then I saw two shoes dangling just above the floor. I stifled a scream, but my fearful gasp echoed through the quietness. Sol heard it and whirled around.

Sol saw what I saw. He threw himself forward, clutching at pieces of furniture for support. "No. Joey."

Joey lay sprawled out in an overstuffed La-Z-Boy in its full reclining position, his feet dangling off the footrest. He stared straight at us, his mouth open, his lip bloody and swelling, his eyes glazed. He raised one arm as if to point to where his assailant had fled.

"Are you all right? Did he hurt you?"

I steadied myself against a tall chest of drawers and began searching around the bottom of my pocketbook, trying to find my cell phone.

"Please, Sol. *Please* let me call someone."

Joey looked first at me and then at Sol. He shook his head.

"Why not?"

Joey shook his head again, this time not to protest, but to bring himself around. He held on to the chair arms and strained into a semi-upright position. He was so diminutive that he seemed swallowed up by the cushy velour of the chair. Sol pushed the footrest down, bringing the chair up straight. With his help, Joey slid up to the edge of the chair. Seeing the slight young man, I thought that only the most heartless criminal could want to do him harm. His growth of dark stubble didn't make him look tough, just unkempt. In truth, a stiff breeze would've knocked him over.

"Water," Sol commanded, as he pulled a handkerchief from his pocket to dab the blood running down Joey's chin. I looked around in vain for a glass or one of those upside-down water jugs or a spigot.

"The desk." Sol pointed to it just a few feet away.

On Joey's desk lay another one of Sol's beloved figures, this one broken. Her ivory arm lay a short distance from her body. Near it was the tambourine she had once held in her hand. There, too, a water pitcher was knocked over, the glass broken. Books were scattered about. Obviously there had been a scuffle and Joey had been on the receiving end. If his attacker had a scratch or a bruise, it was only because he had hit poor Joey, not because Joey had put up any resistance.

"I think he took the figures, the ones in the window," Joey moaned as the old man helped him to his feet. "I didn't know what to do." He looked as pitiful as he sounded. "I'm sorry, Sol," Joey said, swaying forward. "I told him he couldn't take the figures. Not without paying."

"Sit back down and forget the figures, Joey. It's you that's important. How badly are you hurt?"

"He only hit me once." Joey chuckled softly. "All it took, Sol. All it took." He touched his lip ever go gently. "Ouch." Leaning forward, Joey opened his mouth as best he could. "My teeth?" he asked.

Sol laughed. "They're there. Wouldn't take much to put you away, little man."

I was so relieved at the lighter turn in the conversation that I sighed out loud. Hearing me, they looked my way.

"The water's spilled. The glass is broken." I threw my hands up in the air.

Sol's eyes rested on the broken figure. "Bring her to me," Sol said.

I picked up the figure and the pieces and put them in his outstretched hand.

"Who do you think did it?" I asked Joey. "What happened?"

"It all happened fast. So fast. I was in the back when I heard the doorbell ring. I came up to the front of the store and buzzed him in. Thought I recognized him. He started asking about the figures and walked over to the front window. I followed him, but he didn't wait for me. He reached right in, took two of them out. That one"—he pointed to the broken figure—"and another one. I told him to be careful. Do you think *that* was my mistake?" he asked as he raised his hand to his mouth again.

It was then I noticed Joey's huge ring. Four wide rows of diamond chips were set down deep between high parallel gold ridges. The ring covered his ring finger from his middle knuckle to his fist. The sides were so thick that his third and fifth fingers were spread apart, making his hand appear deceptively large.

"What happened then?" Sol asked.

"He wanted to know how much they were, so I started over toward my desk to look up the prices. I didn't want to cheat you, Sol."

Sol shook his head sadly. "Go on."

"I starting looking up the prices and he put one of the figures down. I guess it was that one." Joey motioned toward the broken one. "That's when I think I heard the doorbell again," he added.

Sol gave me a knowing glance. His calmness was reassuring. "That was us," he said.

"He grabbed at me and asked where I was getting them. It

all happened so fast. That worried me. I didn't want him to see the list. I thought fast, didn't I? I didn't want him to know, so I told him I didn't know, but he grabbed for the book."

"Did he get it?"

"I don't know. I hit at him." Joey thrust his balled-up ringed hand in the air. "That's about all I know for sure. I don't know if I hit him or not."

Joey stopped and looked around him as if trying to reconstruct what happened.

"I *think* the doorbell rang again, but he hit me so hard I'm not sure. And then the next thing I knew I saw you . . . I'm sorry about the others."

"Don't worry, Joey. Those figures he took from the window—" Sol wrinkled his brow.

"There were two of them. Plus 'Scheherazade,'" Joey said. His eyes searched Sol's for forgiveness.

Sol laughed. "That's right. They weren't the fine ones. They weren't worth much. And 'Scheherazade' is still in the window. Two figures? What are they? Nothing. No. It's you I'm worried about."

And the book, I started to say, but didn't. I hardly knew Sol, but I couldn't stand the thought that anything bad could come to this dear grandfatherly gentleman. If the intruder, whoever he was, took the book, he would know Sol's name by now, maybe his address and phone number, too.

I stepped over to the desk, this time under the pretense of straightening things up.

"Come, Joey," Sol said gently. "We'll get 'Scheherazade' now. You and me, we'll go home. Everything will be all right." Sol looked over at me. "You should go now," he said.

"No. I'm fine. I need to help you straighten up," I said, thinking how I wasn't about to go out in that dark street with no taxis around and God knows who lurking in the alley? Not in this life. Or the next one.

"Bring 'Scheherazade' to me, please," Sol said, taking me up on my offer to help. "See, Joey, you're fine, or you will be when your lip goes down. 'Scheherazade' is still here. Everything is going to be okay."

So much for looking for the book.

Sol took the precious figure carefully, lovingly from my hands. He ran his hand over her exotic Persian costume and bejeweled headdress, then clasped her to his chest. He looked up at me, his eyes clear, his face calm.

"This is my finest figure. She's beautiful, like the story. Bold, yet graceful, like Rimsky-Korsakov's great music. Melodic. Seductive." He held the exquisite statue away from himself and tilted her toward me. "And mysterious," he said reverently. "Look at her."

He laughed. "It took me one damn week to get all those parts together! Didn't think I would ever find that feather for her headdress."

Remembering the many boxes filled with tiny pieces back in the factory building, I understood.

"Once I have a figure assembled, I bring it to Joey. He sells them. We split the money."

"How much does Joey sell them for?"

"Now 'Scheherazade' costs a lot. Four hundred dollars. Some of the smaller, plainer ones, like that one"—Sol nodded to the broken figure—"not much. One hundred, two hundred."

I started to say that four hundred dollars was nothing. Even at four thousand dollars, the figure would be a steal. For a split second, I was even tempted to say I'd buy her. Oh, *how* I was tempted.

Get real, I thought to myself, remembering the life-threatening events of just minutes earlier. Funny, even those chilling memories couldn't wipe away the vision of Sol's four-hundred-dollar 'Scheherazade' as the cover of a Layton's auction catalog.

"They sell quickly," Sol was saying. "Other people have asked Joey where they come from, haven't they?"

Joey, who by now seemed much more confident that he wasn't badly hurt, nodded. "We've never told anyone where they come from," he said.

"Do you call him? The one who was here tonight, when you have one finished?" I asked.

Joey perked up. "Oh, he's not the only one who has bought them. We—"

"No. We never tell anyone," Sol interrupted him. "I never know how long it will take to find the right parts and bolts and then put it together. Anyway, not knowing if there'll be one here or not, that keeps customers coming back to the store. Sometimes they will buy other things. Joey gets some real good stuff from these old Brooklyn families when the last one has died out," he said. "I tell him he sells too cheap, but he says he likes to move things out, not keep them around. That's good for business, you know."

"I've got a good lead for tomorrow," Joey began.

I glanced around, wondering what Joey did with the good stuff. His repeat business was the last thing I was interested in at the moment. I was amazed at how Sol and Joey had seemed able to quickly dismiss the night's happenings and settle back into everyday life. Guess that was the difference between living in Brooklyn and Leemont.

"Do you think whoever that was tonight will be back? What would you two do then? Will you sell more figures?" My mind was racing forward.

"Now we have you, we won't need to. I'll just sell the molds and be set for life." Sol smiled contentedly.

I groaned to myself. I wanted to tell him to forget the molds, damn it. It was the figures. That was where the money was. Lots and lots of money. Why couldn't Sol understand that the gold mine he was sitting on was the figures, not the molds? Obviously now was hardly the time to launch into Economics 101 and Antiques 202. I did the next best thing: I smiled, albeit rather weakly, back at him.

"But *you* need to go, Sterling," Sol said. "All that can wait for another day. Joey and I live close to one another. We'll be okay."

I glanced out the window into the darkest night I'd ever seen. "Then let's leave together," I said.

"We can do that," Joey said, rising to his feet again, this time without help. He paused a moment to get his bearings, then went to his desk. Triumphantly, he held up a black composition book.

"It's here," Joey said, tucking the notebook that I had overlooked in my state of fright into a tote bag. "Give me 'Scheherazade.' We don't want to leave her here."

WHILE JOEY DOUBLE bolt-locked first the shop door and then the protective metal door, I plastered myself flat against the building. I'd once read that to have shadows you must have light. There were plenty of shadows, but as far as I was concerned not one bit of light. Or at least not enough to do any good. In the distance a lone, dark something slunk slowly along the street. My heart pounded against my chest. Only when I realized it was nothing but a dog did I dare to breathe again.

We walked silently along until we reached a lighted intersection. It seemed forever before a cab turned the corner down the way and headed in our direction, and I walked out to the center of the street to be sure he saw us.

While Sol opened the door for me, I gave Joey a big bear hug.

"Thank God you're okay," I said.

"Sol, I'm going to be tied up a lot of the day tomorrow, but I'll call you as soon as I can," I said, opening my arms to encircle the old man. He eagerly returned my embrace.

"Take care of her now," Sol said to the cabbie, as he closed the door after me.

Always the gentleman, I thought.

I turned for one last glimpse through the back window of the cab. They stood huddled close in the darkness. While Sol pulled his scarf up around his ears, Joey held him by his arm. Then, as one, they began trudging along.

I tugged my coat tight around me in an attempt to settle down for the ride. We had pulled away from the curb and were starting toward Manhattan, or so I assumed, when abruptly the cab made a sharp U-turn in the middle of the block. I had no idea where I was. I looked out of first one side of the cab, then the other, straining to see a street sign, a store name, any kind of an anchor to ground me.

It was then I saw a dark-clad figure standing in the alley between two buildings.

I jerked my head around to see better. The cab slid around
another corner. In this black maze, everything looked alike.
Where were we? That building looked like Sol's. So did that
one. And that one.

I cowered in the corner and closed my eyes. Was I dreaming
this whole thing up?

Chapter 9

Dear Antiques Expert: I recently overheard an antiques dealer talking about provenance to one of her customers. Exactly what does this mean?

Sophisticated antiques collectors love the term "provenance." It helps give a piece credence, and sometimes, a pedigree. "Provenance" most often refers to where the object originated, but it can also refer to who once owned a particular piece. And that association can influence the piece's value. For example, people will pay more for a diamond worn by the Duchess of Windsor, or a baseball touched by Ted Williams, or a Shaker desk once in Oprah Winfrey's collection. Ultimately, knowing a piece's provenance, whether its origin or who once owned it, can make the difference of thousands of dollars.

I TOSSED AND TURNED all night and finally awakened long before the hotel clock radio alarm went off. On the street below, midtown Manhattan had come alive much earlier, way before dawn.

By 8 A.M. I had taken my bath, wolfed down a muffin from the corner deli with some lukewarm tea, and had gotten dressed.

Problem was, the New York I needed wouldn't come alive for another hour. I tried reading and rereading the *Times* left outside my door, but yesterday was all I could think about. Unfortunately, I hadn't dreamed it up. Not any of it.

I tried to put the events at Joey's store out of my mind and concentrate on Sol's problem. I figured I had seen maybe twenty of Sol's figures completely assembled. There were parts for . . . how many? Scores—maybe hundreds—more? Who knew how many molds Sol had? Outside of Europe, one person knew more about these figures than anyone else outside of Europe— Richie Daniel, head of modern decorative arts at Layton's. Seeing him was my first order of business.

I'd come to know Richie when he was just beginning at Layton's and I had found a Baccarat black enamel and crystal liqueur set in a backstreet antiques shop in Venice, California. One look at the set and I was transported to Fred and Ginger twirling to "The Carioca" on the balcony of the Copacabana in *The Gay Divorcee*.

Not everyone had seen what I saw because the set was dusty from neglect. It was mixed in with some old Revere Ware skillets and a rattan picnic basket in such bad shape that it should have just been left in the woods. Obviously, the tattooed shop owner either hadn't bothered to check the decanter or glasses for a mark or had never heard of the world-famous French glasshouse. Each piece was clearly marked with a long-stemmed goblet encircled by the words BACCARAT, FRANCE. The tag looped around the neck of the bottle dated the nine-piece set from the late 1950s and would cost me twenty-five dollars. But actually the set had been made in the 1920s and easily was worth a thousand dollars. Today, it would sell for triple that.

Richie Daniel was a Texan who preferred his nickname to his given name, Richardson. And he couldn't have been any more unlike Nigel Rhodes if he were from the planet Bakelite. Richie was the black-turtleneck, designer-jeans, Ralph Lauren tweed-jacket type. He kept his dark hair buzzed, not too short, not too long. I'd never seen him pass by a mirror, old or new, without giving himself a sideways glance. Though Richie was way past the forty mark, maybe even at the half-century mark, he would have had people think he was a boy wonder, which he was back when he started writing articles and books on anything related to the Art Deco period—furniture, glass, silver, and bronze figurines. Before then, no one in America paid much heed to the style. After all, Art Deco wasn't all that long ago. Even now it still couldn't truthfully be called "antique."

Little matter. Art Deco was now *the* look for Hollywood stars, TV personalities, and anyone whose house was a backdrop for a *People* magazine personality photo. As they said in the trade, Richie Daniel *made* the market. His success even landed him a one-night stand on *The Larry King Show* and a guest appearance on *Oprah* when she did a segment on what the stars collected.

The moment 8:59 turned over to 9, I rang Richie. Yes, he would be happy to see me anytime in the morning. American antiques held center stage this week, he said, so he was pretty free.

I caught a cab right over. But unlike yesterday morning, when Nigel had whisked me upstairs, this morning I had to jump through Layton's hoops. I gave my name to the Versace-clad blonde receptionist wearing knockout gold earrings. For a brief moment I wondered who she might be. Or might be kin to. Society girls with gilt-edged lineages practically killed to get jobs in the New York auction houses. It was a status thing to say you worked there. You didn't have to know anything about antiques; just being there was sufficient. In the waiting room alone, she was surrounded by a pair of nineteenth-century Venetian blackamoors, each holding a flaming torché. On the high-gloss walls, huge color posters touted Layton's record-breaking sales. An eighteenth-century American Queen Anne dressing table. An early Staffordshire polychrome salt-glaze arbor group. A second-century Roman marble sculpture. A nineteenth-century Navajo wearing blanket. A 1928 Le Corbusier chaise lounge. Just by being there one was anointed, by association, to all this wealth.

The pretty young thing punched in Richie's extension and said a few throaty words. Meanwhile, I paced about, worrying how much of what I'd seen I should reveal.

"Sterling. Sweetheart!"

I turned to see Dana Henchloe escorting a blue-gray-haired lady walking with a gold-tipped cane off the elevator. I groaned. Right behind them Richie bounded off the elevator and sprinted toward me. Anyone watching would have thought that I was the family attorney waiting to hand this man a check for his rich grandmother's entire estate. His enthusiasm triggered my caution button. I knew he couldn't care less about me.

Richie whisked me onto the waiting elevator up to the third floor and his corner office. At the desk outside his sanctuary sat another one of those gorgeous anorexic young things. She didn't have to stand up for me to know she was probably five feet ten and weighed no more than 120 with a heavy fur coat on. Everything about her was long and narrow—her hair, her face, her dangling earrings.

"Sterling, this is Anna. Anna, anytime Sterling Glass calls me, buzz her through," he said, winking.

Anna, who had no last name, peered up at me through eyes that suggested she'd had a little too much fun last night. When you've got those kind of deep-ocean blue-green eyes that guys get lost in, what do you expect? But other than her stare, she made no attempt to acknowledge my presence. My mother would have banished me from the house for such poor manners. She must *really* be someone, I thought to myself.

Once in his office, Richie seemed to turn it down a notch. Thank God. But when he asked me, "So, what do you have for me?" I felt more uncomfortable.

On the top shelf of his mahogany bookcase I saw the figurine of a dancer delicately balanced on an onyx base, arms outstretched, and dressed in a halter and shorts—remarkably similar to one I had held in my hands in Sol's basement. But this bronze and ivory figure was posed on both feet, not just one, and she wore a bandanna-style headband rather than a tight-fitting cap.

"Have? Ahhh." I had to tear my attention away from her. "Actually, I brought Nigel an exceptionally fine Paul Storr tea urn," I said.

Richie gave a low whistle. "Guess that made his day."

"He seemed pleased enough."

"But on the phone you mentioned some Deco pieces, right?" Richie hooked his left thumb into the waist of his jeans. Were we at Layton's or Texas? Richie tossed me a playful, come-clean-with-it look. I noticed the Ace bandage on his right hand. He caught my glance.

"Squash. Went for the ball. So did my partner. Nothing like stumbling over your own feet and getting hit with a racket." Richie laughed and I saw the light bruise on his lower left chin.

"Sorry," I said.

"So, back to why you called."

"Oh. Right. To pick your brain. That's why I called." I glanced back at the figurine. The resemblance between the pieces was truly remarkable. "Well, you see, Deco's not exactly my field. I'm more the eighteenth-century cherry chest and English silver sort. But then, you know that." I laughed, trying to figure out the best way to broach the subject of Sol's figures and molds. Back when I was a kid, I was the one always in trouble in grade school because I couldn't fib. When I did, it showed. Maybe that was what had kept me honest all these years. I tried again. "But you can always learn something new, right? Forget that old dog, new trick stuff. We're in the twenty-first century. It's about time I caught up with the twentieth century." I hoped I just sounded silly.

"Take that Deco figurine, for example," I said more seriously, and pointed toward his shelf. "Are there lots of fakes of those out there?" I nodded in the direction of the world beneath his third-floor office.

"You seem to know enough about Deco to be able to spot a Baccarat liqueur set without any trouble. Come," Richie said patronizingly, ushering me toward his desk. "Sit down. Now, I must say I'm a little disappointed. You bring Nigel a high-five-figure goodie and from me you want a lesson in Deco figurines?

Tell me. Have you read any of my books?" I detected a mildly cynical tone to his voice.

Boy had I stepped in it this time.

"To be honest, I do have your book on Deco glass and china, but—" I tried to look penitent—"I haven't read it. Checked out all the pictures, though. That's exactly why I wanted to ask you some questions in person. You only write about and show examples of the real and very *best* objects. I'm curious about the new ones. The fakes."

"Ah, compliments. Can't get enough of them." Richie smiled, just a hint suggestively. "They always get results."

He took the captivating figure down from her high perch. Gently, he placed her on his desk between the two of us and settled back in his chair. He glanced at his Cartier tank watch.

"There's nothing new about *this* little girl," he said, the corners of his mouth curling up as he spoke. "Lesson number one: she's as good as they get. Original. Undamaged. The ivory is perfect. Not discolored or cracked. The bronze? Unscratched. And she has a perfect provenance. Came straight from the estate of a high-ranking family in Germany."

"Oh? Do you know which one?"

Richie hesitated. "I can look it up."

He made some motion toward a bottom desk drawer but stopped midway.

"Hmmm. Come to think of it, they had *lived* in Germany or maybe it was Austria—somewhere in Europe—but the figure came to us by way of Argentina." He flashed that maddening smile again. "One of those smart Jewish families who migrated while they still had wealth and could get their things out in the late 1920s."

"Back to the fakes," I said, trying to reel him in, only to be interrupted by his ringing phone. Obviously another client he had told Anna to ring through at any time.

"May I?" he asked politely.

"'Course." I smiled understandingly.

"Alicia! Sweetheart. How are you?" Richie spoke into the phone as he winked at me. Everyone who followed the movies knew who Alicia was. Of course she could ring through.

"How's the filming coming—ahead of schedule? Unheard of, but with a professional like you," Richie cooed. "Say, I have a good friend here in the office, someone you need to know. Sterling Glass. Yes, it *is* a great name, and she's a hotshot appraiser, too, knows her stuff. You might need her sometime. An ounce of prevention, you know." He laughed. "No, Alicia, no robberies, *please*. But your goodies *are* getting more valuable day by day."

Please is right, I thought to myself. Me and Alicia? I stifled a laugh.

Even more fascinating than hearing Richie selling me, an eighteenth-century girl, to a fleeting media darling stuck somewhere in the 1920s but worth zillions of twenty-first-century dollars, was watching him work her. That was what he was paid to do; it brought in the high rollers and kept them coming back.

"We *do* have some great things coming up, looking at one right now. Perfect piece for your bedroom, on the nightstand, your dressing room, anywhere."

I wondered what he would say. "A cute little figurine that'll cost you a day's wages but would send a kid to an Ivy League school for a year or longer?"

He reached over and pulled the figurine closer to his side of the desk.

"It's an exquisite female figure, a dancer. Oh, 1926 or 1927 I'd say. No, it's not as finely modeled as your Chiparus 'Miss Kita.' This one has more of a coy look, flirtatious, but at the same time sophisticated. Reminds me of you, Alicia," he said. His voice turned as smooth as silk. "I'll send you the photo and dimensions. Want it by e-mail or a hard copy? And by the way, speaking of 'Miss Kita,' " Richie paused for effect. "I did a little checking. One recently sold just shy of $140,000. You got quite a steal."

I waited anxiously, hoping to hear how much Alicia had paid for hers, but I never found out. One thing I'll say, though. Richie didn't talk down to Alicia. She obviously knew her Art Deco stuff. More than I did, that was for sure.

The moment he hung up, I jumped right in.

"Look. The reason I'm asking about these figures is, well, I've come upon a whole group of them. The real ones. I'm sure of that."

"Oh?"

"Yes."

"Where?"

It wasn't the question I expected. "That's not relevant, is it?" I asked.

"Remember, provenance. If the figures are in Europe, it's one thing. If they're around the corner, that's something else."

"I'm not really free to say where they are." I smiled sweetly. "Appraiser-client confidentiality."

Richie shrugged and licked his lips. What choice did he have? He whipped out his overlaid silver and mother-of-pearl pen and began scribbling notes.

"Okay. How many are there?" he asked tersely. Richie's silky voice was gone. It was all business now.

I didn't like the sudden shift in our conversation. I had an urge to pick up the phone and call Peter. He'd know what to do. Damn. I hated it when I needed to rely on someone besides myself.

"How many did you say there are?" Richie asked again.

I swallowed hard avoiding giving him a straight answer. "Several."

"Come on, Sterling. What's several to you—three, four, ten, fifteen? Good Lord, how many? Couldn't have been but so many. Was it a collection? Couldn't have been in a shop. A museum?" He fired his questions at me, nonstop, his eyes cold. I could almost see his brain spinning around, all the while trying to wear me down. I wondered if he knew that the dollar signs were swelling in his eyes, more like Richie Rich, cartoon character, than Richardson Daniel, international auction house expert.

I stiffened. "Whoa." I held up my hands as quick as a Park Avenue traffic cop standing in the course of a speeding limo. I took a deep breath.

"Okay. Okay." Richie backed off.

He twirled his pen around and around in the air. Most people would have tapped it on the paper. But he didn't want to bend the 14K gold nib.

"I understand your responsibility to your client. But I'm assuming you've come to me because you want to dispose of them."

He didn't wait for me to answer.

"One thing we must be careful about. You don't want to

overload the market. As you know, too many of one thing and not enough collectors—and the bottom drops out."

Considering the situation, I wondered whether I should say anything about the molds. I knew I shouldn't, but my curiosity was burning. Only *I* knew where the figures were.

"Very interestingly," I said slowly, "the owner also has some old molds of the figures. Original molds."

"Molds? Really, now." His voice and face showed his surprise, but he quickly regained a more casual demeanor. "Oh well, *they* wouldn't do anybody any good," Richie said flippantly. "There are already scores of repros and fakes out there. Even if you had the original molds to make the bronze bodies, you wouldn't have the ivory. And can't get it. That's one way I can tell the new figures. The faces and hands and the other parts that originally were made from ivory now are nothing but plastic or some other synthetic."

He put his pen down, carefully, and clasped his hands together. I could see his knuckles go white. His face remained calm.

"On the other hand, it *could* be interesting to have a couple of the old molds for historical purposes. They surely wouldn't be worth anything—except to some museums, and how many can they display?" he asked parenthetically, his tone casual and practical. "So, let's say your client is ready to sell some figures—and, oh, throw in a few molds just for good measure."

"I'm not sure if my client *is* ready to sell."

"Testing the waters, eh?" Richie cleared his throat, ripped off the sheet of paper he'd been scribbling on and put it in the center drawer of his desk. He stood up, went to the door, and closed it. He returned to his desk, sat down, and stared straight at me with his moonstone blue eyes.

"I'll make it worth your time to bring them to me. But only one or two figures at a time. Can't flood the market. And a couple of the molds that we might try selling to a museum or," he said nonchalantly, "to a collector with a historical bent."

Richie stopped abruptly, and ground his teeth together. "This is tricky, you know. Those molds, those molds." He shook his head nervously. "They can't get in the wrong hands. Not if they're the true, original molds. That would blow the market wide open." His eyes narrowed. "We'll have to do this together, Sterling," he said, more calmly. "Can't have any duplication or even close facsimiles of the figures in the same auction."

Methodically he rolled his eyes toward the phone. "Of course," he began softly, the corners of his mouth slowly curling upward, "there are also private collectors."

"Of course," I acquiesced, numbly repeating his words to be sure I had heard him correctly, "private collectors." So he was thinking about cutting the auction house out on this deal, was he?

I stood up. I didn't want to hear any more. I had a lot of thinking to do.

"So," Richie said, pleased as punch, "seems like you might *have* brought me something after all."

Following my lead, Richie started toward the door. He placed his hand on the knob and left it there.

"Not bad for a day's work? So when are you going back? Is it Virginia or North Carolina? Been too long since I've seen you. Can't remember. It is Virginia, isn't it? Say, how about dinner tonight?"

Don't think that I'm so honest that for about one-tenth of a second I wasn't tempted to take him up on the offer. Rack of lamb in the Grill Room at the Four Seasons? Noisettes of organic Niman Ranch pork at Chanterelle? Miso-glazed Chilean sea bass at 71 Clinton Fresh Food? No telling where Richie might take me to wine and dine—all the while pumping me for information.

"Thanks. I really wish I could, but you know how it is when you don't get to the city often." I said sweetly and a tinge regretfully.

"Sure. Oh, of course! How forgetful of me, the auction starts tonight."

Richie finally opened the door. We stepped into the hall.

"You got me so excited thinking about this new prospect that I forgot why you're here," he said. "Anything I can do for you? Have a seat reserved for you? It's going to be a big crowd. The lookers have certainly flocked in for the preview, and the girls manning the desk tell me they're swamped with absentee and phone bid requests."

"One thing you *can* do," I said, taking Richie up on his offer while he couldn't back out. "Do you have the catalog of your last Deco sale? I'd like to study the prices and bring myself up to snuff. It's sort of embarrassing to have come upon such a treasure and not know as much as I should."

Richie stepped back into his office, took two, then three, catalogs from the bookshelf and flipped through the pages. "These will keep you busy for a while. And by the way," he said, opening one to a full-color photograph of a large bronze figure of a bare-chested male in blousy pants standing on a marble base and holding a bow and arrow. "See if you have one like this. 'The Archer' by Alex Kéléty—$186,700. Alicia bought it for the front entrance of her pool house."

I thought of Sol's four-hundred-dollar "Scheherazade."

"Hope your hand gets better," I said.

Chapter 10

Dear Antiques Expert: I recently tried to purchase an ivory figure in an English antiques shop. When the owner realized I was American he wouldn't sell it to me. When did it become illegal to have ivory?

The story behind that law goes back to the 1920s and 1930s. During the height of the Art Deco era, 60,000 or more ivory tusks were shipped yearly from the Belgian Congo to Liverpool. From just one tusk, scores of heads, torsos, legs, and other body parts used in the Art Deco figurines were carved. The ivory was inexpensive, but millions of elephants were being killed. Realizing how severely the elephant population had dwindled, the 1989 Convention of International Trade in Endangered Species made it illegal to trade in ivory, and America accordingly banned the importation of ivory.

FOR YEARS BEFORE she died, Mother chanted a litany. "I'm worried, I'm confused, I'm worried," she said. Day and night. Night and day. It drove me crazy at the time. Now I understood how she felt. And I still had my wits about me. I was disappointed, mad, hurt, betrayed. Never, in all my years of appraising had I been so blatantly asked to take a bribe. Did I appear so stupid to Richie that he thought I'd go for his scheme? Did I look that dishonest myself? Back home I would've said, "Hey! I didn't just fall off the turnip truck."

What to do now? Call Peter, call Sol Hobstein?

At the hotel, calling Sol, I wondered just what my chances of finding him would be at 10 A.M. on a Friday. I knew nothing about his habits, what his day would hold. But luck was on my side and he picked up. I told him I'd be there as soon as I could.

Even in the bright day-after-a-snow sunshine, Winston Place looked the same. Dark. Inside, the building wasn't much brighter in daylight than nightfall. We walked back to Sol's office, passing rows of boxes. "What are these, anyway?" I said.

"Eh. They come and go. Change now and then. Never paid them any mind. I rent the space out to the guy next door. He and some of his friends use it for additional storage. I don't need it anymore."

"So you own this building?"

"Bought it at a good price back in the seventies," he said. "The guy upstairs had some sort of mail-order service, and I had a small sewing business here on the first floor—women's lingerie. Slips mostly. Don't wear them anymore, do you?" He laughed his coughy laugh. "When he gave up his business, nobody moved in upstairs. That's when I bought the building. I never did use the whole place. But I was glad to have the basement for the figurines. You're only the third or fourth person ever to go down there, other than Joey and my wife. She died years back. We had no children. Joey's like my boy."

"How is Joey?" I asked.

"He's okay. He's little, but he's tough. A good spirit with a good heart to match." With that, Sol dismissed the whole incident. "So, what did you want to see me about?" he asked cheerfully.

"It's two things really. The figures and the molds," I said.

Sol chuckled. "Well, that's all I have, young lady."

I smiled. "Let's start over with some questions. You're putting the figures back together one by one, right?"

Sol fished around on his desk until he found the same crushed pack of cigarettes he had retrieved yesterday. I wondered how long they had been there. Just as he had yesterday, he put one in his mouth and let it dangle there, unlighted.

"Yes."

"How many would you say you have"—I paused, looking for the right word—"assembled?"

"I haven't been doing it for long. For years the memories were too unsettling. At one time I even thought about destroying them. Just throwing the boxes out for the trash. Never even opening them up." He looked at me. "But I couldn't do that either. And so they sat. Just like me. Guess I wasted a lot of years."

"We all do the best we can at the time," I said.

"What's done is done," he said, drawing an end to those thoughts. "How many?" He began drumming his fingers on the desk one by one, counting as he did so. "Including the ones you saw downstairs, maybe twenty-six, twenty-seven, oh . . . thirty or so, all total."

"Have you sold all of the figures—other than the ones that I saw yesterday—that you put together?"

"Most are gone, yes. Do I have any more ready to sell? Right now, no." He took the cigarette from his lips and laid it on the desk. "You see, I didn't sell them all. Some I have given to friends, or what friends I have left. I'm old, you know." He looked at me, disheartened. "It's such a bad habit, you know, growing old." Sol began one of his coughing spells that I'd come to expect but still found painful.

Old age were never kindly, Mother whispered in my ear.

"I understand," I said to dear Sol, waiting for him to regain his composure. "You know, when we spoke over the phone, all you'd tell me was that you had some molds, not what kind of molds. Truthfully, I know more about seventeenth-century Delft pottery than I do twentieth-century sculpture. I feel I should tell you that you have the wrong appraiser, except for one thing. I am honest. I do care about the sculptures. And you."

He brightened. "Honesty. That's all I ask."

"Do you realize that the figures you are assembling are worth much more money than the molds?"

"How can that be?" His face showed his disappointment first, then his disbelief. "With the molds someone can make new figures."

"But do you know how much the old figures, the ones you have here . . . the ones you have the parts for . . . are selling for?"

"Joey has no trouble getting one, two, four hundred dollars for them. But take a mold and make more figures and sell those for fifty or seventy-five dollars, and then you're talking money. Real money," Sol insisted, growing impatient with me, as if I couldn't do the math. "I told you. Kidders will be interested."

"Kidders hasn't seen them, have they?"

"I *told* you, only family—and you. That's why I need you. So I know what to ask when I take my deal to Kidders."

The only thing I disliked about being an appraiser, other than listening to people tell me about their things at cocktail parties, was having to disappoint people. And Sol, like many older people, had the value of his things backward, thinking that one thing was a giveaway and the other was valuable, when it was just the reverse. That was one reason why it was so pitifully easy to bilk the elderly.

Chances were, Sol was not going to believe the facts that I'd just picked up from Richie. Knowing that the figures he had assembled could bring thousands of dollars would be of little consolation; he was obsessed with the molds.

"Let's look at the bright side first," I began gingerly. "Just one of the figures, one of your simple ones, will probably sell for eighteen to twenty-two hundred, maybe even three thousand dollars."

I pulled one of the catalogs and opened it so Sol could see. I turned to a page showing figurines typical of those I'd seen in his basement—exotically costumed women in provocative poses.

"A rarer one will bring ten thousand on up. But I can't tell you right now which ones of yours are the low thousand-dollar figures, and which are the ten-thousand-dollar ones." I was careful not to mention the six-figure prices the rarest ones could bring. "Trust me, please, when I say that I feel certain that you're going to get a great deal of money for the figures themselves. You are going to be very, very rich, Mr. Hobstein."

Sol listened to me without comment or coughing. He glanced at the pictures with only vague, fleeting interest.

"You see," I continued, "not only do you have great objects, you have a great story here. Their provenance—where the figurines came from—that's a story in itself. Your grandparents. Your parents. How you brought all those parts and pieces here so long ago, and only now have opened the boxes after so many years." I laughed cheerfully. "Why I expect you might hear from Wendy Moonan or John Berendt once the word gets out."

"Who are they?"

"Oh." Of course he wouldn't recognize their names. "Wendy Moonan writes about antiques for the *New York Times*. John Berendt wrote a book about an antiques dealer," I explained.

"I was well read once," Sol said earnestly, quickly adding, "but can't say I would have read anything about antiques, even then. But Sterling, the *molds*, they—"

"Sol. The thing about the molds is that there are *already* copies being made of these figures—not from *old* molds—from molds people have made from buying the figurines and making *new* molds to reproduce them."

"Kidders?" he asked between wheezes, a worried look on his face.

"No. Not Kidders. But that aside, the manufacturers—whoever they are—can still make the metal parts out of bronze, but these days they can't get the ivory to make the ivory parts. So even if a company did have an old mold and used it, the new figure wouldn't be the same."

"But *I* have ivory," Sol said indignantly, his jaw stubbornly thrust forward. "If Kidders or someone wants ivory, I have it. I'll sell it."

"*You have ivory?* How?"

"When my family packed up the figures and molds, they packed the ivory as well. Little pieces. Parts of big tusks." Sol frowned and began rubbing his forehead. "I seem to remember something about selling some ivory. Maybe in the thirties? It got old and brittle. Ahhh. Yes." He lowered his hand from his brow. His gentle eyes sparkled as yesterday's life came clear. A better time for him than the present, I was sure.

"Yes, yes. Now I remember," he said excitedly. "It was *another* sculptor who had some ivory that was old and had become brittle. Ivory needs moisture," he said to me in a teacherly way. "My family always kept ivory wrapped in the softest bunting. Father had extra ivory. Beautiful, white ivory. He shared his. He was that kind." Sol, happy in the memory, smiled gently. "And then, before the war, when we were packing up the figures to hide them, Father said to me, 'Wrap the ivory carefully. It mustn't dry out.' I did as he instructed."

Sol got up and crossed the room. He pulled out his watch chain and with the smaller of the three keys he unlocked a file cabinet drawer. He took out a white box freckled with dark brown stains and laid it on his desk. He opened the box and brought out what looked like a thick wad of cotton. Wrapped inside, like a babe in swaddling cloths was a figure—her face, arms, and legs all of ivory. I recognized her face immediately. Her features and expression were, if not identical to, at least the sister of the figurine I'd seen in Richie's office. While Richie had described the figure over the phone to Alicia, I'd studied her, following Richie's every word.

"Coy," Richie had called the figure. "Flirtatious, but at the same time sophisticated. Reminds me of you, Alicia."

"I'm very proud of this little figure," Sol said, turning her over and over in his palm. "I carved it all to practice how to make the ivory parts. I wasn't as promising as my grandfather as an artist, but I had talent. I might have made something of myself had I been born at a different time or in a different place, but that was not so." There was no hint of remorse in his voice. Rather, his face shone in pride. "Of late, I have so much time, that I began trying my hand so I would have all the right parts for the figures. See? Not bad," he said, lovingly gazing at his creation.

"May I?"

Sol handed the figure to me, face down. Not face up, as I was expecting.

"See," he repeated, this time excitedly. "Here, at the nape of her neck, where her short bob curls around. See. I have put my signature. S. S." He pointed. "The *H* wouldn't work, so I used S. S. for Sol Stein. That works beautifully, like little extra curls or waves." Sol beamed. "Just unfortunate that it happens to be the infamous SS, but . . ." He shrugged the coincidence off.

"You're a master," I exclaimed. "She's exquisite. How many like this have you carved?"

I studied the figurine carefully, noting every detail I could. It would be important to recognize those that Sol had carved in order to tell them from those he had assembled from the pre-existing parts.

"This is my first. I kept her. For the others I just carved the parts I needed. I've carved the parts for four others. I've carved five figures altogether; the other ones were better. I gave three away. Joey sold the other one."

"Tell me something. Did you copy this face exactly? Would there be another one just like it? An old one?"

"Well . . . yes, and no. Many of the faces tend to resemble

110

one another. They were done in the style of the day. The poses
and costumes make them look very much alike—very Deco.
Still there are little subtleties. Differences. Those show the in-
dividual touches, the—" Sol paused. "The preferences each
artist had." He smiled. "Some carved noses better. Some liked
high cheekbones. I like mouths. You have a pretty mouth, Sterling." The old man stopped to muffle a cough. "Especially when
you smile. You don't hold back. Your whole face smiles."

I was concentrating so hard on the figure, it took a moment
for his words to sink in. When I didn't immediately respond,
Sol frowned worriedly, as if afraid that I might have taken offense at his comment.

There are three things you must learn to say, Sterling,
Mother had drilled into me. *Say, "I was wrong," when you've
made a mistake. "I'm sorry," when you're remorseful. "Thank
you," when you receive a compliment. Most important, you
must mean those words when you say them.*

"Why, thank you, Sol. That was the nicest compliment I've
ever had." I had never meant words more sincerely in my
whole life. "And I can't say enough about your carving, your
talent. I'm, well, speechless."

My mind was racing round and round. Could it be possible
that the figure I had just seen in Richie's office was actually one
of Sol's creations?

Provenance.

Richie had told me that it had come from Argentina. But,
thinking back, he'd also begun saying something about a German or Austrian family. There was only one way to be sure.

"You did sign them all, the ones you carved the parts for," I
said for confirmation. "All five. This one and the other four."

"Oh yes. Remember, I have no children, Sterling. These are my progeny in my old age. I gave them my name. Well, almost."

"Sol, tell me something. Could the same face be used with different bodies to make a figure?" I asked.

"Of course."

He made it sound so simple.

"When you're assembling the figures—" I was doing my thinking aloud.

Sol finished my thought. "How do I know what parts go together? Sometimes I do it from memory. I remember the figures I worked on long ago, even ones my parents and grandparents worked on. For some I use pictures from the old catalogs . . . the few pages I still have. Others are trial and error." He chuckled to himself.

"That's why I haven't done more," he said. "It's a long procedure. Fitting this head with that body, getting two arms that match up. I make many mistakes along the way. And once the parts are right, then there is still the process of putting them together with the bolts to hold them in place. It is very tedious. But then! But then!" His hands and arms danced through the air like a conductor's. "But then!" His exertion brought on his cough. He stopped and wheezed. "It was because I was having trouble fitting parts together and I grew impatient. That is why I began to carve the ivory parts."

I turned the little ivory figure over again, taking in every detail. "All this work. How long did it take you to carve her?"

"Too long. Weeks. Oh . . . don't be mistaken, Sterling. That's not the way it was done back home. That wouldn't have worked. Figures had to be turned out. Money had to come in. Back then the ivory already was partly carved."

Sol stopped. He rubbed his head. "Not carved with the features. The ivory was, well, shaped." Again he paused as he sometimes did when searching for the right word. He started again. "It was *formed* by machine first. The carver was given pieces of ivory that already had been formed to be the right shape and size. Round for a head. Long, thin to make an arm. A larger, thicker piece from which to shape a torso. Whatever."

As he talked, Sol's hands outlined each different shape for me. In the light of day, I saw that he had the graceful, expressive hands of an artist.

"Then the artists finished the parts off," he continued, his hands still moving in the air. "They carved them down from an outline they had to follow. A template. But they added the details on their own. That's what made the figures come alive. The details. It was the carvers, the masters. *They* made the little figures perfect."

I nodded. "The finishing touch. I understand. That's how they used to carve furniture legs and feet, too, from a block of wood and an outline. Then a carver would turn it into a plain, padded foot, or a masterful ball-and-claw foot."

Sol clearly wasn't interested in what I was saying, but I knew furniture much better than sculpture. My explanation helped me to understand the process.

"So tell me, Sterling. What do we do now? I must work hard to assemble the ones I have. Perhaps not spend time carving."

"No. You *must* carve." To deny Sol his craft was wrong. "You must continue to carve. Just don't mix the figures up." I spoke slowly. Emphatically. "Sol, *don't* put the figures that you are carving the faces and parts for in with the figures that you are putting together, assembling—the ones you already have *all* the parts for. Keep the two separate. Understand? You see, there are two stories here. The story about how you are assembling the old figures and then how you are *carving* lost parts for these masterpieces from scratch. It's a lost art re-born."

"I shall. I will keep them separate," he said, tapping his chest to keep his cough down. Then, with renewed vigor he said, "I know. I'll do both! Both processes are tedious. When I grow tired of assembling, I will turn to carving. And when my eyes grow dim from carving, I will turn to assembling. I like that."

"And don't give Joey any more figures to sell," I said. "At least not right now."

"No. I didn't think I would. If he doesn't have the figures to sell, then he can't get hurt again, can he? But I have two almost finished," he said. There was a tinge of disappointment in his voice. "You see, putting them together . . . carving the new parts . . . well, it gives me something to do. What's an old man to do with his life when the world and time have passed him by?"

"Oh, you can keep working," I said. "You should. You must. You're doing something wonderful. *No* one else could do what you're doing." I had no trouble sounding persuasive. What I was saying was true.

"Just save all your figures now, the ones you assemble and the ones you create," I told him. "I still have research, and thinking, to do. I've spoken to someone who may be able to get a great deal of money for the ones that are already put together. You don't want to sell—" I started to say a fifty-thousand-dollar piece for a few hundred dollars, but changed my mind.

"You don't want to sell one of your treasures for less than it is worth."

Sol opened his mouth as if to protest.

"You must promise me that," I pleaded. "Let's just wait."

Sol's eyes met mine. "There's that pretty smile again," he said. "I'll do what you say, Sterling."

Chapter 11

Dear Antiques Expert: I just learned that my Windsor chair is American. Doesn't the name Windsor denote an English origin? If my chair is American, is it less valuable than an English one?

Yes, Windsor chairs originated in England during the Middle Ages when the chair symbolized authority—so much so, it could only be sat in by its owner, or with permission, a distinguished guest. By the later 18th century, though, things had improved, and comfortable spindle-back "Windsor" chairs became popular on both sides of the Atlantic among the emerging middle class. American Windsors are actually rarer than their English counterparts. Today a really good single Pennsylvania Windsor chair can easily cost $3,000–5,000. A pair can bring $10,000–15,000—on up to $65,000 or $75,000 for the best of the best.

BEFORE I LEFT Sol I got his work and home numbers. I had to explain that I probably would not see him again on this trip but would call him from Leemont. If he had had his way, I would have moved to New York right then to help him match up his molds and assemble figures.

Realizing that he knew his time was running out made it doubly hard to leave Sol, but I had to move on, to decide what to do next. I could go back to Layton's and look at Richie's figure one more time, which is what I really wanted to do, or I could begin scouring the galleries and shops for more information on Art Deco figurines, old and new, which is what I felt I really should do. But my growling stomach was voting for something else entirely.

A light came on in my head. Lunchtime. No New Yorker ever passed up a lunch hour except under the most dire circumstances. What were the chances Richie would be at lunch? Pretty good, I decided. Or, if not at lunch, at the gym. It was worth risking a try. Anyway, there was a deli near Layton's that served a great Reuben with slaw and extra pickles. I would drop by there after checking out the figure in Richie's office. Myself, I never skipped lunch, or any other meal, unless it was absolutely necessary, and I avoided all gyms like the plague.

But how to get back to Richie's office? I thought. I'd visit the French Decorative Arts exhibit on display in the public gallery for just long enough to be able to comment on a couple of the pieces and act like I'd been there for hours. If Richie was in, he would never know I'd left the building.

For the second time in ten minutes, I approached the front desk. "Great exhibit." I smiled. "Oh, I have a question for Mr. Daniel. If he isn't in, I'll speak to his secretary, ah—" I fished for her name—"Anna."

How could I forget it? When Richie had pronounced Anna with a broad "ah," Anna sounded as long as she looked. I crossed my fingers for good luck that Richie would be out and Anna would let me come up.

"No. He's there. He just hung up from another call, " the receptionist said, punching in his extension number and cooing into the phone.

Drat.

"He said you know the way." She pointed toward the elevators.

Some contrast to this morning's zealous greeting.

I walked past tall, silent Anna who was busily doing who-knows-what, other than looking fabulous, and stuck my head in Richie's door.

"Sorry, Sterling," Richie said, looking up from the book on the desk in front of him only long enough to give me a cursory glance. "Had an important call. Looking for a reference. Expecting another call. Any minute." He spoke in shorthand while turning the pages.

I fidgeted about. It was a little past 1 P.M. Going against traffic, the ride out to Brooklyn had been a breeze, and my visit with Sol had been short. I wondered what Richie had been doing during that time. For starters, he had moved the figure in question from his desk onto a table underneath a window. It looked out on to Madison Avenue and suddenly I saw my way over to the figure. Small-city girl watches big-city traffic.

Richie, his head still buried in the book, muttered something indistinguishable, and pointed to the chair.

"I'm okay," I motioned back to him. "Take your time. I love looking at the city. Especially in the winter when you can see all the coats. I'm a fur watcher," I half-sang, giving him a flirtatious shrug.

"Un-huh," Richie snickered.

I went to the window, fur watching. After a few minutes, I

knelt over and began inspecting the figurine's neck. S. S. No doubt about it.

"Ah. There it is." Richie marked his place, then turned my way. His blue eyes were as large as a wild cat stalking her prey. Looking into the sunlight behind me, he blinked quickly. Then his eyelids slowly returned to their usual sleepy, half-opened state. Either way, half-closed or fully opened, Richie's eyes could conceal more than I, in my small-town ways, could decipher.

"Sorry about that," he said. "You're back so soon?"

"Been looking at the French—"

His phone rang. "Sorry." He threw me yet another apologetic look and picked up the receiver.

"Yes, Anna? A what? Have you called Tracey to go down and take a look at it?" he asked impatiently. "She's where? Oh, I forgot. No, I can't take the time right now. *You* go down and look at it. Huh? What's the condition? Okay. Unsigned? Probably isn't anything. If you have any questions, get the information. Ask them to leave it and I'll look at it later. My bet is that you can make a judgment call."

Richie hung up, rolled his eyes, and said, "Just somebody who *thinks* he has something. How *do* you stand it? Don't you get calls day and night wanting to know what something is worth? Tracey Hollins, my assistant, usually handles these walk-ins, but she's out in the Hamptons chasing down some really old Lalique pieces. Anna says she wants to learn, so I'm throwing her to the lions. Just hope she doesn't"—he paused, clearly rethinking his choice of words—"*mess* up. Now where were we?"

"I was on my way out, when I realized I have another question," I said. "Where did the artists sign their pieces? I thought

I'd read that signatures were on the bases. May I?" I let Richie see that I was closely examining the figure on the table and wanted to pick it up.

"Of course. Go ahead." He nodded agreeably. "That's right. Usually the artists signed the base of the mold before the figure was cast. Then again, many molds were never signed. Believe me, I wish they'd *all* been signed." Richie laughed. "The absence of signatures has led to a lot of confusion," he said, shaking his head regretfully. "It can be hard, even impossible, to know exactly who made some of the unsigned sculptures — even the best ones. I don't have to tell you that knowing who the artist was can mean big bucks."

"So what do you *do* when you find a great figure with no signature?"

"The same thing Liam Wellington down the hall does when he finds a great unsigned painting: I call in people who have spent their whole lives studying nothing else. It's those experts who decide if the sculpture is —" he laughed — "well, hopefully, the real thing *and* sculpted by the right artist. There's always the outside chance it can be a fake, or a copy, of course, but we usually catch those right off." Richie rolled his eyes. "Bottom line, when it comes to identification, we identify an unsigned sculpture the same way the art experts identify a Rembrandt or Renoir."

"But surely the artists knew that the base with their signature or mark could be broken or possibly replaced." I hesitated, gave the figure a quarter-turn, then asked, "Did any artists ever sign the figures themselves?"

"Not that I know of." Richie stopped. "Of course, having

said that, new discoveries are being made every day. You know that. That's what makes antiques so much fun. When your friend Nancy Evans wrote her book listing the names of the Lancaster, Pennsylvania, Windsor chair makers, prices skyrocketed. Now *every*one's looking for a Windsor chair signed by D. Danforth or Calvin Stetson."

I bowed in Richie's direction. "Now it's my turn to be impressed. How do *you* know so much about Windsor chairs?"

"I keep my ears open."

Richie grinned that maddening grin. "Who knows? I'm always snooping around used furniture stores. I might find one! Ears and eyes. That's what it takes in our business. Luck comes to those in the know."

I smiled back. "To the prepared mind," I said, intentionally flattering him. I turned my full attention back to the figure I was holding. "The reason I was asking about the signatures is," I began tentatively, "well, what do you make of this?" I held the fetching figurine toward him.

"What?" His curious look told me what I wanted to know; he hadn't noticed anything unusual.

"Oh, I don't know if it's anything," I said innocently, "but see where her hair waves. Right there. If you look real hard, those first two waves look a lot like two *S*s. And is that a period? I just thought maybe those were initials. Or a signature."

Richie frowned. "No. I don't think so."

"Oh good. That's all I was wondering. Well, see you tonight?"

"Nope. Next week's going to be a bear. I'm clearing out as soon as I can today. Good luck to you, though. Bidding?"

"Yes. For a client. We'll see how it goes."

Richie said nothing else. As I turned to go, I saw him rotating the figure, carefully examining her.

In the elevator, I started to think. Odd that Richie had made no mention of our first conversation of the day, had said nothing about the figurines and molds. He acted almost as if he had never even seen me before. Or it could just have been Richie's powers of concentration. One thing was for sure—he was totally focused on the figure when I left him.

BY THE TIME my Reuben arrived I was famished. On top of that, the morning's events had taken its toll. If I was going to be alert at the auction, a nap was in order. I headed back to the hotel. I'd rest, then leave early to go back to Layton's. Thanks to my late lunch I wouldn't need supper; I'd have a glass of wine and some nibbles after the auction.

Back in my hotel room, the urge to know if I had any messages back in Leemont began gnawing away. I dialed 9 to get an outside line and hooked up with my home phone. Five calls were waiting. Funny what boosts your self-esteem when you're on your own.

The first call was a throwaway from a telemarketer.

Number two was a request for an appraisal, which gave me a little surge.

Number three was from my daughter, Lily, bless her heart. She asked about the trip but managed to get in a few hints about new clothes. My mind wandered back to the many trips Lily and I had taken to New York when she was a little girl. At least she was thinking about me.

Call number four gave me pause.

"Matt Yardley from Babson and Michaels. I'm in the New York office, Ms. Glass. We have a large and unusual claim for some very fine antiques down in your area. The claim went to the Richmond office first, but they sent it on to me. They also gave me your name. If you could return my call. Again, it's Matt Yardley. Babson and Michaels Insurance. That's 212 . . ."

I replayed it twice.

Number five was from Amelia Nottoway, my best friend, checking in after returning from a trip herself, calling to let me know that all was fine at my house, which was right down the way from hers.

Two jobs out of five calls. Not bad.

Of course, instead of taking the nap I'd promised myself, I called Matt Yardley. I figured my being in New York was a good omen. When I told him where I was, he insisted that I come right over. "It's worth it," he said. "This is a major claim."

This time the dollar signs were ringing up in *my* eyes.

I agreed to be there by three thirty, just enough time to wash my face, put on fresh makeup, and do a quick clothes change —I'd go straight from Mr. Yardley's office to Layton's. Nothing drastic, just a different top and dressier pumps to go along with the classic go-anywhere black jacket and pants. I put on my discount-house winter white silk blouse. The knit pants would make the blouse look considerably finer than its $59.95 original price, discounted to $22.95, less the 25 percent sale mark-down off that, which meant, with tax added in, the blouse had cost a little over eighteen bucks. I slipped into the Prada pumps that I'd splurged on in the fall, finished off the outfit with pearls (fake ones in the city, of course) and onyx and pearl earrings (real, since I figured no one where I was going would yank them out), and was out the door.

The prospect of a new job had miraculously revived me. But it was a state of mind that would prove to be short-lived.

Chapter 12

Dear Antiques Expert: My neighbor's house was robbed and many valuable antiques stolen while they were on vacation. But the police told her she hadn't had a robbery, she'd had a burglary. What on earth is the difference?

Most people whose homes have been broken into say they've been robbed. But the police and insurance companies are sticklers for using the correct terminology. To them a robbery occurs when force is used to relieve a person of his or her valuables—as in you're walking down the street and somebody sticks a gun in your ribs and says, "Give me your money and your jewels." You do, and you've been robbed. But when someone breaks into your house and steals your things without bodily forcing you to give them up, then you've been burglarized.

SEATED ACROSS FROM Matt Yardley in the high-rise conveniently located on Sixth Avenue, I began poring over the million-dollar-plus fine arts insurance policy he handed me. He sat quietly, arms folded, watching me. I had to concentrate hard to keep from glancing up at him. When I felt a warmth creeping up my cheeks, I prayed that he wouldn't notice. Though any man that handsome was probably used to blushing women.

If I hadn't thought Peter and I had missed our window of opportunity, I wouldn't have been swooning over this man. Then again, a girl *can* dream, can't she?

Matt was one of those men who looked you straight in the eye when he talked to you and kept looking you in the eye as you talked. Most guys' eyes wander the moment a woman opens her mouth. The ones who appear to hang on to a woman's every word melt her heart in no time. The fact that Matt's eyes were a deep gray green and his widow's peak gave him an elegant, sophisticated look didn't hurt matters.

I tried to focus as I turned to the pages where the jewelry and decorative pieces were listed.

"Look carefully at the starred items," Matt was saying. "Those are the ones that are now missing."

I ran my finger down the list, glancing at the headings, pausing only when I came to a starred item. There were several of those.

> *Copeland Spode dessert set, circa 1850—$7,800*
> *Chinese Export punch bowl, circa 1770–1790—$4,200*
> *Victorian silver-plated tilting water pitcher—$1,250*
> ** Modern Cartier ruby and diamond bracelet—$15,000*
> ** English Derby shell serving dish, circa 1830—$3,200*
> *Pair of 19th-century Dresden candlesticks—$2,800*
> *Swiss gold and enamel watch, circa 1780—$6,500*
> *Art Nouveau French silver gilt embossed cigarette case—$1,200*
> *Sterling silver water pitcher by Steiff, Baltimore Rose pattern—*
>   *$2,800*

Shirvan prayer rug, late 19th century—$2,700
Victorian brass chamber stick—$500
Sevres lobed dish, circa 1773, restored—$1,400
Bronze figure of Minerva mounted on onyx base, 19th century—$1,750
Georgian pearl and diamond floral brooch—$8,500

I'd been skipping from one page to the next, just getting a feel for what was what. The brooch stopped me cold. I carefully read its longer, more detailed description.

Georgian brooch fashioned as a floral spray consisting of three large blossoms, each blossom with a center single pearl (approx. 7 mm each) encircled by old mine-cut diamonds (approx. .20 carat each) and accented by small, diamond-set leaves. Gold mounting with silvered prongs. In original fitted leather box. Circa 1850. $8,500.

At the back of the appraisal, photographs corresponded to each object's written description. Though the appraisal said the pin came with a fitted leather box, and the box was clearly evident in the photo, the picture left little doubt that this was the same pin.

"Matt," I said, finally looking up, "I think I've seen this."

Matt ushered me into a conference room where I could spread the appraisal papers out. He returned to his office to call the Richmond branch to see if they had obtained any more recent information on the theft. I wasted no time making a call of my own.

"Peter. Thank goodness I reached you."

"Sterling? Did you get my message?"

"Listen, I'm calling you from Babson and Michaels, the insurance company, from their home office. But wait, why did you call? It wasn't about the pin, was it?"

"No. I was just calling to see how you—"

"You still have the pin, don't you, Peter? At your house," I broke in.

"Yes. Is something wrong?"

"Well, I'm dead sure to positive that the pin LaTisha found is just one of several pieces listed as missing on a huge insurance claim. It's not your usual burglary. It's complicated. See, it wasn't in Leemont, which makes it all the more confusing. The claim came from one of those huge estates just outside of Charlottesville. Old money. Old people. People named Hanesworth. Originally, the claim went to the Richmond office, but it was so large that Richmond sent it to New York, along with my name." I paused to catch my breath.

"The pin? We *are* talking about Sarah Rose Wilkins's pin," Peter asked.

"Well, it *wasn't* hers. It probably belonged to the Hanesworths. Just keep it safe for now. I need to verify that it is the exact same pin, but I'm positive it is. Thank God I didn't put it on that night!"

"Keep it? Where?" Peter asked, talking over me. "It's Friday afternoon—getting close to five o'clock, Sterling. It's too late to get to the bank to put it in my safe deposit box. What am I supposed to do? Guard stolen goods over the weekend?"

"Oh dear. When you put it like that . . ."

In my panicked state I shook my head, thinking that might help me to think more clearly. I would have given anything for my Magic 8 Ball.

"Sterling. I thought this was Sarah Rose Wilkins's pin and I was just holding on to it for safekeeping till you and Roy could get together. What you've just told me changes the situation. I'm not about to harbor stolen goods," Peter replied quietly and calmly, but sternly. "I'm not exactly worried about any, let's say, unexpected callers looking for hot goods at my house, the way it happens in the movies." Peter's long-distance voice was a blend of slight bemusement mixed with concern. "But I do have the Salvation Army shop to think about. Its reputation. There's only one thing for me to do—call the police. Tell them I inadvertently have something that may be stolen. Then leave it up to the insurance company and the police to sort it all out."

"Oh dear," I said again. "I don't know what to do. For *you* to do, I mean. I told Matt how the pin turned up at the Salvation Army. I thought that was the right thing to do," I said, now second-guessing myself.

"The truth is always right," Peter said, his now calm voice reassuring. "You did the right thing."

"I hope so."

"Sterling. How much longer will you be at this number?"

"I don't know. Matt—Matt Yardley—is calling Richmond right now, but I have to be at the auction by a little after five so I can bid for the Katzes."

"I'm going to call Lieutenant Pavich. I've had some dealings with him. Can I reach you on your cell phone?"

"You can try, but I'll have to turn it off once the auction begins. Call my room and leave a message. How late will you be up?"

"If I can't reach you, I'll stay up until you call me."

I thought I discerned a sweetness in his answer. But then, that's me, always hoping.

I was placing the phone back on the receiver as Matt came back in.

"No luck on my end. The Richmond office has only what they've sent me." He walked over to the table. "You've opened up some real questions here. Of the things on the list, you've only seen the pin, right?" He spoke cautiously.

"From what I've seen, yes. But," I quickly added, "it's a big appraisal."

I had checked some of the starred silver pieces indicating that they were stolen items, but no Paul Storr pieces or eighteenth-century tea urns had surfaced. No reason to tell the story about Sarah Rose's tea urn now.

Matt sat down across from me, ready to take notes. His hair was beginning to show an occasional hint of gray, and he looked the role of a New York executive.

"It's not totally unheard of for members of a wealthy family like the Hanesworths to file a claim after their parents have died and they start dividing the silver and jewelry. When there are so many valuable items in a home, only then do they discover something is missing. We usually get two or three, sometimes more, claims like this a year," he said matter-of-factly. "Most times, though, the piece or pieces will show up. Some family member will already have it, or it was overlooked when going through the things. People, or should I say, rich people at least, are generally very honest about their possessions." A quick smile flickered across his face. "Makes my job easier."

I couldn't imagine that Matt Yardley knew anyone but rich people.

"It's the large number of items, and the variety of different things—everything from the pin," he said, flipping through the papers, "to the Shirvan rug—that makes this claim different."

"All easily transportable," I said as I began scribbling some notes myself, partly to keep track of our conversation, and partly to keep focused. "You'd think, though, that over time someone would have missed some of the things. The prayer rug, for example, even though it is small and thin enough to fold and slip into a bag. Or"—I stopped on the page where the thirty-two-hundred-dollar English Derby shell-shaped server was listed—"a fine piece of porcelain."

I found the corresponding picture in the index and turned it so Matt could see. "I'd imagine this piece would be displayed on a sideboard or in a corner cupboard. Then again, they have so many fine pieces . . ."

"Exactly. Plus the children weren't in and out of the house every day. Who knows how often, or how seldom, they might have gone into the dining room. Mrs. Hanesworth had died four, no, five years earlier. Mr. Hanesworth wasn't well either. He was so distraught after his wife's death that the children decided not to disturb anything at the time, even though she had willed many items to them. I think they were more concerned about their mother and father than they were about their family's things."

"Mr. Hanesworth simply hung on longer than the family thought he would," I said.

"True."

"Which means it was possible for many items to, shall we say, leave the premises, perhaps one at a time?"

Matt nodded his head to one side in regretful agreement.

"So it might seem. Especially now the pin has shown up off the premises."

"Yes," I said, "but I'm jumping to conclusions. I need to verify that this is the *same* pin, and of course I'll need to go over the claim more thoroughly. There's something wrong, but right now I don't know exactly what it is. What's the old saying, I just feel it in my bones."

"I have no doubt that you'll figure it out, though," Matt Yardley said confidently. More confidently than I felt. He began gathering up his files. I did the same as I snuck a glance at his hands. No gold wedding band. Not that that meant anything. Hank had never worn a wedding band, nor had my father.

"You realize that I won't be back in Leemont until Monday night," I said.

"You're on the clock, Ms. Glass. If you can do any research while you're here, talk to anyone, telephone calls, whatever. You've been here, in this office"—he glanced at his Piaget, the sort I've seen advertised but seldom glimpsed in person—"a little over an hour. Taxi fares. You took a taxi to get here. You'll need one to go, you said to Layton's, I believe. Just keep a log." Matt Yardley held his hand out to shake mine. "My card's in the folder. Have everything else you need?"

"For now."

Not quite, a voice inside me said. Oh well.

Chapter 13

Dear Antiques Expert: A friend and I are going to New York and she plans to go to an auction at one of the fancy auction houses. I've never been to a live auction and I don't know much about antiques. So the other day when she told me she was going to bid on several lots at the auction I didn't know what she meant. Could you please explain this?

A "lot" is simply the numerical way auction houses identify their merchandise. Each auction begins with "lot 1" and proceeds through the items, lot by lot. A lot can be one piece, or a group of items. For example, lot 115 might be a "Victorian arm chair, circa 1855, with rose carved crest rail," whereas lot 126 might be "Four hand-colored botanical prints dating from the early 20th century, plus two landscape scenes." Grouping similar items or sets together in one "lot" keeps the auction moving along.

NOW YOU TELL ME, how, after all that had transpired in the past seven or eight hours, plus the Joey fiasco of the night before, I could have enjoyed an auction. I myself don't know. But once seated in the chair at Layton's, with paddle in hand and the bidding about to start, my memory of the last two days faded away, and the thrill of the chase took over. Even when not buying for myself, bidding was still a rush. Some folks like the roulette table. Others prefer the racetrack. I find a night at the auction quite exciting enough. They're all high-stakes games. Once you've placed your bid, *les jeux sont faits.* Your fate was sealed.

Ten or fifteen years ago, I wouldn't have been in New York bidding on American antiques for a young doctor and his wife from Leemont. The Katzes wouldn't even be living in Leemont. But things had changed all over the South. People who once thought Charleston was in North, not South, Carolina, now were buying houses in Jamestown—a suburb of that fast-growing metropolitan area, Greensboro, North Carolina— and nowhere near Williamsburg, Virginia. *Reconstructed Yankees,* Mother called the new breed of folks who began moving south in the mid-1960s. She loved twisting that bit of history in the South's favor.

My mission was to bid on, and win, lot 37, a circa 1805 Sheraton curly maple candle stand with delicately turned pedestal estimated at twelve to fifteen hundred dollars; either the group of six Sheraton chairs I'd casually walked past the day before—lot 39 and estimated at five to eight thousand dollars—or lot 58, an important Philadelphia schoolgirl's sampler, circa 1800, estimated ten to twelve thousand; and lot 123, a nice five-piece Boston coin silver service, circa 1820, estimated at three to five thousand. I liked the chairs, but the sampler had the greater charm and more investment potential. I did the math. Only if the chairs stalled considerably below their low estimate would I enter a bid on them.

Around the room I spotted the heavy hitters: Billy White,

chairman of White, Cross, White, and Jordan, held paddle 32. Asher Berg, the premier New York antiques dealer sat at the back with his son-in-law, Sam, who would do Asher's bidding for their East Fifty-eighth Street gallery.

I was thumbing through the catalog one last time when I heard Richie's voice outside the auction room.

"Sweetheart! How *are* you?"

I leaned forward to see who he was calling sweetheart this time. Luck was on my side. Richie's back was to me. Next to him stood Anna, looking even taller and thinner standing up than she had while sitting down, thanks to her long black cashmere Chesterfield coat she was wearing.

Richie was greeting Margaret and French Everett who were looking eternally young in their matching ankle-length black diamond mink coats, despite their seventy-plus years. The Everetts were legendary interior designers who bought perfect pieces for their Westchester and Southhampton clients. Richie finished pumping French's hand up and down, then kissed Margaret's hand, bowing as he did so.

"You must meet Anna," he said, "my new secretary. Anytime you need me, just tell her to buzz you through. You'll remember that, won't you, Anna," he said, looking up at her. He didn't give Anna a chance to answer. She just stood at his elbow, half a head taller than he, looking stunning.

"And by the way—" Richie turned his head ever so slightly from side to side as if to check to be sure no one could eavesdrop, but he didn't lower his voice. "There are going to be some great pieces at my Deco sale week after next. It's a hot market and it's getting hotter. You've heard of Alicia?"

"How could we not?" French said. "She's plastered every-where. Wasn't she in the last *Town and Country*? We were. Never seen any of her films . . ."

"And can't say I want to," his wife said.

"But we *do* know the name," French went on. "Think she was at one of Warren and Annette's parties that we went to. Or was it at Michael and Catherine's?"

"Think she was," Richie said, cagily neglecting to say which party. "A word of advice. Alica's getting into Deco in a serious way. She's posing for the cover of *Vanity Fair*, and guess how she's doing it?"

"Not like Demi Moore, I hope." Margaret let out a disapproving groan.

Richie took his cue from her. "Wasn't that over the top?" he gushed, then laughed. "Not to worry. Alicia's doing a *Deco* pose. Wearing an authentic thirties outfit. She's even going to have the dogs. Two beautiful borzoi decked out in diamond collars. Just like one of those irresistible Poertzel bronze fig-urines. The market's going to go *wild*." Richie licked his lips.

The Everetts looked at one another and raised their eye-brows. "Thanks for the tip," French said.

The Everetts, with paddle 50 clearly visible, slipped into their front-row seats.

The Katzes had given me a limit of twenty thousand dol-lars—give or take a little. Between my straight twenty-five-hundred-dollar fee, whatever I would bill Sol and Roy Madison for, and now the money Babson and Michael would chip in, I was feeling flush.

I was tempted by a couple of items in the early lots, until the prices began soaring 20, 25, and even 50 percent over the pre-auction estimates. I could find better deals at Saks Fifth Avenue's January sale . . . or at the Salvation Army in Leemont.

Eventually, the curly maple candle stand came round. I won it for $1,350, right in the middle of its presale estimate. I passed on the Sheraton chairs when it became clear that there was plenty of competition for them. Anyway, I had decided the sampler was the better choice. There was a momentary lull as some Currier and Ives prints sold at their low estimates, but then the prices kicked back up. Obviously getting the sampler wasn't going to be as easy as I'd hoped.

Within five seconds of the opening bid, I could see the competition—Asher Berg *and* the Everetts. I decided to let them battle it out first. If I jumped in too soon, I'd just drive up the price as one more bidder. Twenty seconds later, the bidding reached fourteen thousand dollars, then stalled.

The sampler was wonderful and worth every penny it was garnering. The scene depicted a family standing in front of their two-story, early Federal house. Its colors were still vibrant. It was signed and dated and had an ironclad provenance—all factors making it highly desirable. Either the Everetts or Berg—whichever one got it—would add at least 50 percent over the sampler's final price before selling it. If the auction price ended up being fifteen thousand dollars, after Layton's tacked on its 20 percent buyer's premium, and then the 50 percent (or more) dealer markup was added, and taxes were put into the mix, somebody would be paying upward toward twenty-eight or twenty-nine thousand—possibly more—for it. That made the sampler a steal for the Katzes at anything under twenty thousand.

After a couple of hesitant raises from the Everetts against

Berg came the inevitable lull. I raised my paddle against Asher Berg's $16,250 high bid. It was greeted by several turned heads.

"Sixteen thousand five hundred to the lady. Sixteen five. Sixteen thousand five hundred dollars."

The auctioneer looked pointedly at Berg. Sam disgustedly turned his paddle upside down and placed it on his lap.

"Fair warning," the auctioneer announced to the room. "I have $16,500 bid for lot 58, the fine Philadelphia sampler. Are the bids all in?" His eyes quickly swept the room one last time. "Sold. To paddle number . . ."

I held my paddle high.

". . . 61." He smiled as he noted my number in his ledger. I smilingly nodded back when he glanced back up.

By the time the auction house tagged on the buyer's premium for the candle stand and sampler, I would have spent over twenty thousand dollars of somebody else's money, been paid to do it, and loved every minute of it. The Katzes could wait till another day to buy a nineteenth-century coin silver service.

I was tempted to stick around and see how things ended up, but I was more anxious to hear from Peter. I told the young fellow at the desk I'd be back tomorrow, turned in my paddle and completed the paperwork, and caught a cab to the hotel.

The Katzes had paid for the ride, but I could also charge it to Matt Yardley with a clear conscience. Just three lots before the sampler, a Victorian brass chamber stick, not identical but comparable to the $500 one on the Hanesworth's list cited as stolen, was sold. The one tonight had sold for $650. And one of the lots that had far exceeded its estimated selling price was a pair of shell-shaped English Derby serving dishes. The

Hanesworths' single dish was appraised at $3,200, a top price, I'd thought. This pair had sold for almost $10,000. Pairs always sell for more than double the price of a single piece. Still, I needed to keep my eye on the market for fine English porcelain. Obviously, prices were going up and it was my business to stay on top of them.

Giddy with success, I scribbled "Research" next to the I ♥ New York logo on my $6.25 receipt.

Chapter 14

Dear Antiques Expert: I recently found an Art Deco figure identical to one I inherited in an antiques shop. The difference was that mine is small, just 10 inches tall, and the one in the store must have been 20 or 24 inches tall. Does this mean that one of them is a fake?

During the 1930s, wall "niches" became a popular architectural detail. The bronze, or bronze and ivory, Art Deco figurines were perfect for these spots, but since a small figurine could get lost in a large niche or a high-ceilinged room, many manufacturers produced the same figurine in a variety of sizes. So size alone does not denote a real or fake piece. (Incidentally, some figures came with a hollowed-out stand containing a colored electric lightbulb to add a glamorous touch to the niche, but these seldom survived.)

IN THE MORNING I felt as if I hadn't slept at all. Again, I'd thrashed about all night. Some way to spend my time in New York. Twice during the night I had awakened, having dreams about Barefoot Bagman back in Leemont.

No one knew much about Bagman—how old he was,

where he got his money, if he had any family. He'd just always been a permanent fixture, walking barefooted up and down the streets of Leemont. Rumor had it that Bagman went barefooted because he said Jesus did.

His real name was Shaw Bagwell. Bagwell became Bagman since he toted a burlap bag around with him. What he carried in the bag was the real mystery. Some people said it was all his worldly goods. Others said it was nothing but empty aluminum cans and glass bottles. But others swore that it is the Confederate gold purported to have been buried somewhere around Leemont during the last days of the great siege.

In real life Bagman lived in the basement of the old Sandusky mansion on River Street. The Phillipses, a doctor and his wife, who'd bought the Sandusky house some fifteen years ago, inherited Bagman with their purchase—the way someone inherits an outdated refrigerator left behind by the former owners. Apparently Bagman had never bothered them.

If the Phillips, or anyone else, had ever been in Bagman's hovel, no one knew about it, which made the aura surrounding him all the more legendary. The few who had dared to talk to him said he wasn't stupid, so he couldn't be labeled the town's idiot. I was always told he was "touched," or "tetched," as some folks say.

Pixilated, Mother had said. *That's a much better, more descriptive word.*

On occasion Bagman went to the Salvation Army to buy somebody's discarded sweater or get a hot meal. Peter had tried to get him to move into better quarters, but Bagman said the furnace kept him warm in the winter and the red-dirt floor cool in the summer.

In my dreams, like an old peddler out of a nineteenth-century English novel, Barefoot Bagman was loaded down with valuable silver, antique jewelry, and bronze figures. And in the way things occur in dreams, Bagman was riding an elephant with four huge ivory tusks on his way to his basement room home.

I looked at the clock. It was 7:15 A.M.

I leaned over the side of the bed and retrieved one of the auction catalogs Richie had given me and began to flip the pages idly. I stopped at the Art Deco silver. I thought again of the Paul Storr tea urn. From the moment it had surfaced in the brown paper bag hidden in the moth-eaten blanket at the back of Sarah Rose Wilkins's closet, it had nagged at me. Finding the pin inside the oven mitt raised *more* questions and suspicions. But about whom? Sarah Rose Wilkins? She was certainly above reproach.

One unexplained valuable piece could be overlooked—and could be a fluke. Two unexplained valuable pieces could not—especially since women *wear* jewelry. Though the pin was exquisite, it wasn't flashy. If anything, it was understated. Truth be known, I doubted if many people would realize they were looking at valuable diamonds. Because the pin didn't scream "Notice me," I just couldn't believe that Sarah Rose Wilkins, modest though she was, could have resisted wearing it, if in fact it was hers. But now I was sure that the pin hadn't been hers.

Things just weren't adding up. And what if some other piece also had been hidden in her apartment and gone undiscovered? It, too, could have ended up at the Salvation Army. I wondered if Peter had searched Sarah Rose's other things sent there? I reached for the phone.

"You can't do that," I scolded myself out loud. "He already thinks you're blowing this thing all out of proportion."

But like it or not, I was involved. The time had come to do some serious thinking.

Sarah Rose's family was small and didn't live near Leemont, and no relatives or heirs had gone in or out of her apartment on a regular basis. She had been able bodied and independent until a week before her death. It wasn't all that unusual for an eighty-year-old woman to be hospitalized, released, and then die unexpectedly. Doctors didn't know everything. That was that. The end. The police had resolved the issue of her death to their satisfaction the day Roy and I had gone to Sarah Rose's apartment.

When the urn had surfaced and there had been no record of her owning such an exceptional piece, I had asked some questions out of curiosity. Now they seemed more significant.

Okay, so the pin was really Mrs. Hanesworth's, or had been at one time. Was there a possible connection between Sarah Rose Wilkins and the Hanesworths? I thought hard, trying to remember everything I could about Mrs. Wilkins. She had taught school. That ruled out the chance that she might have worked for the Hanesworths, who possibly could have given her valuable pieces in lieu of a paycheck.

She was not known to be kin to any fine aristocratic, or filthy rich, family. Nor her husband. People in Southern towns like Leemont knew all about one's lineage or, in the case of blue bloods, their pedigree. Or at least people of the Wilkinses' generation did. Nope, the Wilkins weren't kin to the Hanesworths. Inheritance did not seem at all likely.

The presence of both the pin and the urn was puzzling

enough. Since the urn wasn't anywhere on the Hanesworths' appraisal, the idea that the two things might have come to be in Sarah Rose's apartment from two different sources . . . that was the kicker. I would have to get in touch with whichever Hanesworth heir had sent their claim in to Babson and Michaels. Maybe they had missed listing a Paul Storr urn.

What was I thinking? If I was determined to worry myself sick over something, I should have been fretting over Richie Daniel. Now that was a suspicious situation if I had ever seen one.

It was time to lighten up a little. I laid out a sensible plan that suited no one but me. Breakfast. Saks. Antiques shops. Auction. Dinner.

There was no reason to rush back to Layton's right away. The morning session would feature nice, but not exceptional, items—pieces ranging from the low hundreds to mid thousands, on up to maybe ten or twenty thousand. After lunch, the merchandise always kicked up a notch. The occasional twenty-five- to seventy-five-thousand-dollar piece was offered. But come the end of the day, the stars came out—the pieces expected to bring one, two, or three hundred thousand dollars and on up. The real humdingers, the ones that everyone—the sellers, the onlookers, the auction house, the media, even the buyers (they figured the prices would go higher next time)—hoped would go through the ceiling, maybe even reach the million-dollar mark, were saved for the grand finale. Or the dismal fizzle.

I'd shop in the morning, go to Layton's in time for the real show.

* * *

FIRST STOP WAS SAKS. I wove my way around the willowy wannabe models handing out pungent perfume samples. An hour later I was back on East Forty-eighth Street, content that my mission was accomplished with Lily's periwinkle silk cardigan and tee, and the cashmere crewneck sweater that I couldn't believe I found in Ketch's size in hand. I wasn't interested in shopping for myself.

If I grabbed a pretzel from one of the sidewalk vendors, I would have time to check out the huge Metro Antiques Mall a few blocks up before going on to Layton's. If I couldn't be tempted by Ralph Lauren tweeds at 35 percent off, I could keep focused and walk past row after row of red Bohemian glass decanters, shelf after shelf of cloisonné vases, and rack after rack of silver-topped walking sticks—reminders of the day I was tempted to break one over my ex-husband's head. I was determined to whiz through that microcosm of dead people's lives, pausing only for bronze and ivory figurines.

I wasn't disappointed. In stall after stall, from the mall's first to its fourth floor, small tabletop bronze sculptures of ladies, gladiators, dogs, angels, and nude and virile Italian boys abounded. But only the occasional booth was manned, making it hard to gather much information. When I heard voices, I headed in that direction.

"It's not a question of its value," an older woman was saying. "It's a matter of *my* cash flow."

I didn't have to see what was going on to know that those were the words of a dealer. *That* old song and dance, I mused. How many times had I heard those very words spouted by a seasoned dealer trying to get a good deal.

"I think I'll have a quick sale for it, but," the woman continued, "before I can buy it I have to get in touch with my customer. I'll leave a message on his machine. Look, he's probably out; he usually comes by here on Saturday afternoons."

That's when a younger-sounding voice chimed in. "I can't wait around all day." It was that high-octane speak that seemed the norm among the twenty-somethings.

"Look, honey, these are *antiques,* not Hershey bars. You don't just buy expensive antiques on a whim. If you need money in a *hurry,* take your ex-boyfriend's ring to the pawnshop. What's your rush, anyway? It's not hot, is it?"

For a moment I expected everything to go black and white. The exchange was right out of a 1940s film noir. So that's where they got the dialogue: real life.

I was dying to see what was being peddled. I sauntered along, careful not to draw any attention to myself. Out of the corner of my eye, next to an oversized Gucci handbag, I glimpsed a delicately balanced silhouette of an Art Deco figure. Holding on to the inanimate figure for dear life was an equally angular young woman. I edged to my right to get a better view. It was Anna, Richie's secretary, dressed in the same stunning cashmere coat and the same long gold earrings as yesterday. She'd pulled up her blonde hair beneath a black fedora. She wore little, if any, makeup. She looked like a million bucks.

The dealer was a seventyish, heavyset redhead wearing oversized red-rimmed glasses that rested low down on the tip of her nose. She had multiple chins. Her hand, crippled with age but adorned with bright red fingernails, was wrapped around the base of the bronze statue like a cobra. For a second, I wondered if I was going to witness a tug-of-war. If so, my bet was on the septuagenarian dealer who was wearing enough 18K gold bracelets to choke an airport metal detector.

I hung back. One of the great things about antiques shops is the number of natural hiding places they provide. An almost eight-foot-tall English mahogany secretary-bookcase gave me perfect cover. If need be, I could drop to my knees to examine the piece's feet and legs more closely.

"What's the *most* you can give me for it?" Anna asked.

"Seven hundred. Seven twenty-five," the dealer replied.

"But I paid more for it than that!" Anna's tone turned desperate.

"Ever buy any stocks, honey?"

That slowed her down.

"No, no. Not yet."

"Is this your first antiques deal?"

"No. Yes. Well, the first real one."

"All right. Truth's out. Now listen. First rule, don't play. Second rule, if you're gonna play, have a sure sale before you buy. All right?" The dealer let out a sympathetic groan and heaved her heavy shoulders. "Maybe I can go $850."

I thought I discerned a sigh of relief as Anna dropped her hold on the figurine.

"Why'd you buy it?" the dealer asked her.

This time I heard a sigh for sure.

"I probably ought not to tell you. I work at Layton's." Anna slowed down, dropping her voice to a confessional pitch. "I see these things come in. They sell for eight, ten thousand dollars. More. I found this one and thought—"

"Layton's, huh? Thought you looked the type." The dealer made a clinking noise with her tongue against her cheek. "So you thought you could play with the big boys. All right. What happened?"

I peeked around the back of the secretary-bookcase. The dealer, clearly a woman who'd heard and seen it all, was standing with one hand on her ample hip. With her other hand, she pulled the little figure toward her and squinted at it over her glasses. "Where'd you get it, honey?"

"At an estate sale out in Queens. I go to them on weekends."

"You did good. It's real. And in good condition. What's wrong with Layton's?" She dropped her chin to her chest and peered over her glasses. "Why didn't *they* want it?"

"Well, they did at first. Said it would go in the next Deco sale," the young girl said. "Then . . ." Her voice trailed off.

"What changed their minds already?"

The shoulders of Anna's coat moved up and down when she shrugged. "My boss said they had too many of them for the upcoming sale. Now I'm stuck with it."

"So why don't you just keep her? Show her off? Bet she'd look good in your digs."

When there was no reply, just another shrug of Anna's shoulders, the dealer pressed on.

"So that's it, huh? You really *do* need the money. What'd you do? Buy something you shouldn't've? Get Mumsey and Daddy-O to help you out."

"It's not like that." That desperate tone was creeping back into her voice.

"Look at you. Rich girl. Cashmere coat. Job at Layton's."

"It's not like that," Anna repeated. "I have . . . other responsibilities." Her voice dropped to a whisper in this empty place. "A little girl."

"Tell your husband to get a second job."

Anna said nothing.

"Oh."

"I want to make a life for her."

The old dealer turned and placed the bronze and ivory figure on the shelf behind her, her bracelets clanging as she did so.

"I'll give you a thousand," she said. She whipped out her pocketbook and counted out ten one-hundred-dollar bills.

"Take my advice. Find yourself a nice young rich lawyer, honey. New York's full of 'em. All right? Forget trying to buy and sell. That's for the pros. Play up what you've got. Your looks."

I waited until I heard Anna's heels thumping on the steps before emerging from my hiding place. I watched her start down the stairs, tall, straight, glamorous, even from the back. Her voice had that husky Marlene Dietrich mode, except when she seemed desperate—then it had a certain shrillness to it—but whose wouldn't under the circumstances?

Chapter 15

Dear Antiques Expert: I am beginning to look for a mahogany secretary-bookcase for the living room. I found two in a really nice antiques shop. What puzzled me is that they looked almost exactly alike, but one tag read "American, circa 1780. $75,000," and the other tag "English, circa 1780. $25,000." Since they are so much alike and even made about the same time, why is there such a price difference?

Many more secretary-bookcases were made in England in the later 18th century than in America. That was America's Revolutionary period, and even once the war was over it took years for the young country to become established. England also had a much larger well-to-do population who could afford such pieces at this time than did America (secretary-bookcases have always been expensive). In this instance, rarity explains why the American one cost three times as much as the English one.

THE DEALER WAS rearranging a group of gold charms inside the display case where the figurine had stood just moments before. Her heavy bosom rested on the top of the case while she fiddled with the objects laid out on red velvet beneath her.

"Excuse me. Do you know anything about those things over there?" I pointed to my former hiding place.

"What do you need?" she asked, without glancing up.

"The secretary-bookcase over there. Do you know if it's English or American?"

From her humped-over position the dealer glanced around me, toward the other dealer's booth.

"Oh!" I exclaimed, as if noticing for the first time the Art Deco figure. "That statue behind you?"

The woman straightened up and turned around.

"That one. There. On the second shelf. The thin, kinda slinky one. With the shawl."

"She's a beauty," she exclaimed, taking the figure down. "Just came in, in fact. Won't be here long. Have a fellow coming in to see her this afternoon. The good things never last any time. She won't last the day."

So all these *other* things aren't very good, I was tempted to say, going after the logic—or lack of logic—in her sales pitch. But, of course, I didn't. It's just that antiques dealers' selling ploys have always amused me.

"You know, my grandparents had a figure that looked like this one," I said.

"Honey, *every*body's grandparents had one. Everybody who was *any*body, that is. And if they didn't have one, you *need* to have one to prove your grannies *were* somebody."

I smiled inwardly, remembering the many nineteenth-century oil paintings of anonymous men and women I'd been called on to appraise as my clients' great-great-grandparents. It had always amazed me, how, after years of hanging in the dark, dusty recesses of some hidden-away country antiques

shop those very paintings quite miraculously could be identified as the long-lost portraits of my clients' dear, dead ancestors. Ironically, this discovery coincidentally happened about
the time those ancestors' "descendants" had socially arrived.

There was one thing people had in common, Mother once
told me: the craving to claim blood kin to somebody well-to-
do. *If they can't do it in the present, they'll do it in the past,*
she'd added.

"These figurines? I don't get it," the dealer rattled on. "But
if it's your taste . . . Me, I lived through Art Deco once. Back
in the twenties and thirties. No reason to do it again. I sold all
that stuff back in the fifties, figures included. Nobody thought
they were *art* then." She drew the *r* out as long as she could.
"And they didn't when your grandmother bought them either.
Nothing but set-around stuff then. Whatnot decorations."

The old woman threw her head back and laughed. "Oh,
these days the highfalutin art critics have a lot to say about
these little darlings. I read in some antiques magazine that no
other art form expressed the new women's movement of the
1920s like they did. Humph. Hogwash."

Running one finger along the figure, she raised her eyebrows
and gave me that woman-to-woman look that knows no gen-
erational bounds.

"*Art?* Ha. Those dirty old men back in the 1920s couldn't
believe their luck. After all those years of women in high collars, buttoned-up shoes, and laced-up dresses . . . and suddenly
they could have a figurine of a girl with her skirt up to her
crotch and perky little boobs sitting out in their living rooms?
Wasn't anything 'arty' about it. I sold all my Deco stuff. I was
glad to get rid of it."

Her heavy bust heaved. "Shows how much I know. About that time, Deco got hot again. *Que será, será.* But this one?" She squinted over the red rims of her glasses at the figurine in her hands. "Yeah . . . I can see why you think it's art, if you want to call it that. Specially compared to the stuff they're making these days. This one took some skill and time to make. Not like that computer crap they're calling art nowadays. Nah. Don't get me going on that."

"May I see her?"

"Sure, honey. Sorry. I get going sometimes. At my age, I can do it." She laughed as she handed the figure over to me.

"You say she just came in?"

"Yeah. Pretty young thing, the girl who brought her in. Seemed to know what she had, but needed cash worse. I got a deal. Bought it cheap. I can let her go for . . ."

The dealer hesitated while giving me the once-over. She glanced at my hands to see my jewelry, but I still had my gloves on.

"You aren't from around here," she said, stalling.

"No. My accent always gives me away. Virginia. But I know a little something about these figures. I need to learn more," I said for no reason at all.

She looked at me quizzically, no doubt wondering why I had let her go on so, if I knew what I was looking at. "I have to make a profit," she said defensively. "Ones like these are selling for ten thousand dollars at auction."

While she'd talked, I'd examined the figure. This one was quite different from the ones I'd seen assembled at Sol's, but I had seen some similar parts in the boxes and lying around. This was a girl right out of the 1920s in her fringed skirt, high

heels, and Spanish shawl draped around her shoulder in a seductive, come-hither way. The tilt of her head, her playful pose,
the way she hugged one arm about her reminded me of a picture of my grandmother in her college yearbook.

What was the saying? Your parents have atrocious taste. Your
grandparents have acceptable taste. Your great-grandparents
have superlative taste. These figures from my grandmother's
generation were just old enough to hold a fresh charm for me,
even if my mother had pooh-poohed them in my youth.

Ha! Mother said out of nowhere. *Your grandmother used to
wear short skirts like that. You still have her shawl somewhere.
You'll probably want to wear it now. Your grandmother was
quite a looker. Wore her hair in a bob. Learned the Charleston
and Lindy, too. They called them the Roaring Twenties. Well, she
told me even though she looked the part, things sure didn't
roar where she was.*

"I guess it's the romance of it all," I said.

"I could let her go for $6,250," she said.

That would be a cool $5,250 profit in just a matter of min-
utes. But what were the chances of my biting? Of her making
the sale? Next to none.

I thought about most of the dealer's inventory that hadn't
moved in weeks, months, even years, not to mention the
monthly rent she likely paid for her twelve-by-twelve-foot stall.

"That's a fair price," I said, carefully putting the figurine
down. "She's worth it." I looked the dealer straight in the eye.
"If I had the money, I'd buy her. Right now I don't."

"If it's the money, have you thought about a repro?" she
asked, smoothly shifting gears, trying to salvage the deal.

The dealer was already starting to ease her way down to another bay of shelves. She returned with a slightly larger figure, this one a dancing girl with a long green pleated skirt swept up and held in her hands at her sides. She put the figure between us.

"Six hundred ninety-nine dollars. You can buy her for five hundred from the manufacturer off the Internet or twenty-five thousand from a dealer who's trying to pass her off as being old—as being the real McCoy . . . in a shop *or* on the Internet." She laughed.

I was tempted to buy the figurine so I could show Sol what even the fakes were selling for. There was no way I could convince him to come see for himself, I was sure of that. Right now, though, I was more concerned with learning everything I could from my new friend.

"You know, I don't even know what your name is," I said impulsively. "I can't tell you how helpful you're being. Like you said, lots of dealers would try to slide this one by me as real . . . like it was a real steal."

The dealer drew herself up. Obviously I'd struck a nerve.

"I'm Sterling Glass," I said, extending my hand.

"Look, honey, *all* antiques dealers aren't bad. We aren't *all* like the con men out there on the streets trying to sell fake Rolexes and Chanels. In here, if I make a mistake it's one thing. But I'm *not* a crook." Her yard-long collection of bracelets hit against one another as she shook her pointer finger with its bright red fingernail at me.

"I meant it as a compliment," I said, drawing my hand back.

"Just checking." She sneered slightly, then smiled. The years certainly had not made this crusty gal any gentler.

"Maribelle Mason. Been in the business since I was twenty-five. Been in business fifty-plus years and, in life, eighty now and counting. And you know what?" she asked, shifting her full weight toward me, "I learn something every day. And so can you if you keep your eyes open. Look here," she said, taking up the reproduction figure she had just brought out and shaking her good. "Know where I got her?"

I shook my head.

"From a collector. *Big*-time collector. He got taken but was so humiliated he wouldn't take her back and retrieve his money. His pocketbook could afford the mistake. His pride couldn't."

"How could you tell she was a repro?"

She waved my question away like it was child's play. "Told you. I've already lived through Art Deco. The first time round." The dealer took off her glasses and with her crooked finger pointed to her eyes. "I've got the eye. Like an artist's eye. I can tell. Here, let me show you."

Maribelle adjusted her red glasses, pushing them higher on her nose, and placed the two figures next to one another.

"It'd be better if we had the real one just like the repro," she said. "But this will do. All right. Look here, now." She pointed to a tiny line running along the side of the reproduction figure's face. "See that? It's a mold mark. This is poured plastic."

Maribelle traced the line along the figure's face. "Why that line makes this little doll look like she's been under the knife for a face-lift." She ran a finger along her own face, pulling her skin tight. "Think I should have one?"

She let out a hearty laugh, let go of her skin, and kept talking. "Just kidding. See? It's not carved. You won't find that line in the real one, see?"

She tilted both figures toward me.

"What about the difference in the sizes," I asked. "Does that have any significance?"

"Nah. Not really. Lots of the original figures came in several different heights. But here's something that *does* matter. See, the plastic one is starting to have a little yellow tinge to her complexion. Like she's a smoker. That happens to plastic. It gets creamy. Lemon yellow. Not ivory. Now feel the bodies," she said.

"But what about piano keys," I asked, taking off my gloves so I could touch the figures. I could hear Mother calling me to come inside to practice those dreaded scales and arpeggios when I was a child. "Wash your hands, first, Sterling," she'd always say.

"Nice," Maribelle said, nodding toward the cabochon ruby and diamond ring that Hank had given me one Christmas.

"Thank you."

"Soap and water. Just wash the keys off with soap and water. Now feel along here," Maribelle instructed me, pointing to the reproduction figure's profile. "Sometimes this can be hard to tell if you haven't had a lot of experience, but the crevices and edges in the new figures are rounded, smoother . . . less sharp. They aren't as deep. That's because the old molds were better made. Better defined. Better crafted. The new ones? Pffff." She blew them off in disgust.

My thoughts ran back to Sol and his obsession with the old molds.

"How can *I* tell?" Maribelle laughed as I ran my fingers first over one, then the other, like a kid learning Braille. "*I* have the eye and the touch, and the years. Lots and lots of years."

Maribelle reached into her pocket.

"Here, take my card. Who knows? You might find yourself in the money one day. I'll still be here."

A COLD WIND was whipping up off the East River when I left the mall. For some reason I was no longer the least bit interested in lunch. Layton's was a good nine or ten blocks away, but I hated to waste the three or four dollars it would cost me to get there by cab, no matter how cold it was. There was no real urgency to get to the auction quite yet. Just walk fast, I told myself. And I needed time to think. I stuck my hands in my pockets and tucked my head down. Block after block I passed watch and camera shops, then more antiques and finery shops: crystal chandeliers, Oriental porcelains, and embroidered tablecloths, and all at unbeatable sale prices. Half the stores were going out of business—the same way they have been for the past umpteen years.

Between the cold air and the brisk walk, it didn't take long for the hunger I hadn't felt just minutes earlier to kick in. I stopped at the pretzel cart near the corner. I was counting out my money when who should walk next to me and wait for the light to change but Anna.

With her was a man, a head shorter than she and stocky in that squared-off, thick-shouldered way. He obviously was not happy.

"I told you you wouldn't find anything here," I overheard him say. "You shoulda hit another of those house sales. No good steals are gonna be along here, not in this high-rent district."

"Well, I'm tired of getting up at 4 A.M. to hit another house, Ralph."

"Okay. You've told me that already."

"And you've told me ten times that I wouldn't find anything along here," Anna snapped back. "But listen to me. Some of these guys fence all sorts of things in their back rooms."

"Okay. I'm tired of fighting about it. Look, you try one more place, then we're getting out of here. I'm not wasting any more of my time. We'd be better off hitting junk shops out in Yonkers."

The light turned red.

I had turned my back to Anna and her companion, the moment I'd recognized her. But half of me wanted to get a good look at him. My other half wanted to bolt out of there.

Only when I felt the swish of rushing bodies moving past me off the curb and onto the street did I dare look up and search for their backs in the fleeting crowd. Anna and Ralph Whoever-he-was had stepped out from the pedestrians moving up the street and stopped in front of a store in the next block. When Anna went in, Ralph hung back, paced around a few seconds, then moved up to the next storefront and blended in with other window shoppers. If only he'd turn around so I could see him.

Clearly Anna was the front. With her looks she could charm an Alabama buzzard off his roadkill.

It didn't make sense. From their conversation, it sounded like they were trying to *buy* goods. But Anna was *selling* the figure in the mall. I filed the thought away while I craned my neck to see what Ralph would do next.

His outline I thought looked remarkably like the thick blob of darkness that had swept past me in Joey's alleyway.

I lost any appetite I might have had. I'd walked five blocks already. Only five more to go. Forget the money. I'd figure some way to charge the cab to Babson and Michaels. I stepped into the street and stuck out my hand.

Chapter 16

Dear Antiques Expert: I recently saw a mirror with a highly polished black frame decorated with birds and butterflies and Oriental scenes. Some of the details, such as flower petals in the scene, were raised, which I'd never seen before. When I told the owner how much I liked it, he wrote down the description and price for me. His note said it was "japanned." Did this mean it was from Japan?

Though the mirror's design is Oriental, the term "japanning" refers to the technique used to paint and decorate the frame. To achieve the shiny finish, several coats of varnish or lacquer are applied to the wood. Bits of gesso-like material are then affixed to the lacquer to give some of the details their "raised" look. Finally, the scenes are hand-painted. Japanning originated in the Orient, but became popular in Western countries during the 16th and 17th centuries. Because paint flakes and chips, antique jappaned pieces in good condition, especially American ones, are rare and costly.

TALK IN THE antiques world before Layton's January auction sale had been that one piece might bring over a million. When the hammer fell for the last time, a Philadelphia tea table and

Newport secretary-bookcase had hit that golden mark. A pair of ball and claw-footed Queen Anne console tables had just missed it. And I was there to witness it all.

It was almost 6 P.M. when the auction was over, but that left a little time to scoot over to Park Avenue and East Sixty-seventh Street for a walk through the Seventh Regiment Armory Winter Antiques Show. My original plan had been to treat myself to a nice, albeit lonely, meal at Oscar's, the legendary meeting place tucked away in the Waldorf's Madison Avenue entrance. I'd eat around 8 P.M., while everyone else was at the theater, try to get a good night's sleep, then hit the antiques show on Sunday.

But ever since my meeting with Matt Yardley at Babson and Michaels, I'd had a persistent, gnawing urge to get back to Leemont to get to the bottom of Sarah Rose Wilkins's *supposed* urn and pin. I hated to leave Sol hanging in midair. But I could do my research at home more efficiently by combing the Internet and making some well-placed phone calls for information about Art Deco figures than I could by aimlessly wandering around New York's antiques spots. God knows I didn't want to chance bumping into Anna and that creepy Ralph Whoever-he-was again.

I'd checked on the status of the early Sunday morning flight with US Air. Everything looked fine.

AFTER A YEAR'S stint at the New York Hilton following the September 11 tragedy, the Winter Antiques Show, the Armory Show to old-timers, had returned to its customary home and usual glamour. More proof that the antiques world survived and thrived, even in the worst of times. Once again things were back to normal. Magnificent arrangements of exotic lilies, orchids, proteas, delphiniums, and bells of Ireland flown in from around the world adorned the booths set up in the vast, cement-floored Armory space. The brilliant array of flowers equaled the beauty of the antiques on display. It really was a glorious sight.

The star of the show, though not the most expensive item, was a completely original circa 1730 to 1750 black lacquered Boston highboy recently discovered in Omaha, Nebraska. Early japanned highboys with exotic Asian designs have long been scarcer than hens' teeth. Sometime in the later 1860s the highboy had traveled west with the son of an old Boston family who was looking to add more wealth to the family's coffers. It had passed down from one family member to the other until a couple of years ago, when the last direct family descendant died and a nephew who inherited the piece called in a local dealer.

The lacquer on the highboy was in such excellent condition that the dealer first thought it was an old copy, only about 125 years old. But when she learned it had arrived in Omaha in 1867 or 1868, she began doing her homework and realized that it was the real thing. When word of the highboy leaked out, a shrewd New York dealer convinced the equally shrewd Omaha dealer to let him show the highboy at this premier show for a cut. No price was given on the laminated sheet citing the highboy's provenance and history through the centuries. Rather, at the bottom of the page was written, "Only serious collectors should inquire further about this piece." Rumor was that the asking price was a little over one million dollars.

The highboy set the tone for the show in quality, age, rarity, and price; rumor was that a great Windsor chair had actually sold at the preview party for six figures, and a Southern quilt, not too unlike the one Peter had rescued a few years back, had sold for somewhere around thirty-five thousand dollars.

And everyone had said the market would be dead.

Every year Lita Solis-Cohen wrote in *MAD* (the *Maine Antique Digest,* that Bible for all serious antiques lovers), that people attended the Winter Show not just for the antiques and a chance to see the array of quirky, obnoxious, and lovable dealers but also to hear the insider gossip. I didn't pay much attention to the trade gossip; after all, Leemont was a long way from New York and the Main Line antiques world that stretched from Delaware up to Maine and Vermont. But I listened to it just for the fun of it all. And that night, things were anything but just "things." The determined buyers, using high-roller phrases such as "investment quality," "blue chip," and "future return," made me wonder if I was on the corner of Park and East Sixty-seventh or downtown on Wall Street.

Eavesdropping on the *serious* shoppers' conversations, I might have thought that despite the exorbitant prices, people were walking away with the steal of the new century. Even among the idle lookers—the beautiful people, the ones there to be seen rather than to buy but so wealthy that I thought of them as above such everyday sentiments and emotions—I overheard gushing comments about "my grandmother's pearl and diamond starburst pin" or "my great-great-great-aunt Margaret's exquisite coin silver water pitcher" or "my great-great-grandfather's gold pocket watch." And to hear them tell it, *Well!* there wasn't one piece being shown in that most glorious of all antiques shows that was half as good as the now lost family treasures owned by their dear, departed ancestors.

Now *you* tell me that stuff is just stuff.

Unfortunately for me, other than a couple of stunning Art Nouveau silver pieces by Martelé, there were very few twentieth-century pieces at the show. And no Deco figurines.

I had no regrets when I left the hotel the next morning to catch a flight back to Leemont.

It felt good to get home.

I waited until after the church hour to call Peter. He said he'd be straight over. Had I noted a slight concern in his voice? Was he as anxious to see me as I was to see him?

"Sight for sore eyes," Peter said when I opened the door.

"I'm probably going to make your *ears* sore, I have so much to tell you," I warned him. "Hot tea?"

Peter settled down in the high-back wing chair to the side of the fireplace, which he'd claimed as his own the very first time he'd come over. While we drank tea I told him about my encounters with Sol and Richie, and then Anna and Maribelle in the antiques mall, and later, Anna and Ralph. And then Matt Yardley and the Babson and Michaels claim.

"*What* a mess," I said, stopping my blathering to catch my breath, but finding enough air to add, "all of it!"

"And you loved every minute of it." Peter smiled.

"I did not. And you could be a little more sympathetic," I shot back. Lowering my eyes in mock guilt I admitted, "Well, yes, I did. But that's not to say that I'm not worried about these things," I added empathically.

"Let me give you something else to worry about, then."

"What now?"

"I called Lieutenant Pavich after we talked. He didn't seem very interested in the pin."

"Why not?" I said.

"Because he was out of the office a lot. Distracted at the time. But there may be a tie-in between why he was distracted and the mysterious pin."

"Oh?"

Peter put his teacup down and leaned forward. He wrinkled his brow and ran his hand over his mouth, the way people do when wrestling with what to say next.

"Well?" I said impatiently.

"For some time now the Leemont police have had complaints about a roofing company that comes to town, goes into the better neighborhoods, and calls on old folks who live there," Peter began. "One guy goes first, hands out his card, and says he sees a problem with the roof. Of course it's an older house and there probably *is* some reason for the people to think their roof might need repair.

"So the man checks out the problem and he returns with a couple of damaged pieces of roofing. He shows these to the people and says he'd like to check the attic to see if there's any sign of leaking or water damage. They let him do that, of course, and he comes back with a piece of rotting wood."

"Obviously he keeps the bad wood and roofing with him," I said.

"Obviously. So once he's convinced them that the job needs to be done, he quotes them a price. Now this fellow doesn't want any time to lapse so they can change their minds. He says that he just happens to have a crew that's finishing up a job around the corner at the So-and-so's house. In several instances, the police learned, the person tries to call Mr. So-and-so."

"Let me guess," I chirped in. "Mr. So-and-so just happens not to be at home."

"Right. Because, the con man says, 'Mr. So-and-so has already paid us and left us to finish the job up. He ran out to do some errands.'"

"Which makes the new victim all the more trusting."

"You got it. These guys haven't even been near the So-and-so's house—except to ring the doorbell to be sure no one's at home. The crew appears at the new victim's house in about five minutes. That poor soul writes the con man a check. The crew crawls all around the house hammering and making noise and not doing much of anything."

"And the business card?"

"When you call the number, an 888 number of course, you get a recording, or, on occasion, a live person who tells you that the fellow isn't in, he's out on a job, but he'll return the call. Now, if you and I were faced with this situation, we'd get to the bottom of it, but remember, it's a con game on the elderly. Sometimes they don't even remember having had the job done. Or they've lost the card. Or they are too embarrassed to tell their kids or friends what has happened when they realize they've been set up."

I nodded, remembering the sad, diminishing mental state of my mother. I clearly understood how it all could happen.

"What does this have to do with Sarah Rose Wilkins? She lived in an apartment house."

"That's coming . . . or at least part of it. So," Peter continued, "it seems that Jenny Emerson, you know her, she's Craig Emerson's youngest daughter, she's an attorney up in D.C. She was coming to Leemont to check on her dad. She arrives, only to find this crew of young guys swarming all over Craig's house. Now Craig was in the construction business for years. If he needed roofing done, he would have called his *own* company, except—"

"Except everyone's known that Craig Emerson has had Alzheimer's for years now."

"That's right." Peter shook his head emphatically. "But the kids have been keeping him at home until he can't function anymore . . . or probably until one of them feels ready to come back and move into their father's mansion. Anyway, Jenny Emerson's a smart gal. She played dumb, greeted her dad and his housekeeper, thanked the roofing guys for being there, told them she had to get some groceries, and came back with the police. The police had had enough complaints that they could question the guys pretty hard about lots of names and addresses. Finally, one of the younger helpers fessed up, which is how they found out how who the ring leader was."

"But the pin? The urn? How does this connect? Were they stealing things from these houses?"

"That's what's not quite so clear. Just listen to what happened. You'll see why Pavich needs your help."

"*My* help?"

I'd moved to the edge of the settee. When I scooted closer I kicked the butler's tray with the tea, almost knocking it over.

"Whoa, there!" Peter said, laughing as I caught myself and the table with one hand. "You're really getting into this."

"What can I say?" I resettled myself and began tapping my foot. "So what happened?"

Peter leaned further forward himself and clasped his hands in a preacherly way.

"The con man is Dwayne Sloggins from over in the Dixon Springs area, around forty-five minutes from here."

"I know where Dixon Springs is. What's he doing working for people in Leemont?"

"Patience, Sterling. That's coming next. Sloggins's modus operandi was to hang around Leemont's better neighborhood drugstores or grocery stores and wait till some well-dressed old person was checking out. Then he would pick up a candy bar or gum from the racks by the checkout counter and get in line. If the old person and the cashier had a friendly conversation, when it was his turn, Sloggins would ask the cashier the person's name. He'd always do it in a familiar, friendly way, like, 'That old man sure does look familiar. I used to deliver papers around here. He wouldn't be Reverend Andrews, would he? Looks so much like him.'

"Now Pavich says that Dwayne Sloggins is a decent-looking guy, smooth and polite. Sort of a country good-ole boy. Naturally the chatty cashier wouldn't hesitate to say, 'No . . . that's Dr. McFarland,' or whomever. Sloggins would say he'd forgotten the fellow's name, or he didn't recognize the good doctor after all these years, or whatever.

"That's when the cashier would tell Sloggins all about the old man or lady. Apparently, sometimes Sloggins would write down where the person lived, saying he thought he'd drop by and pay a friendly visit while he was in town, you know, for old time's sake. Other times, he'd just look the name and address up in the phone directory after he left the store."

"So they've been able to track it all down. That was quick."

"Well, not exactly *all* of it."

Chapter 17

Dear Antiques Expert: Our home was recently broken into, and we lost silver and jewelry and even some antique prints, plus brand-new electronic equipment. Ours was only one of a rash of break-ins in our neighborhood. The burglars were caught, but when the cases came to trial, they got off with really light sentences. Nobody can believe it. How can that be?

You and I may find those light sentences reprehensible, but I remember hearing New York City's former "art cop," Bob Volpe, explain that you have to expose law-enforcement officers to the arts so they will have an understanding of the seriousness of personal property theft involving art and antiques. Unfortunately, even today not enough police officers know enough about art and antiques and their historical and monetary value to make a strong case against the thieves.

PETER GOT UP and began pacing around the room.

I couldn't resist. "Peter, have you seen Bagman lately?"

"What?"

"Have you seen Barefoot Bagman lately?"

"No. Why? What on earth made you think about him? Especially now."

"I don't know. Doesn't matter. I didn't mean to interrupt. I'm sorry. What were you about to tell me about the roof scammers?"

"Well, the young guy who fessed up said that apparently Sloggins got some leads from a woman, but the fellow wasn't sure who. Sloggins wouldn't admit to anything, of course, but the kid said Sloggins made lots of cell phone calls just before giving them an address or directions to a job. The police ran down his calls and came up with the name of Jane Finn. Interestingly, she sits for old and sick people."

"Makes sense. Does she live out in Dixon Springs, too?" I asked.

"No. Here in Leemont. I'm told she's well thought of. Even Ed Pavich knew who she was. She had sat for the mother of one of Pavich's neighbors a few years back. Pavich had seen Finn around the neighborhood. Talked to her. Nice lady. Or so Pavich thought at the time."

"What does she say? Has she admitted to anything?"

"Not yet."

"Well, what do the victims say? Had she sat for any of them?"

"Just one or two it seems. Pavich's men are checking out the dates of when she sat for those families and when the roofing jobs were done. He hasn't gotten the reports yet. The police have to dot every *i* these days, you know; they still don't begin to know exactly how many people the guys have scammed, or even how widespread the scam is. The way I see it, if Sloggins came into Leemont, he could go over into Norfolk, even down to Raleigh."

"One thing I do know, Peter," I said, "is that these sitters tend to be friends with one another and even switch off jobs for holidays, weekends. When I had to have sitters for Mother they were always giving one another's names as references. Who knows? Many more people than this Jane Finn might be involved. It could be a whole network."

"Or she could have simply gathered information from other sitters and then passed it on to Sloggins," Peter said.

"That's true, too. I know you get tired of hearing my mother's quotes," I said. "But 'opportunity makes a thief.' Sir Frances Bacon."

"Exactly." Peter nodded. "And there are lots of possibilities here for lots of people to have lots of opportunities to steal, I'd say."

He paused, smiling.

"Anyway, it's Pavich's job to sort all that out. Presently, though, Jane Finn seems to be the gal to watch. My gut feeling is that she's the link. She's how I've come to know about all this."

I had been so intrigued with the story that I'd skipped right over asking how Peter had learned all this. "Oh? How's that?"

"The morning I called Pavich, when he called me back we only had a short conversation. As I said, he was rushed. Later, after Jane Finn's name came up in our conversation, I found out that he'd been in such a rush because he was dashing out to try to catch her at home," he said. "She's been working the third shift, so he was reasonably sure he'd find her there in the late afternoon, when night workers tend to sleep. She was at home but up and dressed.

"Of course she didn't have any idea why Ed Pavich was calling on her. He'd arrived unannounced. But since they were nodding acquaintances from earlier times, she invited him in.

"The first thing that caught Pavich's eye was a large silver vase on a table in the living room. It puzzled him, but he passed it off. Then, when he sat down on the sofa, he could see into the dining room. There was a beautiful porcelain soup tureen and a silver ladle that, according to Ed, looked very expensive."

I opened my mouth to ask a question, but Peter beat me to it.

"You're wondering how he would notice." Peter said. "Being a man and a police officer. Well, he told me how. Ed's wife isn't interested in anything except horses and race cars, but his baby sister married money, just like he did, and according to Ed, it didn't take his sister any time to develop *fine* taste so she could spend her husband's money. These days, when Ed and his family visit his sister in Baltimore, she carefully 'educates'— that's Ed's word—him all about her newest acquisitions. Tells him how old they are, where they came from, and especially how much they cost. He thinks that she's secretly trying to get Ed's wife interested in antiques—but it hasn't worked."

"Aha." I couldn't help but smile to myself.

"The clincher, though, came when Ed was talking to Jane Finn," Peter continued. "She never did admit knowing Sloggins, but as they got deeper into the conversation she not only seemed to get nervous and uncomfortable, she began fiddling, messing, with a bracelet. Once she realized what she was doing, Ed said, she immediately tucked it under her sleeve. Pavich is sharp. Notices every little thing."

"A*ha*," I said again, even more emphatically this time.

"Could it possibly have been a ruby and diamond bracelet?"

I asked. The description of the Cartier bracelet on the Hanesworths' inventory of stolen goods came to me.

"I asked Ed what kind of bracelet it was. He's unsure. Jane
Finn was across the room. But he did say that it looked like diamonds. Maybe set in platinum."

"Platinum. White gold. Rubies. Diamonds. Whatever, any
of the above is suspicious for someone living on sitters' fees,
though I imagine sometimes she makes more than I do."

"That's what I thought. About owning things like Pavich described . . . Not that she makes more money than you do," Peter clarified himself.

I let the comment pass. "So what did Pavich do next?"

"Well, he told me that his first thought was to be in touch
with you."

"Me?"

"Ed said he wants to talk to you about the fine antiques he
saw in Jane Finn's house."

"But there are other appraisers in town."

Peter lowered his eyes.

"*Peter* . . . You didn't."

"Not exactly. It just happened." Peter looked sheepish. "Just
shush for a minute and I'll tell you what happened. It's all very
logical."

He took a deep breath. "When Ed Pavich got back to the
station from Jane Finn's house and started thinking things
through, he remembered *my* call telling him about the *pin*."

Peter held out one hand and said, "Bracelet." Then, extending his other hand, he said, "Pin. Naturally Ed connected the
two. That's when he called me back. During our conversation

I told him what you'd told me . . . about how the pin had shown up on a list of items missing from the Charlottesville area . . . and, well . . . here we are." Peter grinned at me.

I frowned. "Why didn't you tell me all this when we talked on the phone?"

Peter looked at me as if I had been out to lunch. "I couldn't have. I didn't know it. You and I talked late Friday, remember?"

How could I have forgotten?

"Ed only called me yesterday," Peter said.

"Oh." I realized I was unconsciously counting the days off on my fingers. "Friday, Saturday, Sunday. So much has happened . . . so much out of the ordinary . . . in such a short time . . . just lost track of time." Plus I haven't had a decent night's sleep since Wednesday, I wanted to say.

"Even if I had known all this, I wouldn't have told you. Why distract you from your fun in New York?" Peter smiled.

"And after hearing about all the other problems with, what's his name—Sol?—I'm glad I *didn't* have the option of telling you what was going on down here. You do need to call Ed first thing in the morning, though," he said. "I told him it would be Tuesday, but I'm sure he'll be happy to hear from you on Monday."

I rose and began gathering up our empty teacups to have something to do. I've never found it easy to sit still for long, and when I'm worried sitting still is totally out of the question.

"Well," I said, "I still don't see the tie-in. Sarah Rose Wilkins didn't live in a house, so the roofing scam can't apply to her. She was very healthy up until the end. She didn't have sitters, so that eliminates Jane Finn. I'm in a fog."

Peter rose and took the teacups from my hands.

"Tell you what, Sterling. Let's don't worry about how Sarah Rose ties into all of this for now. We can think about it, but ultimately that's for Ed and the police to figure out. I say it's time for that glass of wine and I'll take you out to dinner. How's that?"

It was music to my ears.

"On one condition," he added, tossing his comment over his shoulder on his way back to my kitchen. "We can talk about something *besides* the urn and the pin and the bracelet."

"I'll try," I said halfheartedly, for once thinking less about Peter than the problem at hand.

"How about Art Deco figurines?" I called after him.

Chapter 18

Dear Antiques Expert: I was appalled to read where a portion of an antique iron fence around a cemetery plot and two carved sculptures from the graves were recently stolen. Why would anyone do such a thing?

Money. Decorative antiques suitable for a garden or solarium are bringing top dollar these days. Such items found in cemeteries, especially small, unattended cemeteries, as many old ones tend to be, can be easily stolen and sold before they are missed. To illustrate how highly desirable 18th- and 19th-century garden accessories have become, a specialty shop recently featured an iron garden bench for $7,500 and a pair of iron planters for $15,000. Exceptional garden statues are often sold in the $20,000–25,000 range.

EARLY MONDAY MORNING my phone rang. Howard Creighton was the last person I was expecting to hear from, but there he was on the other end of the line.

"Sterling, Martha wants to talk to you," he said.

My heart almost broke when I heard him say to his wife, "Go ahead, dear."

"Hello. We want you to come see . . . " Mrs. Creighton's thin voice trailed off. "What is it we want?" she asked her husband, but spoke into the phone's mouthpiece.

Before he could answer, she said to me, clear as a bell, "And bring back that casserole dish I sent to Sarah Rose Wilkins's house."

The phone went dead.

While looking up the Creighton's phone number, my own phone rang again.

"Sterling. This is Howard Creighton. I'm sorry," he said. "I tried." His voice broke.

"I understand."

"Do you think you could come over this morning?"

I had a million other things planned. Peter had told me to call Lieutenant Pavich. I had planned to call Roy. I needed to call Sol. I wanted to call Matt Yardley. I needed to figure out what was going on.

"I'll be there as soon as I can," I said.

JUST LIKE CRAIG EMERSON, whom the roofing guys had scammed, and the Hanesworths, whom I had never met but who were very much on my mind after my meeting with Matt Yardley, Mr. and Mrs. Creighton still lived in their own home. It was a wonderful, untouched 1870s brick row house in Stuart's Ridge, the nineteenth-century neighborhood overlooking the river and the railroad tracks in the oldest section of Leemont. The Creightons had moved there in the 1950s when Howard Creighton's mother became ill. Some of Leemont's oldest and finest families were still living in Stuart's Ridge back then, but all that was beginning to change. One by one, as the last member of those families died, their houses became vacant. The pattern was always the same. Some younger branch of the family was *going to* move in but didn't. Invariably those younger folks chose to live in an expensive house in Arbor Hills or to buy farther out in one of the newer suburbs or to leave Leemont altogether.

Soon a house would need painting and the slate roof relining. Then a wisteria bush, bamboo tree, or Virginia creeper grew out of control and began to cover the front porch and start its climb up to the second-story windows. Eventually, the heirs would put the abandoned and dilapidated property up for sale. When no one would buy it for a single dwelling (the house next door in the same condition, as the one across the street), some absentee landlord stepped in, paid the back taxes, bought the house for a song, and turned the once-stately residence into a multifamily, low-rent property.

If they were shrewd, the new owners applied for one of those housing assistance deals where they would be paid four or five hundred dollars by the state to rent the property for seventy or eighty dollars to some down-and-out or down-on-their-luck family. Talk about an easy way to double-dip while lining your pockets at the expense of the poor *and* taxpayers. My blood boiled every time I thought about it.

The Creightons had been one of the few families who had bucked the trend, who had actually stayed while everyone else was moving *out*. But then Howard Creighton's grandfather had built the house and I guessed that Howard and Martha had always done exactly what was expected of them, even as young newlyweds.

When the quickly deteriorating Stuart's Ridge neighborhood

reached the point of being unsafe, people gossiped about how foolish the Creightons were to maintain property that no one else would have, even if it were handed to them on a gold platter. Never would anyone have imagined that the Creightons would have the last laugh. For as things always went, the Ridge, as it was now called, had once again become *the* place to live in Leemont—right up there with Arbor Hills—and the grown children and grandchildren of those people who had hot-tailed it to the suburbs were now paying four hundred thousand, six hundred thousand, and more to reclaim the heritage their parents had thrown away for a song.

Turning off River Road, I drove up the hill to the Ridge. The street was dotted with landscaping, plumbing, and electrician trucks parked in front of the proud old houses. Iron posts holding up signs advertising painting companies cluttered the narrow front yards of probably two or three houses per block.

For a fleeting moment it was as if I had stepped back to the plantation days of the Old South. Oh, twenty-first-century workers chatted on cell phones and used the latest chemicals and technology to get rid of the termites and installed the latest high-speed Internet wiring for the Ridge's newly renovated residences, but these workers were just as necessary to the region's economy as were the slaves who kept up the grand houses of that long-ago time. It was the rich landowners or, these days property owners, who kept Leemont's economy buzzing along.

As Howard Creighton had asked me to do, I pulled into the alleyway behind the Creightons' home and parked in their guest spot. The gate to their walled garden was open. I thought about going to the back door to steal a close-up look at the charming nineteenth-century marble water nymph frolicking among the manicured English ivy, but I decided against it.

Instead, I walked down the brick footpath bordered by yellow and purple pansies to the front doorway and about the largest magnolia tree I'd ever seen. I had to duck beneath its limbs to step onto the Creightons' front porch. The boughs, brightly gleaming in the morning sun, hung heavy with dark brown cones dripping with the few deep red seeds the cardinals and blue jays had yet to eat. In almost no time, fragrant white blossoms would grace its waxy green foliage, but right now, as a stiff, late January wind blew past me, May seemed light-years away.

Howard Creighton answered my ring. Peeping around from behind him was Martha, as always neatly groomed, today in a wool coatdress, her hair held in place by a pale gray hairnet like my grandmother used to wear. She pulled at Howard's sleeve.

"Did she bring back my silver casserole dish, Howard? I don't know how I can fix Christmas dinner without it. I never should have let that woman take it to Sarah Rose. And then Sarah Rose had to die. Oh, I'll never get it back. And with all the Christmas shopping to do. What shall I do? What shall I do?" Martha Creighton hung her head in despair. "What shall I do?" she said again.

Howard stood silently by, letting Martha have her say, never taking his ever patient eyes off her. Only when her quivering voice trailed off to a low hum did he turn to welcome me. Hidden from her sight, his look was one of pleading—not for pity but for compassion.

"I know this is an inconvenience, Sterling, but I thought maybe it would help Martha if you came to make an appraisal. I knew you'd understand."

He needed to say no more. The Creightons and my mother had been friends through the museum and other cultural organizations years earlier.

"That's all Martha's talked about for days now. The appraisal. But since this morning she seems to have forgotten about that. Now all she can talk about is her silver dish." Howard Creighton shook his head in despair.

"Martha," he said kindly, turning back toward her, "why don't you go to the library? It's almost time for your show to start. You know, *I Love Lucy.* I'll be there in just a minute. You get settled." Taking her elbow, he gently pointed her in the right direction.

Martha turned and made her way down the hall.

"I'll be happy to do whatever you want done, Mr. Creighton," I said. "Leave. Stay. You tell me."

"I don't know, myself," he said, barely holding back his own emotion and frustration. "Well . . . you're here. Why don't you just wander around?" He shook his head in bewilderment. "Do whatever you usually do. The money's not a problem. Maybe Martha will leave you alone. The children say we need to have an appraisal made anyway. Just . . . just do . . . whatever. I'll be in the library with Martha."

"Yes sir. I understand. I know what to do. But may I ask you something?"

"Of course."

"This silver casserole dish that Mrs. Creighton keeps talking about?"

"Oh, it's nothing. Just one of those silver-plated things that looks nice on the table. Martha used to be so meticulous about appearances. I try to keep things nice these days."

"And you do!" I said, acknowledging the immaculate house with a sweeping gesture. "But tell me, when did Mrs. Creighton send the casserole to Mrs. Wilkins's house? Mrs. Creighton said something about a woman. *You* didn't take it?"

"No. We sent it. It was . . . Now let me think. Sarah Rose went to the hospital. No, Sarah Rose was taken ill, that was it. *Then* she went to the hospital, but she was doing well. Wilma Baker called us. Wilma and Sarah Rose and Martha and I used to play bridge together after Sarah Rose's husband died, you know. Wilma said Sarah Rose was coming home that next day or was it the day after? We were so glad. It was *my* idea that we send something over to the house. Now just how was that?"

He paused, furrowed his brow, then blurted out, "Oh yes! I know. Mrs. Finn, that nice lady who sometimes sits with Martha was here. I had a Rotary meeting at lunch that day. That's why she was here. Afterward, I picked up a casserole from Phil's Deli—their good Turkey Tetrazzini." Howard Creighton smiled contentedly, clearly pleased with himself that he could recall so many details in light of his wife's dementia. I let him talk.

"I remember, because I got some for our supper, too. I was going to let Mrs. Finn take the casserole to Sarah Rose on her way home. But when Martha saw the Styrofoam box, she insisted that we take it out and put it in the casserole dish. I should have had Phil's deliver it," he said ever so remorsefully. "*That* was my mistake."

My ears had perked up much earlier, but I waited for him to finish his say. I had learned from my experience with Mother not to rush the elderly.

"Mrs. Finn? Is that Jane Finn?"

"Oh yes." He brightened. "That's her name . . . Jane. Jane
Finn. You know her? A nice lady. Old, but not as old as we are.
Maybe late sixties. She gets around real well. I told her that she
should sit with Sarah Rose Wilkins when she came home from
the hospital. I told her Sarah Rose would need someone in the
house. Yes, Jane Finn is a real capable woman. A quiet sort, but
capable. She and Martha made the casserole look real pretty in
the silver dish. It kept Martha busy for a long time." He smiled
sweetly. "It was late in the day so I gave her the key we keep
to Sarah Rose's apartment."

"The key? To Mrs. Wilkins's apartment?"

"Why, we've had a key to Sarah Rose's apartment ever since
nice Bob Wilkins died," Howard Creighton said as naturally as
if he were saying it's getting close to lunchtime. "First to their
house. They lived right around the corner when Bob was living. And then, when he died and Sarah Rose moved, she gave
us the key to her apartment."

"Did Mrs. Finn bring the key back?"

"Of course. The next time she sat with Martha. A week or
two later, I'd say. Hung it on the key holder by the back door. It
was after Sarah Rose died. I know that because two days after
we sent the food, Sarah Rose died. I had told Jane Finn to put it
in the cold part of the refrigerator. Oh, that poor dear, her death
was so sudden. And she had just gotten home. Sarah Rose went
home from the hospital too early, you know. We hadn't thought
she was going home until the next week. So sad the way she died.
Those doctors should have kept her in the hospital. Made her
stay. Just because they couldn't find anything wrong with her."
He shook his head in disgust. "Those doctors.

"Then again, Sarah Rose was a strong-willed woman," he

said sprightly. "I heard that she insisted on going home. Sounds like something she'd do. Yes, Mrs. Finn brought the key back, but there was no rush. But," Howard Creighton heaved a heavy, regretful sigh, "in all the sudden sadness, I completely forgot about the silver dish . . . Martha calls it a silver *casserole* dish." He smiled tenderly, as if remembering an earlier time in his life.

"When we heard that Sarah Rose had died, we were still glad we had sent the food because Sarah Rose's niece came to take care of things. I hope she enjoyed it. I wanted to get over to see her, but Martha didn't do well when I told her the news of Sarah Rose's death. Sometimes it's better for other people not to see Martha when she's not herself."

"I'm sure her niece understood," I said to comfort him.

"I don't think I'd ever have remembered the silver dish if Martha hadn't gotten it on her mind of late." Howard Creighton nodded his head up and down, over and over, then swayed, bracing himself against the chair he'd been leaning against. "That's the way it is, you know. They get one thing on their minds and can't let it go."

"Come, Mr. Creighton, you've been standing for a long time," I said. I had been so eager to gather all the details and information I could that I hadn't realized how taxing this was on him. Poor man, he probably hadn't had that long a conversation with anyone in . . . who knew how long.

"Yes," he agreed. "I need to check on Martha, too. Well, you do what you need to do, Sterling."

"I'm just going to make a quick swing through the house and see what's what," I said with false cheerfulness. "I'll find you if I need you."

"Yes. That will be fine," he said, his voice trailing off as he started down the hall.

I wasted no time finding the Creightons' kitchen phone. I could feel my heart beating as I called Peter and asked if he could meet me for lunch.

"I'm seeing Ed Pavich this afternoon, but I want to go over everything with you first," I said after giving a much abbreviated version of what I had just learned. "Do you think that if Jane Finn had the key, *she* might have been who Sarah Rose was telling to get out? I don't like this. What if Jane Finn killed Sarah Rose?"

"Now Sterling, don't go jumping to conclusions. We'll talk it out," Peter said.

As soon as I hung up, I started jotting down notes about the Creightons, Sarah Rose Wilkins, and Jane Finn. My mind was racing with questions for Howard Creighton—whether Jane Finn sat for them regularly, when she'd be back again, if they had had their roof repaired lately. But clearly now was not the time. For now I'd have to settle for telling Peter. Later, I'd tell Ed Pavich what I'd learned so far. I wondered if Matt Yardley had learned any more about the Hanesworths' theft?

Right now, silver and furniture were the furthest things from my mind, or at least appraising the Creightons' china and silver and furniture. But I couldn't let Howard Creighton down. I slipped into the formal rooms of the house and for the first time gave them a quick once-over. Usually I would have the entire room almost memorized, or at least the major pieces, within just a few seconds. Not today.

I found myself staring into space. It was then I realized how distracted I was.

I forced myself to look around. The Creightons' home was like the Creightons themselves, tidy but tired. The rooms had a pale haze about them, even with the sun streaming in. The silk damask upholstered chair and sofa were worn at the arms. The patterned wallpapered walls had faded from a vibrant red to a pale burgundy. The house reminded me of so many old houses I had visited. Dreary and drab.

Still though, there were *so* many objects, *so* much furniture—the accumulation of generation added on to generation—that I knew that this job would take several long hours, even days, of detailed, on-site work. Under normal circumstances, right about now I would be figuring out how to best handle the Creightons' appraisal, considering Mrs. Creighton's condition—a complex and extremely delicate situation for me and for them. Today, though, my only thought was how I could get out as quickly as possible.

Any appraiser knows when it comes to authenticating valuable antiques, a picture really *isn't* worth a thousand words. But, when all else failed, a photograph could at least be a starting point. Given the present circumstances, there was no doubt that taking some pictures was considerably simpler than looking for hallmarks on silver, signatures on paintings, and accurately measuring and describing piece after piece.

I passed over my digital camera, took my old-fashioned Minolta out of its case, and started the four-corner routine—standing in one corner and shooting the opposite side of the room—until I had good panoramic shots. Next I took really close close-ups of some of the details of the major pieces, those details that could add, or take away, hundreds, sometimes thousands, of dollars. I'd drop the film off for one-hour photo finishing on the way to lunch and have the pictures ready to look at immediately.

I opened a few drawers to see what lay in store for another day. Each time I did so, I moaned. Every drawer and cubby hole was crammed full with the sort of treasures that naturally accumulate over the years when no one moves out of a house and discards the family mementos that we wish *our* families had held on to. There were Christmas cards from the 1890s; gold-rimmed glasses from the 1860s; old campaign buttons for Roosevelt—Theodore, not Franklin Delano; gold fountain pens from the 1920s that would make Richie Daniel's hair stand on end; a set of twelve late-nineteenth-century Tiffany sterling silver nut picks in their original silk-lined case—that was just the three top drawers in the circa 1800 Virginia inlaid Hepplewhite walnut secretary-bookcase in the living room. Even the brasses and beautifully splayed feet were original. The secretary-bookcase alone was worth well over $50,000. The silver nut picks would easily fetch $750-plus at a fancy antiques show. Heaven only knew what I'd find in the dining room.

I looked around the corner. There was another Virginia treasure—a period walnut hunt board worth twenty or twenty-five thousand if it was worth a penny—and that was just a quick guesstimate. No telling what valuable and historically important silver pieces undoubtedly lay in wait in its drawers. And lay in wait they would, until another day.

I worked rapidly for a little over an hour. When I realized it was getting close to noon, I slipped into the library. Maybe I could ask Mr. Creighton a few questions before I left.

Both of the Creightons had drifted off to sleep.

Across the room, an exasperated young Dick Van Dyke paced back and forth across the TV screen trying to cajole Morey Amsterdam and Rose Marie into writing the scene for *The Alan Brady Show* his way. Martha Creighton, seated at one side of the sofa, a gray shawl tucked around her shoulders, wasn't moving a muscle. Seated in the lounge chair beside her, Howard's portly chest rose and fell in rhythm with his muffled snores.

When you are old and grey and full of sleep, Mother would say, quoting W. B. Yeats when she, herself, would awaken from a daytime nap that she had drifted into unexpectedly.

I had never felt the words more poignantly. I gazed at the old gray people complacently dozing in front of the gas logs in this library, once the scene of lively conversation. My eyes moved from one gentle soul to the other while Yeats's words played in my mind, drowning out the canned laughter coming from the TV set:

How many loved your moments of glad grace,
And loved your beauty with love false or true,
But one man loved the pilgrim soul in you,
And loved the sorrows of your changing face.

Fighting back tears, I jotted a quick note to Mr. Creighton telling him I'd left, but would call later. I put it on the kitchen counter where I felt sure he would see it, and slipped out the back way, past the marble water nymph without giving it a second glance.

Chapter 19

Dear Antiques Expert: I bought a 1920s decorating book at the library book sale. The author suggested that "beehive" candlesticks be used in the living room on the mantel piece or a side table. What exactly are beehive candlesticks?

The name "beehive" came from the ring design used to decorate the columns of many brass candlesticks in the 19th century. It resembled the ringed cone shape of a natural beehive. Hundreds of thousands of brass beehive candlesticks were made in those days before electricity. The style never went out of fashion and reproduction beehive candlesticks are still being made.

OUR LUNCH FOR two turned into a powwow for three. Peter had called Ed Pavich and asked him to join us at the Dixie Café, a soup and sandwich place on the edge of where Stuart's Ridge meets Leemont's downtown legal district.

I'd not met Ed Pavich before, just heard of him through idle town talk. When he, a Northerner, had married Molly Stone, the daughter of a rich peanut grower from over in the Suffolk area, her daddy had built them one of those new huge, beige and gray stone houses with lots of high-pitched rooflines way out in the county so Molly could have land and horses. Some folks said that Daddy Stone picked the land around Leemont because he didn't want his half-Yankee Pavich grandchildren hanging around him down in Suffolk.

In Leemont, the Paviches kept to themselves. That meant that they didn't run in any of Leemont's social circles—even though Molly was supposedly worth millions. She preferred sports cars to bridge parties, and most weekends she could be found racing her Porsche Boxster at VIR (shorthand for Virginia International Raceway)—something Leemont's ladies couldn't quite comprehend. The Paviches seldom entertained, but someone who had been in their home spread the word around town that everything in their house was new. Not the Leemont way.

But what made the situation even more weird to Leemont's unrelenting way of thinking was that Ed, who obviously didn't have to work, hired on with the police department even while their house was being built. Stranger yet, he showed up for work every day. And he'd risen through the ranks to become Leemont's highly respected chief detective. His Godfather-like manner scared away anyone who thought Leemont was just another hick Southern town.

As a rule I didn't go out of my way to meet any police officer. Cops made me nervous. The only blue lights I ever wanted to see were either in front of Martha Stewart's kitchen towels at Kmart, or hanging on someone else's Christmas tree. From a distance, Ed's storm trooper exterior didn't inspire any reassuring feelings. Ed was packed from his bald head to his big toenail with finely chiseled muscles. If instead of a heavy winter jacket and body-hugging jeans he'd had on combat fatigues,

I would have expected his face to be painted in camouflage. He could just as easily have been wearing a Confederate flag T-shirt, or neo-Nazi gear, and looked perfectly natural. Except on Saturday night. That's when I'd heard he went, alone, to Mass at Holy Comforter Catholic Church. Nonetheless, face-to-face, Ed Pavich was sexy as hell. No wonder some sweet eastern Virginia country girl who liked to drive fast sports cars and ride big horses had fallen for him.

Either Peter had warned Ed about my cop phobia or else Ed Pavich took one look at me and summed up the situation as quickly as I summed up a person's taste. As I made my way to the table where he and Peter were sitting, Ed stood, all compact five feet eight inches of him.

"So this is the famous Sterling Glass," he said as he thrust his hand toward mine. (Forget that rule from the Old South that a gentleman never extends his hand unless the lady extends hers first. This is the New South.) "I've been looking forward to meeting you."

Ed Pavich's deep voice was as gravelly as pebbles mixed with ground-up asphalt. It fit his rough masculine exterior like his snug Levi's. Perfectly. But he had an unmistakable twinkle in his eyes. Involuntarily, I began warming up to him.

"Peter says you probably hold the key to this whole case. I can't tell you how much we appreciate your help," he said before I had a chance to say anything myself.

That sealed the deal.

"I sure do hope I can help," I said.

God, that was lame, but I couldn't think of anything else to say as I wedged myself around the square table next to the rough brick wall.

I don't know if it was intentional or a coincidence, but Peter broke the awkward silence as he helped me into my chair. "We've been scheming behind your back, Sterling. Ed and I think it's essential that you get inside Jane Finn's home."

"To check out the things I'm suspicious of," Ed said. "You know, antiques. Stuff guys don't know about."

Ed Pavich gave me a wink and a sideways glance. I'd always been a sucker for guys who flirted with their eyes instead of their words. Then he smiled the sexiest smile since Dennis Quaid's in *The Big Easy*. Quaid played Remy McSwain, a slightly shady detective in that flick. Just a fluky coincidence, I hoped. But I was getting suspicious of everyone.

"Hey, at least you knew they were antiques. That's better than most," I quipped, hoping I sounded more intelligent this go-round. "So, have you cowboys decided exactly how I'm going to check these things out?"

"Sterling, first tell Ed how you found the sitters for your mother when she was alive," Peter said.

I frowned at the question. "References. Word of mouth. Interviews."

"How did you interview them?" Ed asked, shifting his chair closer to the table. "Where?"

"Sometimes by phone, sometimes . . ." I nervously shifted as I recalled memories I'd fought hard to erase.

Just then Lois approached the table, and our conversation stopped. Lois commanded that sort of respect. She was why this little lunchroom had thrived even during those years when Stuart's Ridge was withering away. If she'd ever combed her wiry, short gray hair or bought a new waitress's uniform, you wouldn't know it. And how she could eat the food served up at

Dixie's every day and stay under one hundred pounds was beyond me. Nor had Lois ever aged. She was a great-grandmother and though over seventy, she could still tote, with one palm, a tray that weighed as much as a wet whale. But what really kept people flocking back to the café week in, week out was the way Lois remembered what you ordered last time and always got your order right today.

Well, actually, it was Lois *plus* the food that her husband, Frank, cooked up in the kitchen *plus* the slightly seedy aura of the place itself that gave the Dixie its staying power. On any given day I'd overhear people talking about when the Girl Scout cookies would be delivered and whose wife was playing around with whose husband—all in the same breath. My lawyer friends told me that more deals were made under Lois's nose than in any judge's chambers.

"Same thing?" Lois asked me.

"Think I'll try something different today. How about a bowl, please—not a cup—of Brunswick stew, with a Virginia country ham biscuit on the side."

"You Southerners," Ed laughed. "It's a Vir-ginia, coun-try ham bis-cuit," he said, slowly enunciating every syllable. "The way you all say it, it's all one word. Virginiacountryhambiscuit."

He almost got it right. Except he was still putting the *r* in Virginia.

Peter ordered a bowl of chili and corn bread. Ed, after much agonizing, chose a meat-loaf sandwich with stewed tomatoes and home fries.

"No fried egg today, honey?" Lois asked him.

On second thought, Ed added a fried egg on the side.

"About the interviews," Ed said finally, turning to me. "Peter told me about your mother. I'm really sorry, and I hate to ask you to do this, but do you think you could do it again? Have an interview with Jane Finn?"

I glanced Peter's way. He gave me his sweet, boyish smile. I looked back at Ed. There was nothing sweet about him. Intense. Demanding. Impassioned. But nothing sweet. I looked again at Peter. I'd do just about anything to win his approval, even after all this time.

"We've already agreed that you have to get into her house to confirm my suspicions. I hardly think she's going to bring the goods to us." Ed flashed a terse smile. "Nobody else would know as much about the things she's got sitting around in her house as you would."

"I remember a professor once telling us that ten minutes in the lab can save you a day in the library," Peter said. "Even if I could think up some excuse to get into Jane Finn's house, which I can't, I wouldn't know the objects and their values as quickly as you would, Sterling. I'd have to spend days doing research, or end up calling you and trying to tell you what I'd seen. Ed tells me time is of the essence."

WHICH EXPLAINED HOW I came to be sitting in a floral upholstered overstuffed chair in Jane Finn's 1920s bungalow. There, while peering into pale blue eyes, set off by such thick dark brown eyelashes that they had to be false, all surrounded by a head of enormous, flouncy frosted blonde hair, I chatted on about Aunt Dorothy, my father's sister. The truth was, I hadn't seen her in over a decade.

I'd told Jane Finn I was considering bringing my aunt to

Leemont. I wanted her later years to be more comfortable than if she stayed in the small New Hampshire town with its harsh winters. Jane Finn said she had more business than she could handle, but when I told her that I lived on Bittersweet Trail she had said maybe she could see me after all.

Thank goodness she hadn't known who I was when I called. I really wasn't as famous as Ed Pavich said. I had cautiously worked our conversation around until she finally agreed that I could meet her in her home that very afternoon around five. Luckily this didn't leave her much time to check up on me, but with my former husband's last name and my current address, I don't think she would have.

Very quickly I learned that Howard Creighton was right. Jane appeared to be a quiet woman. Sitting on the low-slung sofa across from me, she stared at me without ever changing expressions and speaking only when spoken to. I made nervous small talk about my aunt. But glancing around, I saw that in her eagerness to impress me, Jane Finn had pulled out even more of her pretties—a Rose Medallion tea caddy, a nineteenth-century brass beehive candlestick, a slim, leatherbound copy of Dickens's *Old Curiosity Shop*. Or else Ed Pavich's sister just hadn't gotten around to "educating" him about those pieces yet. Either way, this display of fine antiques was in stark contrast to the 1960s oversized orange pebbled glass lamps on the 1980s cherry-veneered and particle board end tables flanking the 1970s Mediterranean-style sofa. I wasn't the first person to observe that every man's house is his unwritten autobiography. In Jane Finn's home, the story was a screwed-up life. Or else she was living a lie. In her case, both were probably true. She definitely needed a visit from the *Queer Eye* gang.

When I complimented Jane Finn on her pretty pieces—especially the silver vase Ed had noted on his visit—her demeanor changed abruptly. She babbled forth like water gushing over a dam.

"I really came from good stock," she insisted, and apologized, all in the same breath. "If I hadn't been orphaned first and then widowed so young—just a bride, really—I wouldn't be in this line of work. Not that I mind. I like old people a lot. I really do. We'll all be old ourselves one day. Maybe even really sick. I've known people who were—"

She was interrupted by the phone ringing. Her eyes darted first to the front door and then back at the black plastic digital clock radio sitting next to a handsome Imari rice bowl.

"'Scuse me," she muttered. "Hello?" After some time she said, "Yes," then walked out of the room, taking the portable phone with her.

I wanted to get up and snoop around, but I didn't know how long she would be, and the wall-to-wall carpeting in the house's small rooms would cover the sound of her impending return.

A good thing I didn't, too, for she was back in no time. Jane crossed in front of me and sat back down and fell silent. It was as if the floodgates had slammed shut as rapidly as they had opened. She sat perfectly still, her hands tightly folded in her lap, her feet flat on the floor. Now that I had been there for a few minutes and adjusted to the weird situation, I couldn't take my eyes off Jane's tiny face, made smaller by her big hair. Her thick beige foundation, which was supposed to take off the years, only added to them by bringing out the lines around her smoker's mouth. But once I got beyond the hair, the false eye-

lashes, and layers of makeup, it was her lips that really fasci-
nated me, bright orangey pink, outlined in a deep mahogany.
If Jane Finn had her way, she would put off the telltale signs of
age as long as possible, even if it meant no lunches at the Dixie
Café for her.

Jane's garish appearance, her guarded demeanor, and the
hodgepodge assortment of things in her house just didn't jive.
I remembered then what my friend, Cyndee Moore, once told
me. "One's shoes are the windows to your soul." I had laughed
at the time. Now I stole a quick look at Jane Finn's feet. She
wore clunky heeled, open-toed, baby blue sandals with ankle
straps. (How could I have missed them?) Her stockings were
the reinforced-toe type that, like her choice in foundation, were
two shades too dark for her complexion. Summer shoes. A
fake tan. Good lord! It was a cold, damp twenty-eight degrees
outside. Who was she trying to fool?

With a little more time, I could have analyzed the dickens
out of the situation. Right now there were pressing questions
and I needed answers. Fast. This was a one-shot chance.

Jane Finn just sat and stared straight at me. I dug in and re-
sorted to the sort of chatter I'd always complained about hearing from my clients and moved into territory I felt more
comfortable in than shoe analysis.

"My grandmother had a pretty candlestick like that one," I
offered.

Jane Finn, the orphaned-as-a-child, widowed-as-a-young-
woman, now past-middle-age sitter for the sick elderly, nervously brushed at some speck on her navy blue slacks. Watching
her I didn't notice the bracelet that had set Ed Pavich off, but
her diamond ring caught my eye. The center diamond was at

least a carat, but it looked even larger, thanks to the sparkling diamond baguettes set in a circle surrounding it. The setting and its era were unmistakable. Daddy had given Mother a ring exactly like it when I was born in 1954. Well, not exactly like it. Mother's center stone was closer to a half carat than a carat, and instead of fully cut baguettes her diamond was surrounded by deep blue sapphire chips, my birthstone. I filed the information, especially the era of the ring, away.

"Was the candlestick your grandmother's, too?" I asked.

Jane Finn clearly had reverted back to her quiet self. She only half-smiled at me with those lips of hers. The silent implication was yes.

"You're so lucky to still have yours," I chattered on, fighting off the temptation to steal another glance at her feet. "Isn't it funny how something as simple as a candlestick can mean so much? I don't know what happened to my grandmother's. The last time I saw it, it was on the top shelf on the whatnot in the front hall. Those family pieces mean so much."

I searched for something more to say.

"I remember one night we had a storm and the electricity went out," I fibbed. "Mamma, that's what I called my grandmother, lit all the candles in the house. Yes, that was the last time I remember seeing it. You are *so* lucky to have yours. I've looked around in some antiques shops. There are plenty around, but they're getting more and more expensive."

Jane Finn finally responded. "I wouldn't think that would be a problem for you," she said.

After a moment or two she asked, "When do you think you'll be bringing your aunt to Leemont, Mrs. Glass?" punctuating first the "Mrs.," then "Glass."

When was the last time I'd been called Mrs. Glass?

"Of course I have to convince Aunt Dorothy," I said, "but they just had another nine inches of snow earlier this week. I think Mother Nature may have done my job for me." I was trying to keep the conversation light, but Jane Finn was all business.

"This spring, then? I have other clients, you know, so I'll need to know when you might need me."

"Yes. I understand."

I thought fast. Flattery almost always worked; it did on me. It had on Richie. It ought to work on Jane Finn. But she was a mighty tough cookie. I tried anyway.

"That's why I was so eager to see you, Mrs. Finn." I was careful to make her "Mrs." as clear as she had made mine. "To find out when you would have free time. You're awfully popular. Everyone says such nice things about you. Howard Creighton speaks *so* highly of you. I know Alzheimer's patients take special attention. He especially admires your patience with his wife."

If the Creighton name set off any warning bells, Jane didn't acknowledge them. We chatted a little longer about Aunt Dorothy, our general time frame, Jane's wages, and, as I rose to leave, the porcelain soup tureen that Ed Pavich had so astutely noticed.

"What a gorgeous Meissen soup tureen!" I said, meaning every word of it. The body was gracefully shaped, and on the lid a playful putto sat astride a cornucopia overflowing with exquisitely painted, hand-modeled flowers. In a fancy shop it would have sold for four or five thousand, or more.

"Thank you."

I gave it yet another try.

"Yes, nineteenth-century Meissen is getting harder to find. The Onion pattern, isn't it? The red and gold overlay is what makes your piece so unusual." The appraiser in me came out. "Why a piece like this is worth thousands of dollars. People search all over to find porcelain of this quality and beauty."

"It was one of my grandmother's things."

"Your grandmother had wonderful taste!"

"Thank you," was all Jane Finn said, moving toward the front door.

"Do you know anything about when she got it? Where?"

Jane Finn smiled weakly and gave a little shrug. Her body language said what her silence didn't.

"Oh well. You probably got off easy," I said casually. "My grandmother talked her head off about her things. I remember being so bored at the time. It was always *this* had come from there, and *that* used to be your great-great-grandmother's. Or I got *this* from such and such an antiques shop. Or I remember buying *that* when I would go shopping with Mrs. Easley on Saturdays. You know, come to think of it, Mrs. Easley was Mamma's age, and I don't even know what her first name was. Mamma just always called her Mrs. Easley. Of course, *now* I wish I had listened to all those stories," I rattled on.

I swallowed hard. I knew what I wanted to say next. But I'm no Kinsey Millhone or Stephanie Plum. Did I dare? Saying the wrong thing could blow my cover. On the other hand, if I didn't get some answers, I would have wasted my time and let Ed and Peter and maybe Matt down . . . possibly even Roy Madison . . . and what about Sarah Rose Wilkins? I had to get her talking somehow.

Damn it, I thought. Most people talked their heads off about their grandmothers, and now when I needed somebody to, this lady was clamming up. Then again, Jane wasn't telling any grandmother stories because she didn't have any—at least not from the grandmother, or grandmothers, who had once owned these things sitting all around her. She didn't even know who they were. They sure weren't any kin to her.

"Even if I *did* have to listen to my grandmother's stories," I said, "at least *you* have these wonderful *things*. Oh well. You can't have everything in life. But your things are so *valuable* these days. In fact . . ."

I heaved a long, long sigh and tried to hide my excitement. I decided to push just one more time.

I hung my head as if sharing a deep-kept secret. Which I was, one I wouldn't have wanted even the Glasses to know. "The truth is, I'm afraid my family had to sell some things. *You* understand that . . . being orphaned and all yourself. When times get hard, well, the best things are the first to go. Can't even *give* the lower-end things away. That's why Mother always told me to buy the best I could. I should have listened to her."

That's enough, Sterling. Back off! Mother commanded. *True. I always told you to buy the best, but don't overdo it. This hard-boiled egg of a woman is starting to get suspicious. You can't pull off the I'm-a-little-rich-girl-but-I'm-so-pitiful act but so well. After all, she knows your last name is Glass and she knows where you live.*

When Jane Finn didn't flinch a fake eyelash—didn't say one word, but just continued staring at me—I took Mother's advice and zipped it. The woman's silence had told me enough.

"Oh well. So much for the past," I said. "You're a mighty

lucky woman, Mrs. Finn, that's all I've got to say. Enjoy your pretty things. Now, let's see." I fiddled around in my pocketbook for a pen and a slip of paper. "I have your number and you have mine. I'm going to talk to Aunt Dorothy tonight. Let's hope they have another big New Hampshire snow this week!"

I gathered my coat around me and said good-bye as Jane Finn closed the door to her house that was like she was. A bundle of contradictions.

I scooted into the cold January night. In my car, I fought the urge to call Peter or Ed on my cell phone. Jane Finn was probably peeping out of her window, watching me. Then again, she might have slipped back into the dining room to examine her soup tureen. She didn't have a clue what Meissen was or just how valuable it was. Of that I was certain.

But not knowing exactly what she was doing, I didn't dare look back. In my state of nervous excitement, I pulled my car away from the curb first, then looked in my side-view mirror to see if anything was coming. This wasn't exactly a main thoroughfare. The mirror was at a catawampus angle. Instead of a view of the street and any oncoming cars, all I could see was some oversized pickup truck just a couple of spaces behind me protruding far out into the narrow residential street. It was one of those new designs that you couldn't see around when one parked next to you. From the front or back, the blown-out wheel fenders made it look like a fat mamma with a big rump and bulging tits. In this neighborhood it didn't surprise me.

What did surprise me was what I saw. In the darkness I couldn't tell for sure, but I thought I saw a head in the passenger seat suddenly duck down.

Chapter 20

Dear Antiques Expert: I hear so much about Meissen china. What makes it so special?

Until trade with the Orient was established, Western countries didn't know about fine china and porcelain. Even during the Middle Ages, wood or metal was used for plates and bowls. The Meissen factory, established by the German king Augustus the Strong in the early 1700s, became Europe's first true porcelain manufacturer. Ever since, the Meissen name has been associated with fine quality, and its pieces, both old and new, are highly sought after.

IF I HAD KNOWN what to do, I would have done it. But since I didn't, I drove around for a while.

After such a busy day, I should have been tired. A fresh rush of adrenaline after I left Jane Finn's had taken care of that. I had a wild desire to go to an antiques shop, the way I had in Manhattan on Saturday. If only I could wander through aisles of beautiful treasures, maybe I could think more clearly, figure things out. Things might not be able to talk, but sometimes they did speak to me. But going antiquing was not an option at 6 P.M. on a Monday night in Leemont, Virginia.

For lack of anything better to do, I drove home.

Arbor Hills seemed to go to bed around 7 P.M. in the wintertime. My house was pitch-dark. I'd forgotten to turn the lights on in my anxious state when I'd left to drive out to Jane Finn's.

Inside I checked my phone messages. There was one of those damn hang-ups from Mr. Unavailable that I hate so much and a quick call from a friend in my garden club reminding me of the upcoming meeting—a bus trip to Prestwould, Lady Skipworth's grand eighteenth-century home just outside of Clarksville—but nothing else. I didn't even have any new e-mails.

If I couldn't go antiquing, I'd do the next best thing. I went into my office. During the day, I could stare out of the bay window and let my thoughts wander among the branches of the azalea and camellia bushes and dogwood trees. At night, especially in the wintertime, I could peer far into the distance and just barely see the lights of Leemont's downtown. In addition to the usual desk and chair and the bookcases that lined the wall from floor to ceiling, in the corner I had a small, 1920s overstuffed chair that was just my size, and an old, fifteen-inch TV that Lily had taken off to college only to bring home again. I gathered up the catalogs I had picked up at Layton's and headed for the chair. I'd brush up some more on the Art Deco figurines that I had pretty successfully put to one side since returning home.

It's good to let ideas ferment in your mind, Mother always said when I was stumped while writing a paper for my high school senior English class. *The body can heal itself, and the mind can figure things out on its own.*

The more I thought about Jane Finn, Sarah Rose Wilkins, and Dwayne Sloggins—plus the urn and the pin, the silver vase, Meissen tureen, beehive candlestick, and the diamond ring, just to stir the pot—the more confused I became. The time definitely had come to put this situation out of my mind, to give it a rest.

And it all seemed so simple on the TV shows. Why, Poirot made it look downright easy. He just *thought* about the problem at hand while drinking tea from fine bone china and then figured it all out. James Rockford cunningly smiled his way through his adventures. His dimples won everyone over to the point that they confessed. Matlock raised an eyebrow and looked confused. In the bumbling process of trying to get the story straight, the solution came drifting to the top. In truth, this detective stuff was hard work. I felt more like Columbo— fretting, sulking about, and worrying the problem. No wonder he was always so disheveled.

And if you don't stop all this fretting and carrying on, you're going to look like dowdy and wrinkled Miss Marple, Mother whispered in my ear.

I laughed out loud. A glass of wine and a little TV. That would help.

I picked up an auction catalog in one hand and the remote control in the other. I flipped through the channels and settled on a rerun of *Green Acres*. It was the best thing on. So much for the glories of cable TV. I glanced down. The catalog I was holding in my lap was the one that Nigel Rhodes had given me of an upcoming general sale, not from Richie's past Art Deco sales. Oh well.

Fatigue was starting to settle in. I thumbed through a few pages. I was ready to switch catalogs when two things happened. The phone rang, and I came to a page showing two pieces of fine Meissen china in the same Onion pattern as the soup tureen. I was so taken by the Meissen that I didn't even glance at the black box to see who was calling.

"Hello?"

"Sorry 'bout calling you at home. Pavich here."

He didn't have to tell me who he was. Ed Pavich's scratchy voice was as unmistakable as Sol's Brooklynized European accent.

"Am I interrupting your dinner or anything?"

"I wish," I said. "I'm just working. Actually, I may have just found something important."

"What's that?"

"Well, it's too early to know for positive. It may be a point of reference about the tureen in Jane Finn's dining room. Ed, you were absolutely right," I said with renewed vigor. "That tureen is absolutely grand. And it is totally out of character with—" An image of Jane Finn's home furnished out of a Sears Roebuck catalog, yet decorated with valuable antiques, flashed before my eyes. "Well, let's say it's out of character with *most* of the things in her house."

"So I didn't send you on a wild-goose chase?"

"Not hardly. There are lots of things in that house that can't be explained." Including Jane Finn herself, I almost added, but didn't. "I just hope I didn't blow everything by asking the questions I did."

He flipped off my comment in his harmlessly gruff manner. "I'm sure you were fine. So what do you think? Can we get together tomorrow morning? You tell me what to do. I want to move quickly, though. These scam people are like gypsies. They pack up and leave in the dead of night. Move on to the next town."

"Is—oh, what *is* his name? Sloggins. Is Sloggins in jail?"

"I wish," Ed said. "He made bail. That's the bad news. But it seems he crossed state lines doing his roofing work—if you can call it work—so there's a restraining order and he's not going anywhere. But now Jane Finn. *That's* another story. So did you get enough on her so we can move in?"

"Whoa! I'm an appraiser, not a lawyer or a detective, especially not a PI. All I can tell you is what I saw and how she acted. Other than that—"

"Ten thirty? Eleven? What suits you?"

"Tomorrow. Not tonight? Right?" I asked just to be sure.

He laughed.

I blushed.

"Yes ma'am. Tomorrow A.M."

"And Peter? Should he meet with us?" I asked.

"Can't say that he's essential to what's going on, but if you'd like for him to be there, sure."

"If you don't mind."

I was treading uncharted waters. Knowing that Peter could be there was instantly reassuring.

"Sure. Will you call him? Or should I?" Ed volunteered.

"Well, where will we meet?" I asked.

"Your place is fine. You could come here, but parking is rough with the construction work downtown. I spend most of the day out in the field, anyway. Your place will be easier. Or how about at the Salvation Army? Does the Rev work there on Tuesdays?"

Rev. I chuckled to myself. I could see Peter's face grimacing at the name.

"I'll call him. Let's say eleven, at my place, if that's okay. Do you know how to get here? Bittersweet Trail. It's in—"

"I know it well," Pavich interrupted.

His answer took me by surprise, not because I didn't think he would know my neighbors—*You snob!* Mother said unforgivingly, momentarily interrupting my thoughts—but because of what Ed said next.

"You'd be surprised what brings me into Arbor Hills," he said, his sandpapery voice mysteriously full of innuendo. "Crime doesn't stop at Main Street or Stuart's Ridge. Vice and corruption know no social boundaries. I've seen it all, believe me."

"And I guess I'm just starting to."

"Till tomorrow then. Get a good night's rest," he said cheerfully.

"Ha!" I scoffed after I'd hung up.

I called Peter, then turned back to the page with the Meissen china on it, glass of wine in hand.

Lot 68. Meissen platter in the Onion pattern with iron red and gold overlays, circa 1880, width 19 inches. Estimate $1,200–1,600.

Lot 69. Meissen sauceboat with attached underplate in the Onion pattern, matching the preceding lot. Estimate $400–600.

I turned back a page or two to see if there might be any mention of their owner. Sometimes when several pieces came from one estate there would be an entry such as "Property of a lady" or "Deaccessioned from such-and-such a museum." Not a clue.

What if all three Meissen items, the platter, sauceboat, and Jane Finn's tureen, had come from the same place, but she had found the tureen irresistible and kept it for herself? An appraiser friend of mine had once gotten into trouble by holding back one piece from an estate, thinking no one would notice. I made a note to call Nigel Rhodes first thing in the morning.

For the rest of the night I did the Columbo thing and frowned and fretted and worried. I had questions but no answers.

What if, I thought now, the Meissen had been among the items stolen from the Hanesworths? Several fine English and European porcelain pieces of this quality and value had been among the items I'd seen on the appraisal. I had yet to read the two-hundred-page-long appraisal Matt Yardley had given me. When I'd scanned it, I had concentrated on the items that were starred, the missing items. I should have reviewed the entire appraisal, especially since Matt had told me I was on the clock, but dinner with Peter had taken precedence on Sunday night. The Creightons had consumed the morning. The afternoon was spent with Ed and Peter and later, chasing down Jane Finn. My guilt was absolved, but my mind wouldn't rest.

I thought again about whether the Hanesworths could have had a tea urn that had been overlooked. For the second time I dismissed the idea that anyone could overlook so magnificent a piece as a Paul Storr tea urn.

But the Meissen? Just a few pieces from an entire set? Now, *that* was possible.

I dug out the appraisal from the pile I'd brought back from New York and tossed onto the top of the heap on my desk. The whole desk badly needed straightening up. Not tonight.

It was only a little past nine, but I decided to go take the

Hanesworth's appraisal to bed and tackle it there. Other than read and fret, there was nothing I could do until tomorrow's business hours. Then I'd begin calling around.

As I turned out the lights downstairs, for the first time I noticed the full moon. It was ghostly white, as only a winter moon can be.

I remembered:

> *. . . the moon,*
> *Rising in clouded majesty,*
> *. . . unveil'd her peerless light,*
> *And o'er the dark her silver mantle threw.*

"Aren't you proud of me, Mother," I asked. "Milton, *Paradise Lost.*"

Never cared as much for Milton as you did, Mother's silent voice in my head reminded me. *Too somber and dull most of the time. God was supposed to be his leading man, but Satan's a much more interesting character. Remember what Keats says about Milton? "Life to him would be death to me." Couldn't agree more. Lighten up, Sterling.*

I looked outside again. It truly was a splendiferous moon. Beautifully round and shimmering in the winter night. A halo crowned it. Portending a coming snow, perhaps?

Lighten up, Sterling. Ah, me. We've lost so much in these modern days. Why couldn't we think in terms of moonlit silver mantles instead of stolen silver urns worth thousands of dollars? I sighed, wishing I'd never heard of Sarah Rose Wilkins, Jane Finn, or Dwayne Sloggins.

A roaring noise that began in the distance and grew steadily louder brought me around. Strange for dark, tranquil Arbor

Hills. At first I thought it was a low-flying prop plane, but not at this time of night. When I heard brakes screeching and saw the glow of headlights on high beam shining across my front yard I instinctively jerked back from the window.

No doubt about it. It was the same hideous pickup truck that had parked down the street from Jane Finn's house. Only after it sped past did I move. And then it was to turn on the outside floodlight.

Chapter 21

Dear Antiques Expert: We have decided to take out a fine arts policy on some of our better pieces. The insurance company said we had to have them appraised. Should the appraisal be for fair market or replacement value? Before I call an appraiser I need to know this.

The simplest way to understand "fair market value" is to imagine a piece being sold at auction. There it would sell for the amount of money someone would pay for it. Now imagine that same piece in a retail store where its price reflects all the dealer's expenses—from inventory taxes and rent to employee wages—as well as his profit. That would be "replacement value," and it is generally considered to be 25–100 percent higher than fair market value. For your insurance purposes, you definitely want your pieces appraised for "replacement values."

I LOOKED AT THE CLOCK: 3:18 A.M.

It was either too late or too early to have a glass of wine. And I wasn't about to get up for good. I turned on the light on my bedside table. A cup of good, hot soothing tea. That would calm my nerves. I blamed my sleeplessness on the wild thought that I was being tracked by some unknown villain.

For God's sake, Sterling, this is Leemont, not Brooklyn, I told myself. Somehow that didn't help. The two places suddenly seemed to have a lot in common. The same choking fear I had felt at Joey's shop that night hit me like a brick.

I put on my robe and slippers, and padded down to the kitchen. So much for the requisite beauty sleep. Waiting for the water in the teakettle to boil, I distracted myself by digging through the Hanesworth appraisal. Trouble was, the deeper I dug, the wider awake I became. There, listed on the original appraisal, but not cited as missing—there it was.

Exceptional English silver tea urn, circa 1810, made in London by Paul Storr. Having fine gadrooning at the lip of the top and along the pear-shaped body. The body of the urn bears the unusual occurrence of two (unidentified) armorials and the whole is raised on finely modeled dolphin-motif feet. Retaining its original hot box with full hallmarks that correspond with the marks on the urn and the removable lid. $65,000.

A fair price, but a little low for replacement value, I mused. It *had* to be the same urn that I had found in Sarah Rose Wilkins's closet. The description of its dolphin motif feet and the presence of not one, but *two* armorials gave it away. I didn't even need to see the photograph accompanying the appraisal, but I turned to the index anyway. There it was.

Of course, Sarah Rose didn't own it. Never had. The poor woman had never even *seen* the thing. It belonged to the Hanesworths, just like the—

The light in my head came on.

I tore at the pages of the appraisal like a drunk trying to get into the liquor cabinet. The Meissen tureen had to be there. I skipped over random listings of rugs, lamps, bowls, until I found what I had known I would find—a full set of circa 1880 Onion pattern Meissen china identical in every way to the platter and sauceboat pictured in the Layton's catalog, including the soup tureen that I was beginning to wish I'd never heard about or seen.

The Hanesworth appraisal valued the Meissen set at thirty-six thousand dollars and listed some 123 pieces including square *and* round serving dishes, three platters, a mustard pot, a soup tureen, two divided vegetable dishes, a sauceboat with attached underplate, and two sweetmeat dishes among the serving pieces. If someone recounted the pieces, there would be only 120. Maybe one or two less, if items in addition to the sauceboat, platter, and tureen had also been lifted.

"Matt Yardley, I'm doing you quite a favor," I said aloud.

A piece or two from a set of china like this Meissen could easily be overlooked, especially if the china had been kept in a pantry and the family hadn't begun to pack things up and move them out of the house yet. It wasn't unusual when a family had an extensive china set, and the Hanesworths probably had several such sets, for the larger pieces to be stored at the back of a shelf. The dinner plates and soup bowls and cups and saucers—the pieces more often used—routinely were kept at the front. You wouldn't use the larger pieces without setting the table with the usual dishes, so it made sense to keep the seldom-used, big serving pieces in the back.

But it would take *time* to move those many stacks of plates and cups to be able to get to the pieces at the back. Something a nighttime sitter had plenty of.

Jane Finn was an overnight sitter.

But *why* would she have put the urn and pin in Sarah Rose Wilkins's apartment?

Even if she had the opportunity and the key when Howard Creighton sent her over there with the Turkey Tetrazzini casserole, that didn't explain why she hid them there. And why did she steal the things in the first place, anyway? What was she planning to do with them? Why on earth would she hide the urn and pin at Sarah Rose's but keep the tureen at home?

So much didn't make any sense. I was drawing a blank.

"... *when a woman is left too much alone,*" Mother often said, "*sooner or later she begins to think; And no man knows what then she may discover.*" *Edwin Arlington Robinson.*

I had more discoveries than I knew what to do with. My head was spinning.

Even more pressing matters began to come at me. Nigel Rhodes would cheerfully kill me when I told him the urn would have to be pulled from the auction. When I told him he'd have to pull the Meissen, too, he would be furious. I sighed.

Roy Madison at the bank would—

The thought of Roy Madison stopped my blood cold. I rubbed my fingers hard across my brow.

Had I ever told him about the pin LaTisha had found? Not that I could remember now, at 4 A.M. The oversight wasn't intentional. I just hadn't. Too much else was happening. Then I remembered. Roy had been out of town when I called to tell him about the pin. Well, it was a good thing that I hadn't.

At least Roy Madison and his cohorts would be tickled pink. No longer would they have to worry about Hope House getting any infusion of real money from the Wilkins estate, which was back down to its twenty-four-thousand-dollar cash value. Without the extra money from the sale of the urn, Hope House wouldn't be able to buy the old sock factory building. Whatever scheme the bank and the politicians were cooking up could move ahead. On the bright side, maybe I'd be back in the bank's good graces.

Matt Yardley already knew about finding the Georgian pin on the Hanesworth appraisal. He would be elated to learn about the urn and to know that the insurance company wouldn't have to shell out sixty-five grand for it. I smiled. And no one had even known it was missing. Now, that was a real twist.

And what about you, *Sterling,* Mother's weary voice asked. She always did look out for me.

Me?

There went my finder's fee and whatever frivolous purchase I would have found to spend the money on. I sighed.

Good Lord. Was that me? Sighing again, and out loud? I always hated it when Mother sighed, and here I was, doing it— sighing with every other breath.

It was at that point that I stopped looking for more trouble. I looked at the clock on the kitchen stove: 4:27 A.M. I'd always done my best thinking in the middle of the night, but it was time to try to get some sleep.

I went back upstairs and crawled into bed.

The same way he had in New York, Barefoot Bagman started trouncing through my dreams. Once again, like a peddler of the olden days, Bagman was humped over, burdened down by his burlap bag full of goods. But this time silver urns and Deco figures were spilling out of his bag. Scores of exquisite Georgian pearl and diamond pins were pinned to his tattered lapels. Under his arm he carried a Meissen soup tureen. Who could sleep through that dream?

A little past five, I trudged back downstairs, boiled water for a second cup of tea, and made a breakfast of a half bag of Pepperidge Farm Double Chocolate Milanos. With no one to talk to.

I went to the window and looked out into the blue-black sky. The moon had long since moved across the horizon, taking its silver mantle with it. Or maybe not.

As promised by the old wives' tale, the moon's halo really had been filled with infinitesimal liquid crystals. A silvery white robe of snow covered the trees and ground.

Chapter 22

Dear Antiques Expert: My decorator has suggested that we try to find a pair of "burr walnut" Queen Anne chairs to use in our living room. What exactly is burr walnut?

A "burr" is a nubby protrusion along the trunk of a tree where a dormant bud grew in diameter but not length. But inside these burrs, the wood has a rich, densely figured grain. Ever since the 17th century, fine furniture craftsmen have used thin layers of this precious wood as a beautiful veneer on chair backs and drawer fronts. Queen Anne chairs with this highly desirable veneer are considered eye catching and are expensive, especially if they date from the 18th century. You should expect to pay $30,000–50,000 for a fine pair.

THE SNOW HAD DWINDLED to a few intermittent flurries by the time I called Matt Yardley at 9:02 A.M. The two or three inches of powdery snow were enough to slow Leemont down, but not bring it to a grinding halt, especially since the streets were still mostly clear. What a shame New Yorkers couldn't see snow-laden trees when they looked out their windows, I thought, as I punched in Matt's number.

"This is a bad-news, good-news call," I warned, before launching into the tale of the tea urn and Meissen china. I explained all that had happened as succinctly as I could and told him to expect two phone calls, one from Roy Madison requesting papers verifying that the urn had really belonged to the Hanesworths and the other from Ed Pavich asking whether or not the Hanesworths had any roofing, or maybe other repair work, done to their home.

"I thought about calling the Charlottesville office directly instead of bothering you," I said.

"No problem, really," Matt said. "Sending the bank the information will be routine. But it may take several calls to find out about any repairs at the Hanesworths' house, and you shouldn't be wasting your time doing that. Tell me, Sterling, are all of your appraisals this . . . this complicated? Sounds like this one could even be a little risky if you have to, well, confront the people responsible for taking the pieces from the Hanesworths' home."

I laughed. "I hadn't thought of it that way. But I have wondered what I used to do with my time before all this."

"Be careful now," Matt said, taking me by surprise. "I'll get back to you after I've checked into the issue of repairs."

He then thanked me so profusely on behalf of the Hanesworths and Babson and Michaels that I was tempted to tell him I'd rather have cash, but thought better of it.

I put the receiver down and picked up my Magic 8 Ball. "Will anything come of this?" I asked, purposely avoiding specifying "this" in my own mind.

I shook the ball vigorously and turned it upside down. A white line appeared in the smoky window. I tilted the ball first one way and then the other, closed my eyes tight, leveled the ball in my hand, opened my eyes, and looked down to find my fortune. *Ask again later.* So much for that.

As well as that phone call had gone, I dreaded calling Nigel Rhodes. He was going to be livid. But time was crucial. I forced myself to take the plunge.

To my surprise, Nigel wasn't so much angry with me as resigned. "These withdrawals are happening more and more frequently these days," he said ruefully.

"Why is that? Surely not all due to thefts, or wild tales like this one."

"Hard economic times?" he asked rhetorically.

"Too many appraisal shows on TV?" I said. "Maybe after agreeing to sell something, people have second thoughts."

Nigel grunted. "Maybe. Who knows. Yes. Well. What's done, is done. About the urn."

I gathered up all my nerve and forged ahead. "Yes. I'll be in touch with the bank about that paperwork at this end. Before we discuss the urn, about the Meissen pieces."

"They will be withdrawn, of course. I assume that this, ah, Matt—the insurance man—it's Yardley isn't it? Matt Yardley will be in touch."

Nigel clearly was only so interested in the Meissen. Obviously, the urn was much more important to him, and to Layton's.

"I'm sure Matt will take care of all the details. But this is something bigger than just a couple of items in an auction. It's tied into a larger scam on the elderly. Any chance you might tell me who brought you the Meissen pieces? I know the Leemont police will be in touch with you, too, but I'm going to be meeting with them shortly. If you could tell me now . . ."

There was a pause.

I pushed my luck.

"I promise to bring you my next big find," I said.

"This is one of Dana Henchloe's deals. Other than that, I can't tell you a name, Sterling," Nigel said, his voice edgy. "Would it help if you knew it was an antiques dealer?" he finally said.

"Yes indeed. From?" I tried not to sound too anxious. There was no way in hell that Dana Henchloe would help me out or even help out Ed and the police if he knew I was involved. And . . . Oh my God! If Dana got in tight with Matt Yardley, he'd steal my business.

"A Southern state."

Dana's territory for sure. I didn't even try to hide my frustration. "Nigel! The South is three, four, *ten* times bigger than the U.K., and that doesn't include Arkansas and Texas."

"It wasn't Arkansas."

"Texas?"

For a moment I thought the beep in my phone was coming from Nigel's eyebrows. Then I realized it was my call-waiting. It had to be either Peter or Ed. For once I ignored the beep.

"No. Yes. Well. All right. South Carolina. Does that help?" he spat.

"Columbia? Charleston? Spartanburg? Greenville? Um, Myrtle Beach?"

"No. Some *little* town."

"Aiken? Camden . . . Cheraw? Bethune?" I asked, grasping at straws. I stifled my urge to tell Nigel that Bethune was home of the Chicken Strut. Instead I said, "Did Dana bring the items in himself?"

"Actually"—Nigel cleared his throat—"if I recall correctly,

all communication has been by phone or fax. Dana was just the go-between. You know. Finder's fee."

"Did you ever meet the person who sent you the Meissen? Ever speak directly to the seller?" After spending the afternoon with Jane Finn, I was beginning to get the gist of this interrogation routine.

"It's a new world out there, Sterling," Nigel said, sounding more like a defensive American college kid than a middle-aged U.K. antiques expert. "You can't expect business to continue to be conducted in the traditional way. It's the twenty-first century, for God's sake."

"Point well taken," I conceded, lapsing into English-speak. After all, I routinely transacted business over the phone, the computer, the fax machine. I tried again. "How about the area code? Do you have an area code?"

"Don't you think I should wait and give this information to your police officer?" Nigel asked.

"You can, but if you have the number handy . . ." I swallowed hard, thought fast, and turned on every bit of charm I could muster.

"Nigel, I know where there's a great Queen Anne side chair. Beautifully figured burr walnut. Period piece and untouched. No repairs. Never been out of the family."

"Really? No repairs? Never? Are you—"

I cut him off. "Never. *And* they're thinking about selling."

"Really? Yes. Well. Oh, I see it now, here's the file. The package came in by U.S. mail, heavily insured, of course. The number? Here. It's one of those toll-free numbers. 888. And, hello! What's this? There's another number here. Ah, that's the fax. It's

804. That's your area code, isn't it? Hmmm. Strange. Yes. Well. You know I don't make all my calls or send my own faxes, Sterling," Nigel said, simultaneously covering up and dismissing his oversight. "Burr walnut, you say. What date? Good condition?"

"Great condition. Totally original. Date? Probably 1715. 1720. Did I mention that it has ball and claw feet?"

I heard a gleeful gasp on the other end of the line.

"I missed that number, Nigel. Could you repeat it? 804 . . ."

By the time I hung up, I was tingling with excitement. Instantly I dialed in to call-waiting to find out whether it was Peter or Ed who had called. Should I reveal now what I had just learned or play coy, I wondered?

That was no longer an issue when I heard the weak voice that had left the message.

"Ms. Glass? Is this Sterling? Ah, I'm sorry I missed you," Sol Hobstein said. "So much has happened. I need to talk to you. You'll call me when you get this."

There was a long pause in which Sol neither spoke nor hung up. Then once again, as if to be positive I would get the message again he said, "This is Sol, Sterling. Call me when you get this. Much has happened." Then he hung up.

God only knew what *that* meant.

I started to lapse into my Columbo mode, adding more issues to my already-full plate. I reached over to pick up the phone, then stopped. I was in a state of panic over Sol and Joey, but what could I do? I was in Leemont; they were in Brooklyn.

"Yes. Well. It will just *have* to wait," I said resolutely, sounding disturbingly like Nigel. "And you, too, Roy Madison."

Fact was, everything would have to be put on hold while I

tried to process the information from Nigel. The Meissen pieces would be coming up for sale shortly. It would be terrible if they were sold. And once the urn was cataloged, it would have a lot number assigned in *that* sale. Pulling items out of an auction always looked bad for the auction house.

I was pacing about when I caught a glance of myself in the long beveled-glass mirror I had hung between two windows. The wild hair. The circles under the eyes. The frantic, worried look and accompanying wrinkles. Only a few short days ago I'd gotten all dolled up for the museum party and looked pretty good, if I did say so myself. My biggest concern that day had been some insider scam the Leemont bank and local politicians were working to put money in their pockets. Now here I was sucked into the middle of a scandal that everyone seemed to think I held the key to unlocking. And some five hundred miles away, where I wouldn't even have had anyone to call on to help or protect me, I'd put myself in who-knows-what kind of danger over a bunch of figurines that the owner hadn't thought enough of to pay any mind to for decades.

What had happened to the good old days when I went into nice peoples' houses to count their Chantilly silver flatware and Wedgwood china? I had to have a screw loose.

Well, I couldn't do anything about *that* right now, either.

I glanced back in the mirror. I really did look a fright. Major repair work lay ahead before the fellows got here.

By THE TIME Ed and Peter arrived at 11 A.M. sharp, I was remarkably well composed considering the circumstances. The curling iron and a little makeup had helped immensely. After my encounter with painted and powdered Jane Finn, I'd started to pay more attention than usual to that daily routine. Less really can be more. I'd seen.

More important, I had the pages in the Layton's catalog and the Hanesworth appraisal clearly marked with Post-its.

On a legal pad I had outlined the sequence of events beginning with finding the urn and ending with this morning's telephone calls. Next I had made a list of the players as best I could, from Sarah Rose Wilkins to the young kid in the roofing crew who had ratted on Dwayne Sloggins. I might have been able to spy a made-up highboy or a married secretary-bookcase across the room, but this kind of detective work was a new game and I wasn't about to make a fool of myself if I could help it.

Nothing beats being ready for any situation, Mother always said. Actually, she would begin by quoting Dante—*I am prepared for Fortune as she wills*—and then launch into a long lecture about how, if you were really prepared, you were in control of your own destiny, invariably ending with *Remember, luck comes to the prepared mind.* In a last-minute gesture, I made a note about the pickup truck I'd seen twice yesterday, then scratched through it. Mentioning such a far-fetched coincidence would make me look dumb.

If anything, I was overprepared when Peter, Ed, and I settled around the antique drop-leaf table.

I went over with Ed all my new discoveries—finding the Meissen pieces that matched the Hanesworths' china in the Layton's catalog. And when we compared information, it turned out that the person who had sent those pieces to Nigel had the same 888 number printed on Dwayne Sloggins's business card and an 804 area code fax number.

Ed was ready to move in on Jane Finn. We went over the

objects we'd seen in her home, items out of place for a woman
of her apparent means—the diamond ring and bracelet, the
large silver vase, the nice nineteenth-century brass candlestick,
the Rose Medallion tea caddy, the leather-bound Dickens volume, and, of course, the soup tureen.

"If we get to her house now, she may be asleep after working all night. Surprise always works in our favor," Ed said.

Despite my outward show of bravado and preparedness,
fear suddenly struck my heart.

"We? Now?"

"Now," Ed said brusquely, standing up.

I hung back. "You don't *really* need me along," I said hopefully. "Surely it wouldn't be, well, legal, for me to be there."

"Smart gal you got there," Ed said to Peter. Then to me he
said, "Actually, I checked with the chief. We don't have an expert on things like silver and china and stuff in the department.
It's not like this was a computer or technology crime that we
could handle ourselves these days. The chief checked with the
museum, and they said you know all that stuff as well as they
do, and values probably better, so it's all perfectly legal. So, let's
get a move on."

I cast a helpless look Peter's way. "Do I have to?"

Ed threw a look at Peter who had been most quiet through
most of our discussion. Caught crosswise between the two of us,
Peter looked uncomfortable. What else could he do but shrug.

"This is *your* case. I'm just a retired priest," he said to Ed.

"Now let me get this straight," Ed snapped. "You're just an
appraiser," he said accusingly to me. "And you're just a retired
priest," he said, looking Peter straight in the eye.

Every muscle in Ed's face rippled when he spoke. "And I'm

just Tinkerbell who happened to fly in your open window. Damn it. Excuse me, Rev," he nodded in Peter's direction, "but you two have helped bust up a whole ring of thieves who are preying on innocent old folks like your parents. And now you're backing down? Hey, this isn't any Jonah and the whale adventure story. We—" Ed stopped and looked directly at first me, then Peter.

"You, you, and me. We're going to Nineveh *now*. This ship's leaving and we're *all* going to be on it, or the whale's going to be waiting in the wings. And I don't have to tell you what happened to Jonah."

"Since you put it that way," Peter said, visibly caught off guard at Ed's apt biblical reference.

I stood helplessly by. Only rarely had my parents made me go to Sunday school—and I didn't take Bib Lit in college. I took my cue from Peter. "Since you put it that way," I said.

When the phone rang, I jumped. "Saved by the bell," I said brightly.

"Make it quick," Ed said as he pulled into his overcoat.

I put my finger up to my lips to silence him when I heard Matt's voice.

"I got the answer on the first call to Charlottesville," Matt said. "Their fax explaining it has just come in. Let me read along here. It seems the Hanesworths had a new roof put on in May of last year. Put in a claim because of, ah, right here it says, ah, something about water damage."

Ed motioned to me to speed it along.

I glared at him and pointed to Matt Yardley's name on the insurance papers.

"Water? On the roof? I wouldn't have thought that *roof*

water damage would be covered," I said into the phone after a moment's silence, while Matt obviously was continuing to read the claim to himself.

"For you and me, maybe not. But with the kind of policy some very rich people have, they can put in a claim if they have a dripping faucet. Whether or not it gets paid—that's a different matter."

"Water? Water damage?" Ed boomed out loudly.

"Am I interrupting anything?" Matt asked.

"Ed Pavich, the Leemont detective I mentioned to you, he and I are going over things, and Peter Donaldson. Peter's my friend who discovered the Georgian pin," I explained to Matt.

"Water damage. Rotting timbers. That was Sloggins's ploy," Ed said, drowning me out halfway through my sentence.

"Do you want to speak to Ed?" I asked Matt.

"I'd be happy to, of course, at the right time. Right now, though, all I see that's relevant is, yes, there was a roofing job carried out at the Hanesworths' house." In contrast to Ed's rough manner, Matt Yardley sounded restrained. He paused again. "If you might give me just a minute here . . ."

I put my hand over the speaker, threw Ed, who was rocking back and forth, just dying to grab the phone out of my hand, a noncommittal shrug, and whispered, "He just says that yes, they did have some roof work done."

"There was money paid," Matt was saying, "paid to, well, looks like it's a reimbursement to the Hanesworths. Wait. There's an invoice here. The letterhead says . . . a Dwayne Sloggins. Just a name. Not a company. No corporation or title listed."

"Sloggins?" I repeated.

Ed lurched forward. I held up my hand to temporarily halt him.

"Matt, here's Ed Pavich. You two had better talk after all." I handed the phone like a hot potato over to Pavich's waiting hand.

Miraculously, Ed managed to slow down, at least until he and Matt had finished talking. That's when he launched into action quicker than Barnum and Bailey's human cannonball flew through the air.

We were on our way to Jane Finn's house.

Chapter 23

Dear Antiques Expert: My grandmother willed a set of 12 Gorham sterling silver goblets to me because they are monogrammed with her initials and those are my initials, too. I appreciate the thought, but they just aren't suited to my lifestyle and I would rather have the money to buy something I can enjoy and could say came from her. I've been told that because they are monogrammed they won't sell for as much as if they were plain. Is that true?

Many centuries ago, when silver was considered the same as money, silver pieces were engraved with the family's coat of arms, or armorial, to provide proof of ownership. Later, in America, where there was no royalty, the owner's initials, or monogram, were used. Furthermore, engraving was considered an art in itself. But fashions change, and today, unless the silver dates from the 18th or 19th century, people tend to want unmonogrammed pieces. While you can probably sell the goblets privately for $350–500, a dealer would more likely pay $200–250 for the set.

DRIVING OUT TO Jane Finn's house, my only consolation was having two men with me—a minister to offer comfort and support; the other, a police officer to carry out the letter of the law. That would have seemed to cover most of life's bases.

We had no more than stepped inside Mrs. Finn's house before the evidence backed up Pavich's claim that, like gypsies, scam artists kept on the move. Jane Finn was taken by surprise all right, but she was hardly asleep. She had scissors in one hand, a marking pen behind one ear, and a roll of bubble wrap half-blocked the doorway.

"Going somewhere?" Ed asked, sparing no words. "Did Sloggins tell you to do this? Or was this your own idea?"

"Loggins? I don't know any Loggins," she said innocently. "Is that somebody from around here? Don't know what you're talking about. I got a good job offer out of town and I'm taking it."

Either Finn had rehearsed what to say, just in case, or else she was a mighty quick thinker on her feet.

"Cut the act," Pavich said. "It's obvious you're trying to get rid of the evidence."

Jane Finn had made no attempt to pack anything in her house except the most precious and expensive items, and those she obviously was carefully packing and labeling for shipping, not for casual loading in the back of a car or a U-Haul.

"So, why are you just taking the good stuff? What about those lamps over there?" Ed nodded in the direction of the pebbled-glass lamps.

"You tell me why you're going to need a silver vase, not a lamp, to read by," Pavich said as he reached into the unsealed box on the floor by the table where the vase sat. He extracted the vase from the box, strewing white Styrofoam popcorn all about as he did so.

He stepped around the box and headed straight to the dining room. The Meissen tureen and silver ladle were still in the center of the table. Next to it was a roll of bubble wrap, tape, a package of address labels, and more scissors.

"And I guess you're going to be serving lobster bisque from your soup tureen to the friends you're planning to make on your new job. Well, let me tell you, Mrs. Finn," Ed said, "it's a good thing they aren't serving bread and water in tin cans in jail anymore, because that's exactly where you're headed, not to some society luncheon with the hoity-toity. Maybe you'll get some Campbell's tomato soup served up in a fancy white Styrofoam bowl. If you're a good girl, they'll even give you a plastic spoon to eat it with."

"You don't have nothing on me," Jane Finn replied, her voice beginning to quiver slightly. "I've worked hard. I saved my money to buy nice things. Just because I have some nice things, you don't have any reason to come snooping around. Rich people aren't the only ones who have things. Now you get out."

This definitely was not my idea of a fun time. I glanced over at Peter. I was expecting him to speak up, to take mercy on this pitiful, defenseless older woman—an orphan and a widow, no less—being beaten by Ed Pavich's bulldog manner. But Peter's usually gentle eyes were cold. His lips were reduced to a thin, white angry line, his jaw set. This was a Peter I'd never seen before.

Before I knew it, I heard my own voice saying, "But Mrs. Finn, you told *me* these were your grandmother's things . . ."

Ed and Peter both swung around. Peter broke in before I could say anything more.

"Mrs. Finn, you told Ms. Glass that these were your grandmother's things, but Ms. Glass has found out differently. Take that big silver coffeepot."

I couldn't believe my ears. Peter, in a voice I'd never heard him use, was heartlessly attacking Jane Finn as brutally and relentlessly as Ed had. What had happened to his Christian charity? If I felt sorry for Jane Finn, why didn't he? And he was calling that precious tea urn I'd spent hours fretting over a coffeepot. What was he doing? He knew better than that.

"Now, if that coffeepot had really *belonged* to your grandmother, then why did you take it to Mrs. Wilkins's apartment and hide it in a paper bag in a closet? Mrs. Finn, you didn't even *know* Mrs. Wilkins."

A flicker of surprised worry flashed across Jane Finn's face. After being up all night on her job and trying to figure out what to do next, she must have momentarily forgotten about the urn. If I'd been in her shoes, I would have known the tea urn was the most valuable piece of all. It would have been front and center in my mind all along. But I was thinking like an appraiser.

Peter wasn't done.

"And that pearl and diamond pin you left at Mrs. Wilkins's hidden away inside the oven mitt. Now you tell me why you'd be hiding your grandmother's fine jewelry inside some other woman's oven mitt."

Again, Jane Finn seemed jolted, but she instantly recovered. She stared at Peter in defiance. For half a moment, though, as her painted lips curled, her eyes silently seemed to ask how he knew about the pin. "You don't scare me. Dwayne's got lawyers. He's a rich man."

"That's Dwayne *Sloggins*, isn't it, Mrs. Finn?" Ed Pavich

said. "The Mr. Loggins that you never heard of. Now you listen to me. All his money isn't going to help you now. For starters he's transported stolen property across state lines. He's used the United States Postal Service to ship the goods—a federal offense. And, most important," Ed said, "he's been scamming the poor, helpless elderly. That's about like an eighteen-wheeler crossing a yellow line to pass a stopped school bus that's unloading a bunch of kindergarteners. We jack up the jail for criminals like that. And you think *he's* gonna be taking care of *you?* Looks to me like you're his partner in this deal. If I were you, I'd start telling all I know. That would help you more than all of Dwayne Sloggins's money and lawyers put together," he said.

The room fell dead quiet. Looking at Peter, who she must've thought was a detective, Jane Finn spoke, her tone growing more defiant.

"You're not going to pin any damn murder rap on me," she said. "I didn't touch that old woman."

Peter and I threw each other startled glances.

"If you don't want that charge added to the list, then you'd better come clean," Ed said calmly. "Tell us just what did happen."

"Phfff," she hissed, shrugging. She turned her back on the men. "All I did was go back to get the silver pot and the pin."

"Why'd you put 'em there, anyway?" Ed said. "Why not bring 'em here?"

"Okay. Look." Jane Finn stepped back and slumped onto the sofa. She heaved a long, heavy sigh. "I didn't know what I was doing. I just saw these things and liked them. Why should those old folks have them? They didn't even use them . . . old people too blind to even see."

"A little bitterness there?" Ed asked.

Jane Finn tossed her head to one side, thought about his comment, then answered, "Guess so."

She stared into the distance. "It was so easy. First a little saucer. A pretty silver fork. A piece of fancy costume jewelry."

Then, in her more usual, arrogant way, Jane Finn began boasting. "After I started sitting for some better people, richer people, one woman *gave* me a silver goblet when her mother died. Said she had twenty-five, and she only needed twenty-four. Think about that! Only *needed* twenty-four silver goblets."

"When'd you start selling the stuff?" Ed asked.

"Selling? I never sold anything," Jane Finn said.

Remembering the Meissen pieces in the Layton catalog that had first tipped me off, I mustered up enough courage to speak. "What about the platter and sauceboat that match the soup tureen?" I tossed my head, motioning toward her dining room. "You're selling those," I butted in.

Ed threw me a look. This was his show now.

"Platter? You mean that big plate? I gave them to Dwayne. He's the one who sells the stuff."

"Just what were you planning to do with the pot . . . or the urn . . . or whatever the damn thing is . . . and the pin? Why were those at Sarah Rose Wilkins's house?" Ed said.

Jane Finn smiled. "I found that big old pot way up high on a shelf in the back bedroom I used to sleep in during the day at Mr. Hanesworth's. That thing was black as tar. Wasn't even sure it was silver. One day I took it down and polished it up that night. I slipped it out to my car. Know what happened?"

Jane Finn seemed to have forgotten she was making a confession. It was as if she were talking to a group of old friends, trying to add some spice to her usually dull life of counting away the hours until her clients died. I glanced over at Ed. He stood quietly by, but the muscles in his jaw were rippling like waves in a storm.

"That very next night," she continued, "I was watching TV and nothing was on. I landed on this show where experts would tell you how much your old stuff is worth. There was this long line of people all standing out in the rain in front of this old castle over in England. They were talking real fast and funny."

Peter and I nodded.

"Then they zoomed in on this old man with a big black umbrella and a big piece of silver. It looked just like that one I'd just swiped. I didn't catch how much they said it was worth at first, but everybody was acting all excited. Then they put some writing on the bottom of the screen." She drew an imaginary line in the air. "It was in English money. There was that funny looking *L* and the number forty thousand." She shook her head in bewilderment. "I figured I had just walked forty thousand dollars out of that big house and no one was ever going to know about it. Hell, I drove around with that thing in my car for weeks while I tried to figure out what to do with it."

"Why'd you put it in Mrs. Wilkins's apartment?" Ed asked.

"I didn't want to get caught with it. Or the pin. I saw one like that on that show, too," she said eagerly. "I'd slipped the pin out two or three weeks before and put it in my glove compartment. Lord, I'd forgotten all 'bout it till I seen that one on TV. These things are"—she paused and drew the next word out into three long syllables—"valuable."

I couldn't stand it any longer.

"But *these* things here are valuable, too," I said, "The tureen. The vase. Your ring." I took a chance on the ring.

"But I'd *seen* things like them," she said matter-of-factly. "I've never seen anything as old as that old teapot and that pin. Old things . . . really old things . . . they're special. Like, really ancient."

"But why hide them in Sarah Rose Wilkins's apartment?" Ed repeated.

"I told you. I didn't want to get caught with them."

"Caught? By whom?"

Jane Finn rolled her eyes.

"Ever seen Sloggins's first wife? Or his second? All beat up. Black and blue. No way I was gonna let him make mincemeat out of me if I could help it. No way. I'm scared to death of that man. He's mean, just plain mad-dog mean." She looked my way. "He got wind of you that night you came over. He was driving by, checking up on me. When he saw your car out front, he called me from his cell phone in that brand-new big truck of his. Wanted to know who was inside my house."

She turned back to Ed. "Look, he was making all the money. I figured it was my turn. He'd come over here and get the stuff and act like he was doing a favor to let me keep a few things around." She laughed. "I didn't tell him about that old pot. Or the pin," she added. "Figured this was my chance. And then I ended up getting the key to Mrs. Wilkins's apartment. I took the casserole in. That's when I had the idea. I could leave 'em there and pick 'em up when I came back to sit for the old lady."

So it *had* been that same truck that I'd seen at Jane Finn's house and then later racing through my neighborhood. I kept silent, trying to understand all that Jane Finn was saying.

But what I was really doing was silently beating up on myself. Why had I shrunk from the truth earlier and tried to come to Jane Finn's defense? Why had I backed down at my moment to shine? Peter had had to do my job for me; my polite, Southern upbringing had stopped me from driving the nail in Jane Finn's coffin. It was a good thing I had a policeman and preacher to go after the truth and bury the bad guy, since I didn't seem capable of doing it myself. Why couldn't I have been as assertive and self-assured as those zealous women prosecutors on TV? Even nice, sweet Della Street on *Perry Mason* had shown more backbone than I'd been able to muster. And the real irony was that I'd *started* this whole mess by finding the urn and making such a big deal out of it.

Damn it, Jane Finn had caused me no end of grief. Her deceit, *her* crimes had put me through torment, distracted me from other work, almost made a laughingstock out of me with Roy Madison. Thanks to Jane Finn, I could have lost good, paying clients. Handling the stuff she was pilfering off of others, I had come close to sullying my good name. Still, only seconds earlier, I'd gone soft, giving her the benefit of the doubt. I had even tried to help substantiate her story. What had I been thinking? I'd let her turn me into a fool.

The more I thought about it, the madder I got.

Remember the time Betsy Anne put the chewing gum in Iris's hair and you took the blame so Betsy Anne wouldn't have to stay after school? Mother asked, an uncharacteristic hint of sympathy in her voice.

But Betsy Anne didn't mean to do it. She couldn't help it. Iris had spilled Coke all over her new dress, I pleaded silently, giving Mother the same answer now, at almost age fifty, that I had given her forty-two years earlier.

And Jane Finn didn't really mean to take those things, now did she? Same old Sterling. Always taking up for the under-dog. It's high time you grow up.

I didn't know who I was more angry at: myself, who couldn't learn life's lessons and who either didn't know when to keep my mouth shut or else shut up at the wrong time, or Peter, for his sudden change in behavior—a change that greatly alarmed me. I dared a sideways glance to catch a glimpse of him.

Ed Pavich's voice brought me back to the here and now.

"Did you hit Mrs. Wilkins?"

"I told you I didn't have nothing to do with killing that woman," she said. "I didn't touch her."

"But you were in her apartment."

"Yeah. I started thinking about it and worried that maybe she'd die in the hospital and then I wouldn't get to sit for her after all. So I went back to get my things. I didn't know she was there. I thought she was still in the hospital. How was I to know? When I heard her in the bedroom I got scared. I was gonna leave, but there she was, coming toward me with her phone in her hand. I left and locked the door. I—" She chewed on her top lip which was still as fresh orangey-pink as it had been when we got there. I wondered if I had on any lipstick at all. "I knew I'd broke something. Knocked into something. I heard the noise, but I left. Next thing I knew, I read her obit."

Ed Pavich was suddenly on his cell phone, telling headquarters he had a case against Dwayne Sloggins and requesting backup personnel to do the necessary paperwork.

Peter was walking around, looking at, but not touching, the objects Jane Finn had collected from others over the years.

Jane Finn, still sitting on the sofa, actually looked somewhat relieved.

I was battling it out with myself.

I was the odd man out.

Chapter 24

Dear Antiques Expert: While shopping for Oriental rugs, I've seen some as small as 2 feet x 2 feet. I've always thought of Oriental rugs as being room-sized. Are these smaller rugs new and being made for our smaller spaces?

Many people envision plush, palatial-sized rugs when they think of Oriental rugs. But for centuries weavers have created small, napless rugs and saddlebags suitable to their traditionally nomadic lifestyle in Turkey, Nepal, Afghanistan, and Eastern countries once part of the Soviet Union. The rugs served as cushions on the camel saddles, and the saddlebags were used as carrying cases. Though called by several different names—Bokhara, Caucasian, Yumut, and Kilim, to cite a few—the general term, Turkestan, also identifies them. Both the rugs and saddlebags are most attractive and their prices often begin in the hundred-dollar range.

JANE FINN WAS more cooperative than I would have expected; Ed had obviously convinced her that it would be to her advantage once trial time came round. As she dragged jewelry, porcelain, silver, and various textiles out from closets and drawers and underneath her bed—thank God there weren't any Art Deco figurines—Jane Finn told us where each piece had come from. She gave a running narrative about how easy it had been to stuff the small Oriental rug in her overnight bag, why she'd taken a vase she liked rather than a bowl that was probably more valuable, how she had left a cheap, green glass pin behind in place of a fine jade pin that Dwayne had sold for eight hundred dollars to an antiques dealer. And as far as my theory about Jane Finn setting out more fine pieces in her home to try to impress me, that had been nothing but my ego talking. In truth, she was getting the stuff out to pack it up.

"So how did you and Sloggins get hooked up together?" Ed asked.

By now Jane Finn had dropped the airs she had put on when I had called on her. She was anything but the "quiet" woman that Howard Creighton had described. She acted the way she looked. Brassy. Braggy.

"Sloggins? One day he showed up at a house where I was the day sitter. While his men were working, we started talking about old people and how they didn't know what was going on half the time. I had listened in while he was making the deal with the old man at the house. I didn't exactly know Dwayne was scamming him when they started to work, but something didn't seem right.

"It was a big house, see. Huge. But his guys didn't look real dirty when they said they finished up, and they had sat around a lot when they'd oughta been working. No tar on their hands.

"I'd had some roof work of my own done a few years back and I saw what hard work it was. I stood over those guys like a hawk—as much as they were charging me. Shoot, I had to work two shifts to pay to get a roof put on that place. So what Sloggins's guys were doing just didn't seem right. No way they could have gotten the work done that fast. Not on *that* house."

Ed Pavich broke off her monologue. "So whose idea was it to team up? Yours or Sloggins's?"

Jane Finn shook her head. "Who knows? It just came to us." "That day?"

"Yeah. I guess so. I said something about the guys goofing off and Dwayne said something about how he bet I saw lots of good stuff in rich people's houses. He told me that he had good stuff in his house out in Dixon Springs. He said he even went to museum parties," she said. "I worked at one of them one time before I started sitting." She stopped, trying to recall the exact order of their conversation. "Then he said something about how he bet I had some nice things myself. He didn't accuse me of anything, but I could see in his eyes he suspected I was taking some stuff home."

"Takes one to know one," Ed said under his breath.

But listening to Jane, I was doing some recalling of my own. Dixon Springs. Hadn't I met someone from Dixon Springs just recently? Now who was it?

For the second time since midnight the light in my head went on. This time it was blinding.

When Peter had told me about the roofing scam he had said Sloggins was smooth, a real talker.

"What does Sloggins look like?" I asked of anyone who would listen to me.

"Not bad-looking. Heavyset," Ed answered. "Why?"

"Hair combed back?"

"Yeah."

"A lot of it?"

"Yeah. You know him?" Ed asked.

"Good God. I think that's the creep who tried to talk to me at the museum. You were there, Peter. He wanted me to come out and appraise his stuff." Why hadn't I made that connection before?

I slumped down on the sofa where Jane Finn had been sitting earlier.

"Huh?" said Jane Finn.

"Yes. It was before you showed me the pin LaTisha found, Peter." I searched his face for some hint that he remembered the exact moment at the museum. "Remember, I was walking away and you came up. There was this man who said he wanted me to come out and appraise his stuff." My voice dropped off as I thought of what might have happened if I had. "No telling what I would have seen at his house," I said.

No telling what scam I might innocently have been part of, I was thinking. Something even worse than what was unfolding right now.

"So *that* was it," Jane Finn said. This time she was the one putting it all together. "Remember how I told you that when you came out here Dwayne called me from his truck when he saw your car? He asked me who you were, but when I wouldn't tell him he said he already knew who you were. I thought he just meant you were one of them rich snobs. When I told him about bringing your aunt down here he didn't say anything more."

"He knew who I was all right," I said.

Jane Finn shifted her eyes nervously from one of us to the other. "Come to think of it. That's when he said we had to mail some of this stuff out. I'd been expecting that for days. That's the way he is. Pushy. Always in a rush. But"—she threw her hands up in exasperation—"he's the boss man."

"Boss man? Are there others? Other sitters?" It was Ed who was speaking.

"What's it worth to you?"

"What's it worth to *you?*" Ed shot back. "You're the one who's gonna need the help."

Jane Finn shrugged. "I don't know their names, other than Tess Elkins. She lives over Norfolk way, but she used to be from here." She shrugged a second time. "Dwayne didn't want his ladies talking too much to one another. Figured we might get some ideas and cut him out, I suppose. Tess told me that one night he just appeared. Started rummaging through her things. Drawers and closets. Like she might be hiding something from him. Made lots of threats to her. I told you," she said impatiently. "He beat up his wives. That's why I hid those things. Don't you see? He's just plain mean."

"A whole ring," Ed said.

I remembered running down the list of all those little towns in South Carolina in my conversation with Nigel.

"Any outside of Virginia?" I asked.

"Yeah. But I don't know where."

"Mrs. Finn, after Sloggins came and got the things from you or Tess or whomever, do you know what he did then?"

"He'd come see what I had, look the stuff over. Then he'd go get the packing stuff and I'd pack it."

"Do you know who he sent it all to?" I asked.

She shook her head. "Up to New York, I think. I told you

Sloggins goes to swanky museum parties. He'd met some guy at one down in—" She cocked her head. "Where'd all that Civil War stuff start? Was it down in Alabama where he went to that party?"

"Fort Sumter?" Ed asked.

"Nah. That don't sound just right. Where's that?"

"South Carolina."

"Nah," she repeated. "It was somewhere in Alabama."

"Montgomery?" I asked. "That's where the first capital of the Confederacy was. Like Danville was the last capital of the Confederacy."

"Yeah. That's it. Montgomery. He went down there for some big Civil War thing. A show or . . . What do they call it when they dress up in the old uniforms?"

"Reenactment?"

"Yeah. That's it. And the museum was having one of them times when people bring things in, like on that TV show I was telling you about."

"An appraisal day?"

"Yeah. I think that's where he got the idea about sending it all off. He met some man who knew all about antiques from up there in New York. I know he was always saying I had to pack the stuff really good if it was going to make it safe up to New York. I figure he was afraid he'd get caught if he sold it round here. One time Dwayne said he was thinking about opening up an antiques shop. Said he used to be a dealer. I never believed him, but he sure did seem to know a lot."

"Mrs. Finn, does Dwayne have a pickup truck? One of those . . ." I didn't have a clue how to describe it.

"Just got a new one. Big sucker, too."

So I hadn't been crazy. I had seen somebody ducking in the truck behind me, the same truck that later had roared through Arbor Hills.

But suspecting Dana Henchloe? The way I was doing now and that I had started doing the moment Jane Finn mentioned some expert from New York at the appraisal day in Montgomery? I had to be careful; my whole professional reputation could be at stake. On the other hand, hadn't Nigel said the Meissen pieces had come in through Dana? Jane Finn interrupted my thoughts.

"So how did you get on to me?" Jane Finn asked abruptly, looking from Ed to Peter to me. "I figured something was wrong when you came to see me," she said to Ed, "but I never thought nothing about you," she said to me. "So. Where did I slip up?"

"It was Mrs. Creighton," I said, bringing myself around enough to speak up, but still remembering the image of Sloggins's big pickup truck, and dwelling on the possible connection with Henchloe, my voice shook a little.

Jane Finn cast me a look of total disbelief.

"Mrs. Creighton? She's got Alzheimer's. That old woman don't even know what's going on. How the hell?"

"You're right," I said, trying to remain calm and collected, despite Finn's hateful look. I wasn't frightened, certainly not with these men around. But the day was taking a heavy toll on me. I was thoroughly exhausted and becoming more miserable with every passing minute.

"You're right," I repeated, "she doesn't know, or understand, much anymore. But she gets one thing stuck in her mind, that's the way Alzheimer's people do. She couldn't get her silver casserole dish—the one you took to Sarah Rose Wilkins's apartment—out of her head. She kept talking about it, incessantly."

Wearily I began recounting Howard Creighton's story about how Martha Creighton had insisted on putting the Turkey Tetrazzini in the silver casserole dish to take to Sarah Rose Wilkins.

"Oh, I remember, all right." Jane Finn's lips turned down in unfathomable anger that the Creightons, of all people, had given her away. "That day they gave me the key to Mrs. Wilkins's apartment, I thought that was *my luck-y* day." She drew her words out as if she were drawing her last breath of life. "Then old Mrs. Wilkins had to come home and ruin it all."

"One thing more," Ed said. "Why didn't you go back to get the stuff out of the apartment again? You still had the key."

"Think I didn't try? I slipped up there after the police were gone. The damn key didn't work. I wasn't about to break in. I'm not *that* stupid."

Ed slapped the side of his head upon realizing his own momentary lapse of logic. "The bank changed the locks."

"You'd have thought they'd have found fingerprints," I half-suggested, half-asked.

"Winter. Gloves," he said.

"It's that damn old silver pot's fault," Jane Finn snorted, ignoring him. "And Dwayne's. I should have been happy just taking little things to keep to enjoy. But he said we could make big bucks if I took some big stuff. I haven't even seen any big bucks yet. Damn old pot."

I cringed at hearing the urn, that masterpiece of craftsmanship and design, being so maligned. Roy Madison's calling it a coffeepot had been sufficiently irritating. Then Peter. Now Jane Finn was blaming her misfortunes on that damn old pot.

But what was really eating away at me now was that she hadn't shown one bit of remorse about stealing somebody else's property, and certainly not about anyone dying—except as it had messed up her own plans.

ED HANDED ME a legal pad. "We're going to need a list of these things. You know the information we need better than any of my guys," he said. Despite my exhaustion, I set to work writing descriptions of the pieces that Finn had stolen and still had in her possession. Meanwhile, police officers began to quiz Jane Finn as they filled out the necessary paperwork.

When I had a half second and Ed was finally free, I again asked him why Jane Finn had confessed so quickly and had chatted so freely, even though she obviously was seething with rage.

"Back there when she was telling about how she stole things . . . it was as if she was bragging," I said, puzzled.

"Her first offense. She was in over her head, so she's gone to the other extreme—trying to come off like a pro. Truth is, I think she's scared to death," Ed told me.

"First offense? That makes it sound like there'll be more."

Pavich shrugged. "Never know," he said brusquely. "Even though she seems to have been doing this for some while and getting away with it, since it *is* her first time getting caught . . . and she has nailed Sloggins pretty well, and we'll probably get more names in the ring out of her down the road . . ." He folded his arms in front of him, gave me a sad, knowing smile, and shrugged. "What happens to that old dame will depend on who the prosecuting attorney is. And who's sitting on the bench that day."

"Ed?" I said, taking advantage of having his full attention. I swallowed hard, eating my pride. "Crow" we call it in the South. The time had come for me to apologize.

I felt close to tears, something that didn't happen to me very often. Maybe it was my tiredness. I couldn't pinpoint the last time I cried, really cried, that is. In the last few days, though, between Mr. Creighton's plight, Sol's surmounting problems, my fright in that dark alleyway and then in Joey's shop, and now my own bumblings, I'd come close to tears . . . how many times? What difference did it make what had brought them on? I didn't like tears and they weren't part of my everyday life. But more and more, they were starting to be.

"Listen, Ed. About what happened this afternoon. I don't know what happened to me."

He shot me a puzzled look.

"Back there when I, well, I . . . I was almost taking up for Jane Finn. Saying she'd told me those things were her grandmother's . . ."

Ed Pavich laughed. "Jane Finn's first offense. Sterling Glass's first hardball. No big deal."

"But," I choked, searching to say more.

"Forget it. You'll learn," Ed said, ignoring my feeble excuse. "You'll get used to it."

"Get used to what? This isn't exactly my line of work. I'm an appraiser. Remember?"

"Yes ma'am, in fact, I do. That's why you shouldn't be feeling guilty. But—" He paused. "You'd make a good investigator," he said, giving me a quick wink for the second time in as many days. "The way you gathered the information, tracked down every clue, stuck with it, kept digging. You're a natural. You just crumbled at the kill. Not that unusual the first time out. Won't happen next time."

"First time? *Next* time? Listen here, Ed Pavich. You may not know about Jane Finn, whether or not she'll do it again, but of this you can be sure . . . Not me. I'm through. *Fin . . . finished . . . finis . . . done* . . . just as soon as you take me home."

Ed looked askance, then smiled. "Until you get the subpoena."

"Subpoena? What subpoena?"

"Don't get feisty. One feisty dame a day." He tossed his head in Jane Finn's direction. "That's my limit. Calm down. You'll just be the expert witness. Jane Finn's willing confession helps, but we'll still need your expertise when the case comes up at trial. Piece of cake."

I didn't like his answer one bit.

Chapter 25

Dear Antiques Expert: When I admired a friend's silver flat-ware, she told me it was the Audubon pattern. I've heard of James Audubon who drew the birds and plants in the South during the 19th century. Is there a connection between him and this silver pattern?

Indeed there is. In 1871 Tiffany, which was already a trend-setting shop in Manhattan, introduced a silver pattern based on popular 19th-century Japanese paintings of birds sitting on tree branches. Because James Audubon was so well known for his drawings of birds and foliage, this lyrical and romantic pattern was named "Audubon" in his honor. It became an instant success and remains Tiffany's best-selling pattern. Collectors willingly pay $350 or $400 on up for a single serving piece, and if it is still in its original box, the price is more likely to be $700 or $800—or more.

I RODE IN THE backseat from Jane Finn's to my house. Ed and Peter both had told me to sit up front, but by sitting in the back I could huddle in the corner and sulk. When we reached River Road, there was Barefoot Bagman trudging along.

"Ever had any run-ins with Bagman?" Peter asked Ed, as he spied Leemont's infamous figure.

"Never a one." Ed dismissed Peter's question, then added, "Thinking about it, there have been a couple of complaints. But when we tried to pin the callers down about what he actually was doing wrong or what law he was breaking, they couldn't say. Either they didn't like the way he looked, or they were genuinely concerned about him."

"Barefoot's quite a character," Peter said. "He comes in the store every so often, and I've chatted with him on occasion. I told you about one time," he said in my direction.

"Well, just last week he came in again. We have a new rule about checking all bags and packages at the cash register. As you can imagine, at first the girls were afraid of Bagman and didn't want him to leave his bag there with them. In fact, they didn't want him in the store at all. One said that she'd heard that he might have a bomb in his bag." Peter laughed. "I suggested it might be a dismembered body or somebody's ashes. They didn't think that was funny."

Ed let out a hearty howl.

I edged my way away from the window toward the center of the backseat.

"Did they look? What *does* he carry around?" I asked.

Peter turned in his seat. "Really want to know?"

To my surprise, even Ed seemed interested. "Yeah."

Visions of priceless jewels, rare silver, tiny objets d'art— anything valuable that you could pack up and put in a bag— these were the sorts of things I imagined.

"Books."

"Books?"

"Yes. Books that he picks up from people's trash. Old magazines that the library puts out for anyone who wants them to pick up. Books and a blanket. And, oh yes, I think he had a can of Vienna sausages or sardines in his bag. He's just lugging around what he values as the important things of life. Warmth for the body and sustenance for the mind," Peter said.

"Well, I never," Ed said.

"He invited me over to his . . . I think he called it 'quarters.' As good a euphemism for a basement as any, I guess. Said it wasn't much, but he thought I might like to see his library. I may take him up on it sometime, when it isn't too hot or too cold or too wet or too dry." Peter laughed. "Actually, I need to do that one day. Bagman's really not a bad guy. Probably very interesting. Yes, I must do that. And Sterling, I'll take you with me."

"Me? Why?"

"Believe it or not, in our conversation he mentioned having a first edition of Thomas Sheraton's *Cabinet-Maker and Upholsterers' Drawing Book*. Let's see, when was that published? In 1791, I believe."

"Good Lord, Peter. Why haven't you told me this?"

"It was just last week. The way things have been happening around here, it slipped my mind."

"Maybe you can hire Bagman as an assistant, Sterling," Ed Pavich suggested.

I didn't mention my dreams about Bagman. "Maybe I should," I said. "No telling what he sees and doesn't pick up. Wonder how much he wants for that book?" I said, thinking out loud. "And wonder where on earth he picked it up. Peter, it *can't* be a first edition."

"Maybe not. Maybe so. Stranger things have happened," he said knowingly. "Or am I preaching to the choir?" Peter leaned back and playfully patted my knee.

No one argued with him on that point. Not after the past few days' events.

By the time Ed dropped Peter and me at my house where Peter had left his car, I was a little cheerier. Still, though, I had mixed feelings about asking Peter in. Any other time, I would have jumped at the chance. I had dreamed of such times. Snow on the ground, a crisp, starry night, a crackling fire in the fireplace, Peter with me. Instead, this night I looked at him, remembered what had happened just a few hours earlier, and wondered if I knew him at all.

"Aren't you going to invite me in? Or would you rather go directly to get a bite to eat?" he asked.

When I fumbled for my key and didn't immediately answer, Peter said, "You're being awfully quiet. Too tired? Anything wrong?"

I still didn't reply.

He tried again. "I know it's been a rough day, but it's nothing you've done. Jane Finn—"

"Oh, but it *is* something I did. It's what I said about Jane Finn's grandmother, and what I *didn't* say about the information I had when I should have spoken up," I blurted out.

And something *you* said, Peter, I desperately wanted to say, but didn't.

"You did falter there for a minute," Peter conceded, "but it all ended well enough." He laughed, then said, "Ended well, except for Jane Finn and Dwayne Sloggins, that is."

He so casually dismissed my painful plight that again his

tone and attitude grated on me. Added insult to injury. Who was this man? I didn't know him at all.

"Didn't you feel *any* pity for her?"

Through the darkness of the night, lightened by the brightness of the white snow, I could see the perplexed look on Peter's face. "Sterling, Jane Finn's guilty."

"I know that now," I said, "but back there at her house when Ed was tearing into her. And then *you* jumped in. I . . ."

I didn't know what to say next.

"Sterling, Sterling. Just how many things have you got going on in that sweet, pretty head of yours?"

Peter reached out, put his arm around my shoulder, and in a brotherly way half-patted, half-hugged it. "Here. Tell you what. Let's go inside, regroup, and call in a pizza. My treat. Look, it's too beautiful a night to waste." He gestured toward the sky.

Mother could no longer resist putting in her two cents' worth. *You know, it wouldn't hurt you to listen to what somebody else has to say, just once in a while.*

I smiled in spite of myself.

"That's a great idea. We can have a fire."

WHILE I CALLED in our order and checked my phone for messages, Peter brought in the logs. Settled in our usual places, he in the high-back wing chair, me in my corner of the settee, we carefully avoided what we both wanted to talk about until the pizza arrived and we were warmed by the fire and a couple of beers.

"You're the only person I know who uses a silver pie server to serve pizza." Peter said, helping himself to another slice.

"Audubon pattern?" he asked, leisurely picking the green peppers off his piece and putting them on my plate, adding, "Your grandmother's or somebody else's?"

"*Grandmother?*" I grimaced. "I don't care if I *never* hear that word again. Not even anything about my *own* grandmothers."

Recovering, I laughed. "Yes, it's Tiffany's Audubon, and no, it wasn't my grandmother's. It was my great-grandmother's . . . on my Yankee father's side. And how you can eat anchovies and not like green peppers, Peter Donaldson, I'll never understand!"

I heard an edge creeping into my voice, but I couldn't stop it.

"So let's clear the air, Sterling. I can tell you're mad at me," Peter said abruptly.

I stifled a sigh at his sudden change of mood. I dropped my eyes and stared into the fire. Only the crackling of a log broke our silence as it shifted toward the back of the grate.

"Well?"

"I'm not mad at you. 'Confused' would be the better word," I said hesitantly.

"I must be guilty of doing something to have *confused* you then, but honestly, I don't know what it is. I really would like to know what I did."

"It was back at Jane Finn's," I said. "First, I made a fool out of myself when I said that she'd told me that her grandmother had owned those things. Of course they *weren't* her grandmother's. I should have confronted Jane Finn right then with the pictures of the Meissen platter and sauceboat in the Layton catalog. That was my fault. I know it. I caved in. But—"

"I understand. You felt sorry for her. You—"

For a split second, it seemed to me that Peter was trying to hide the hint of a smile. That only irked me more.

"Wait, damn it. Let me finish," I said.

I was having a terrible enough time getting my own confession out. Telling him how I felt about how he—dear, virtuous, generous, always patient and kind Peter—had acted was going to be even harder.

I took a deep breath.

"So what I did was wrong. I admit it. But *you* immediately lashed out at her, even more brutally than Ed," I said. "And you looked so mad, almost vicious, like you hated or despised her." I stopped.

The quietness of the moment was unbearable. As I always seem to do, I spoke first, if for no other reason than to break the insufferable silence. "I guess I expected you to be chivalrous, to defend Jane Finn. Isn't that what ministers are supposed to do?"

Peter made no attempt to hide the smile that by now was spreading across his face. "May I speak now?" he asked.

"No. Let me get my side out first," I said. "It's funny that you mentioned the pie server and my grandmother—or great-grandmother in this case. But you see, I have seen situations where people have been left with things, possessions, and no cash, and they have fought hard to hold on to the things they had as a symbol, a memory . . . a vestige of the past . . . not just some material possession, some piece of stuff."

I picked up the pie server and turned it over. Only if you knew what it said, could you read the elaborate, intertwined letters *CET*. Clara Elizabeth Turner, my great-grandmother's monogram. The Clara Elizabeth whose name I bear but am not known by.

"I know there were times when my parents must have been tempted to sell some of the family treasures they inherited when my father lost his job and things got rough. But they didn't, thank goodness. Eventually things got better."

I shook my head, trying to cast off unhappy memories of trying times—only to remember another, more recent, and even more difficult time.

"And I think about the tremendous amount of money that Mother's illness cost. She died before every single penny was depleted, but I've seen *many* times when a family has become so desperate to maintain a parent in a long-term illness that the kids have literally slipped things their parent had loved out of the house at night to sell them to pay for the nursing care or medicine or whatever."

Peter opened his mouth to speak.

I held up my hand in protest.

"*Please*, let me finish. I know you're right, Peter. Jane Finn is guilty. Was guilty. May be guilty *again*, or so Ed has hinted. But for just that fleeting moment," I blurted out, "I had second thoughts. I *wanted* her to be innocent."

I pressed my lips hard against each other. There was nothing else I could say.

"Now, may I speak?" he asked.

I dropped my eyes to avoid his sweet, understanding look. "I guess so."

"I didn't mean to upset you, Sterling," he said contritely. "And I'm sorry if I looked, what did you say, vicious? I'm sure I did."

I looked up. To my surprise, beneath his tousled hair his face was stern. Not angry, but sadly grim.

"I have to contend with that sort of Jane Finn deceit and deception every day at the Salvation Army. I hear one made-up story after the other. There's always some cockamamie 'poor, pitiful me' reason for why somebody stuck that radio in his overcoat, or just happened to have on three sweaters—with the price tags still on them—after going through the checkout lane. Day in, day out, from dawn to dark, it's tale after tale after tale of how Jessie lost his rent money, *again*."

Peter stood up abruptly, as if doing so would cast aside those images, and began pacing, the same way he had done when he had told me about Sloggins, just a day or so earlier. He returned to his chair and settled back, then nervously leaned forward, clasped his hands together, and put his elbows on his knees. He rested his chin on his fingertips.

"It was the same way when I was a minister, Sterling," Peter said, his face taut. "The finest people, the most upright citizens, my parishioners, would come to see me. They'd sit across the desk from me, look straight at the crucifix hanging on the wall behind my shoulder, and proceed to tell me one bald-faced lie after the other. Then expect me to help them out. For God's sake, Sterling, a minister is supposed to help people face the *truth*, to repent, and to go on. Instead, these people—my *friends*—were trying to suck me into believing their lies, to get me to play along with their masquerade, to hide their sins for them."

Peter folded and unfolded his fingers as he spoke. His face had lost its boyishness. It was contorted, filled with disbelief, tainted with deep despair.

My heart was breaking for Peter. If only I could have taken my own disparaging words back.

Then, as Mother had done so many times, she made sense out of it all. I heard Nathaniel Hawthorne's damning words, words that said what I was feeling but dared not express: *when man does not vainly shrink from the eye of his Creator, loathsomely treasuring up the secret of his sin, then deem me a monster for . . . I look around me, and, lo! on every visage a Black Veil.*

So that was why Peter had left the church. The hypocrisy.

It was that vision of duplicity that had led Reverend Hopper in Hawthorne's story to don a black veil and wear it throughout his life, while everyone else's black veils were invisible — like the emperor's new clothes.

When he looks around, lo! on every visage Peter sees the black veil of hypocrisy, Mother said.

But that was almost two hundred years ago, I thought.

What does that matter? Mother answered. *People never change. The question is this: Is it a curse or a gift to have such vision, to see your fellow man in such light? Either way, such an insight is a burden. Peter is a man not at peace with his fellow men. But he is your champion, Sterling.*

"Jane Finn is like so many people I've known, Sterling," Peter was saying, his resolve even more impassioned than before. "She lied. She was guilty. Case closed."

He stood and came over and sat down beside me. He took my hand in both of his.

"I'm not going to chastise you for giving Jane Finn the benefit of the doubt, even though, deep down, you knew differently. Your forgiving heart, the way you look for the best in people, is part of what makes you *you*. You're sympathetic and kind. That's admirable." He brightened and his face softened.

"Here. Look at it this way," he said. "What do you do when someone tells you a piece is . . . let's say an eighteenth-century chest of drawers? You examine it, of course. When you do so, you find all the evidence of why it *can't* be from the eighteenth century. There are new nails, machine-cut dovetails, plywood drawer bottoms—you know the routine."

Like a schoolmaster, double-checking to be sure that his lesson has been understood, Peter asked me seriously, but sweetly, "Now, what do you tell your client?"

"The truth. I explain why it can't be an eighteenth-century piece," I said contritely.

"But your client *insists* that it really *is* from the eighteenth century. You're expected to go along with him, to authenticate it and put an eighteenth-century price on the piece so he can sell it for a great amount of money."

"Well, yes, but that would be *wrong*. And eventually when another expert looked at the piece, I'd be made out to be a liar—or stupid. Plus my client would be deceiving other people," I said.

"Exactly. That's why you would tell the truth to begin with. Why you would refuse to go along with his scheme." Peter smiled. "See? All I was telling Jane Finn was the truth. I was laying the cards, the evidence, out on the table. The only difference between you and me this afternoon is that I've seen too much. I've run out of patience. You're right. I *was* angry and I wasn't going to let her drag her deceit on any longer. Look," Peter said, "if I hadn't jumped in, you would have called her bluff, eventually. But Sterling, I didn't want to play her game.

I wasn't going to let her get the upper hand—especially not at your expense. Pure and simple, she was playing on your sympathies. She's an expert at that. She's as practiced at her art as a poker player is at keeping a straight face."

"Peter," I said, measuring my own words, "remember the first time we really met? The day we ran into each other at the antiques shop and we stopped and had lunch together?"

He nodded.

"You said something then that I've never forgotten. You said that like lost souls, lost *things* need looking after, too."

Peter's whole face shone. "That's what we're doing, Sterling, looking after lost things. Jane Finn's soul is already lost."

"Why do you keep trying?" I said then. "Working there at the Salvation Army? Why not open an antiques shop or . . . volunteer at the museum?"

He looked at me, appalled. Then his eyes grew soft again and he smiled the sweetest smile I've ever seen.

"I just keep on hoping," he said.

Peter let go of my hand and picked up the largest anchovy he could find left on the last piece of pizza. "I bet you an anchovy pizza with no green peppers that when Jane Finn gets up on that witness stand, she's going to claim that she was *given* some of those pieces. And know what? She probably was. Like that twenty-fifth goblet the lady gave her. I'm sure she told poor old Mrs. Gotrocks her tale of woe. That's how she got some of her things."

I nodded in agreement.

"Thank you," I said truthfully. "I feel much better."

"I guess you do, after two, or is it three, Amstels and all that pizza, especially as tired as we both are."

For one brief, fleeting moment, I was tempted to throw my arms around his neck.

I looked into his eyes, hoping I'd see myself there.

When I didn't, I said, "Forget the beer and pizza. I feel better after just admitting that I know more about *things* than I do about people. And," I added reluctantly, "after coming to realize that I still have a lot more growing up to do. Even at my age."

Thank you, Lord, Mother said.

Chapter 26

Dear Antiques Expert: I find Chinese Chippendale furniture with its geometric lattice-work design extremely attractive. Did Chippendale ever travel to the Orient in the 18th century to pick up this design idea?

No, Thomas Chippendale never traveled from England to China, but he was familiar with the geometric lines used in Eastern art and architecture. Eastern designs were introduced to Europe after Marco Polo's famous journey, and once trade routes were established. Chippendale adapted those designs for some of his furniture drawings in his book, *The Gentleman and Cabinet-Maker's Director: Being a New Book of Designs of Household Furniture in the Gothic, Chinese and Modern Taste.* Though other furniture makers combined the Chinese and European designs, the style has come to be known as "Chinese Chippendale."

I CALLED MATT YARDLEY shortly after nine on Tuesday morning. When I told him how Sloggins had a whole band of thieves, including Jane Finn, and that we had recovered many stolen items—and probably not just pieces taken from the Hanesworths—Matt sounded much more excited than I would have thought possible, given our meeting in New York when he had seemed so reserved.

"What I still can't understand is how it was possible for the Paul Storr tea urn to have been overlooked as missing on the appraisal," I said.

"Oh, I meant to tell you about that," Matt said. "I talked to one of the Hanesworths' sons, David, who said he remembered that his parents were proud of that particular piece. The kids, just to goad their parents, used to call it a coffeepot. The kids had no idea it was English or as old as it was. You know how kids purposely ignore whatever they're told by their parents.

"None of the kids remember seeing the piece recently. I think they'd forgotten about it. That the Hanesworths' sitter had found it on a closet shelf makes perfect sense. David said they glossed right over the written description of the Paul Storr tea urn on the appraisal, didn't even connect it with what they called the coffeepot. The family just assumed that it was another piece of silver that they'd turn up somewhere in the house. They never even bothered to look at the picture, if you can believe that."

"I can believe anything," I said. I would've thought a piece valued at sixty-five thousand dollars would send people scurrying to find it, but that was the difference between myself and the fabulously wealthy.

"Yes, especially when you take into account how many, many things, valuable things, the Hanesworths had in that mansion. It's not exactly San Simeon, but it is impressive enough. And filled to the brim. No telling what else may turn up missing," Matt said, then added, "or be found that they didn't even know about." I could hear his smile in his voice.

"So, now that they know about their coffeepot, they can all fight over who's going to get it," I said, relaxing a bit. Just having a friendly chat with someone felt wonderful after yesterday.

"This whole fiasco reminds me of another appraisal," I continued. "One family I worked for sent their two daughters to London to take the Sotheby's course in antiques and fine arts just so the girls would know what they were inheriting and be able to call things by the proper names, pronounced correctly, of course. Why, the tally must have been close to a hundred thousand dollars when you included their room and board."

"There's no room for any Beverly Hillbilly slipups allowed among the unforgiving socially elite," Matt said.

"You're right there," I said. "You never know when some minor European royalty's son is going to take you home—home to Cannes or Bermuda—to meet Mumsey."

"Speaking of trips," Matt said, "when you come up to retrieve the urn, I'd like for you to meet everyone here. I imagine we will be sending a great deal of business your way, and not just out of the Richmond office. Perhaps we can have supper. That's what you Southerners call dinner, isn't it?"

Was there a hint of condescension in mentioning a time-honored Southernism? Or was Matt just being casually friendly? I dismissed it as Yankee-talk. Still, I hesitated before answering. It wasn't because of his comment, though. Rather, it was because my mind had split off into three different directions at once.

Matt had mentioned sending more business my way—that meant more money. Then the comment about the business from places other than the Richmond office. I let my imagination run wild. I'd happily fly out to Jackson Hole, Wyoming, or up to Greenwich, Connecticut, or even over to Malibu to do some appraisals. And while there, maybe drop by to see Alicia's Art Deco collection?

And then the comment about having dinner together.

If only there *were* some way I could cash in on a trip to bring the urn back to Virginia. But Nigel could easily ship it as well as the Meissen pieces.

"I wish a trip was necessary," I said with a tinge of sincere regret, "but I'm sure Roy Madison will be most cooperative and sign whatever papers he needs to in order for Nigel Rhodes to turn the urn over to you. Now the Meissen pieces—"

"I'm a jump ahead of you. Obviously you haven't spoken to Nigel today."

"No." Nor did I want to. Especially with my growing suspicion about Dana Henchloe's involvement.

"The situation probably could be done as you say, by signing papers. However, because these are stolen items, positive identification must be made. I've never seen any of the things. The soup tureen has to get up here somehow. So does the pearl and diamond pin. It would just be simpler if you could handle it all. We are more than delighted to pay your way, expenses, and hourly fee. That is how you charge, isn't it?"

I tried to sound professional and not jump up and down like a child.

"Of course. My hourly rate is $150."

"Reasonable enough. Plus all expenses."

It was too good to be true. Without a second thought, I pushed my luck.

"And when do you anticipate my doing this?" I said.

"That's up to you and your schedule, of course, but I would hope it can be as soon as you can arrange it. Would later this week be too soon? Do you have a favorite hotel, or would the InterContinental be okay? Oh, and tell me, how will you want your reservations made? Our travel department will do that for you, of course. Do you go by Ms. Glass or prefer Mrs. Glass?"

"Ms."

I didn't have a clue if Matt Yardley was married, divorced, widowed, committed, otherwise entangled, or just shopping.

AFTER THAT, I WAS feeling pretty self-important and so I called Sol to find out what his message of yesterday had meant. Had it only been yesterday? "So much has happened," he'd said. To you *and* me, I thought.

I knew no more about the value of his molds now than I had the last time I saw him, but at least I was getting a better handle on the value of his figures, thanks to Richie's catalogs and the Internet. If I took photographs of the statues and did more research, eventually I would be able to guide him toward getting full value for his figurines.

"He came back, Sterling, back to Joey's," Sol said, his voice shaking when I got him on the phone. "It was a little after seven," he said, "just like before. He rang and rang the bell until Joey let them in. Didn't want to, but he was afraid not to. I had told Joey—"

The familiar sound of Sol's wheezing cough interrupted his sentence. He put his hand over the receiver to muffle the sound.

"Sorry," he choked. "I had told Joey not to open the store at all, to just stay away. He didn't have any figures there. The man didn't like that."

"Do you know who the man is, Sol? Was he the one . . ." I realized my heart was beating harder and faster. "The one who . . ." I cleared my own throat for no reason other than to stall for time, to figure out what to say next. The one who got away? The one who beat up Joey? The one who scared me to death lurking in the alleyway when I was in the cab?

"It was the same man who was there before," Sol said. "The man became angry when Joey didn't have any figures. He had a friend with him this time. The other time, Joey had tried to stand up to him. But this time it was two of them." Sol's voice faded.

"Did anything happen?" That same sick feeling I'd had that night came creeping back, first in my stomach and then in my head.

"No fight. Just words. Threats. This time," Sol said, "Joey said the man's friend lurked around in the doorway. Never came in. Like he was blocking it." Though he was speaking so quietly I could barely hear him, Sol began rushing through his words. "The man said he bet Joey had some figures in the back. That made Joey real scared. Joey—"

"Sol, I don't mean to interrupt, but two questions here," I said in an attempt to clear my mind and keep focused and to calm Sol down. "First, what happened to 'Scheherazade'? The last time I saw her, Joey had her. Where is she now? Did he take her back to his shop?"

"Oh, no. After that first night, and then after you said all those wonderful things about my figures, we haven't taken any more of them there. 'Scheherazade' wasn't there. No figures were. That's why the man got so mad. He said he figured Joey had more figures hidden away."

"Okay. Did Joey tell you what the man looked like? The one who had been there before?"

I blew out a long breath in an attempt to regain my composure. When I tried to swallow, I realized my throat was closing up. What to do? I grabbed up a pen and paper and dashed off two stick figures in an attempt to get a grasp on exactly who was who, and repeated my question. "First tell me about the one who was inside Joey's store, Sol. Describe him for me."

"He was the burly one. The other one was WASPy-looking, Joey says."

Despite the tension of the moment, I couldn't help smiling. This Jewish man thought enough of me to speak his mind forthrightly and forget all that PC crap.

"Okay, I need those details about what the men looked like. But one at a time. Please?"

"I told you. The man who had been there before, the one inside, he was thick and burly. Dark."

Hastily, I made heavy square lines around one of the stick figures and wrote "customer."

"Dark? Do you mean black?"

"No. No. Dark. Like me. His friend, the one who stayed in the door," Sol continued impatiently, "*he* was the WASP. You know that place. It's dark inside and it was night. Joey didn't get a real good look at him, but he said he wasn't dark or black. Fair, like you. But big, real big."

I gave the other figure longer legs, and thickened him up so he looked decidedly bigger and wrote "WASP" under it.

"Now, this dark one, the one you say was burly—the one who had been there before—was he just heavyset and dark? Or did he look mean?"

I kept seeing Richie Daniel in my mind. He could never be described as tall and big, nor as dark and burly or thick . . . to say nothing of the sort of guy who would be intentionally threatening, despite his intimidating smile. That smug, cocky smile was as much part of his act as his Texas strut. Then again, I hadn't forgotten the bruise and Ace bandage Richie had been sporting. That hunk of a ring Joey wore could do damage, even accidentally, and Joey had said he'd taken a swipe at the guy—whoever he was. Under the stick figure where I had written "customer," I added "Richie?"

"Burly. *Burly,*" Sol repeated even more impatiently. "He wasn't *real* tall from what Joey told me. More stout. Mostly he was gruff and mean." Sol paused, then said affectionately, "Remember, Joey's a little fellow."

I thought again. Maybe Richie would appear gruff if he didn't get his way, but the physical description didn't fit Richie at all. Then again, it might have, to little Joey. I thought again. No. Just because Richie had wanted to cut me in on a shady deal didn't mean he was guilty of assault and threats. I scratched through his name on the paper.

"They said they were coming back," Sol said.

"But if Joey said he didn't have any more figures . . ."

"Threats, Sterling. Threats. The man scared Joey."

"What did Joey do when they said they'd be back?"

"Joey said he'd try to get another figure. What else could he do? I've told him I'd give him one more to sell to him but then to say there are no others."

Good Lord! The whole situation was beginning to sound more and more like one of those bloodcurdling black-and-white movies. Right now, though, creepy guys like Peter Lorre and Sydney Greenstreet and Claude Rains were getting to be too real to be much fun. I did my best to sound normal.

"Did they say when they would be back?"

"Friday. But Joey said he'd be at services at the temple. So they said they'd come Thursday. Tomorrow. I'll give them a figure. It's my molds I don't want them to get."

Here we go again, I thought. "Thursday?"

"Yes. But they won't get my molds."

My mind was racing. If there were some way I could get to New York faster . . . What was I thinking? Still . . . it wasn't impossible. It would just take some doing. Another idea flew into my head.

"Sol. This is what you must do. Put a figure together for Joey, a new one. Don't give him one that you've already put together. Understand? Make a new one, but—and this is *very* important—when you make it, make something wrong with it."

"Wrong! What do you mean, wrong?"

"Well, like put a head with a hat on or with a wrong hairdo —one that doesn't fit with the costume that's on the body. Or put the wrong legs on a torso. Something. But don't make it real obvious. Sol, do something that only *you* would know was wrong or someone who really knows the figures would recognize. A real expert. Understand?"

"Why would I do that? I'm proud of my work. I don't make mistakes."

"Please."

"Okay. I'll do it for you."

"Thank you, Sol. And I hope to see you very, very soon."

Maybe even on Thursday, I said to myself.

Chapter 27

Dear Antiques Expert: I see advertisements for Mikimoto pearls in glamorous fashion magazines. What makes them so special and just how expensive are they?

Kokichi Mikimoto made jewelry history in 1893 by successfully creating a beautiful, lustrous pearl by implanting foreign objects into oysters. Today we call such pearls "cultured," as opposed to "natural," pearls. Carefully chosen for their color and luster, Mikimoto pearls are considered the finest cultured pearls, since natural pearls are just about unheard of these days. Vintage Mikimoto pearls bearing the Mikimoto mark on their clasps can command upward of $10,000 to $20,000, depending on size and color. That's a real bargain when you consider that some of the new strands can cost over $50,000.

IT REALLY DIDN'T SUIT me to turn around and go straight back up to New York—especially when I only had a few hours to pack and get to the airport. True to my lifelong habit of talking first and thinking second, I'd done it again. On top of that, I was in over my head. But I'd given my word to Sol. There was nothing I could do about it now but follow through. I booked a

direct flight that would get me into New York around 6:45 P.M.
I had been a little timid about suggesting to Matt that I come
that day, rather than Thursday, but both Thursday morning
flights were fully booked and I'd have had to fly standby. With
time of the essence, I couldn't chance that.

Throwing a few things into the suitcase was no big deal.
Getting organized to leave on such short notice was. At least I
didn't have car pools or soccer practice or piano lessons to deal
with, as I once did.

I called Peter on the off-chance that he could give me a lift
to the airport. At an earlier time I might have resisted the urge
to ask him for a favor, thinking I'd appear too aggressive or
forward. But after all that had transpired between us, I felt
strangely comfortable with my newfound knowledge of him,
this very dear and complicated man. And perhaps his com-
plexity explained why he had never been more, well, more
romantic toward me. Certainly, many times he'd shown
true concern, but he always stopped short of the affection I
thought was around the corner. But right now, I couldn't
worry about that. He'd been so open and honest with me;
maybe that was a hopeful sign. Anyway, I needed a ride to the
airport. Finding a parking space there was always dicey, plus
ever since the taxi I'd reserved never showed, I hadn't wanted
to trust my luck. I didn't need any more worries today. I dialed
his number.

Mother calmly said, *You'll be more content now, Sterling.
You and Peter can freely have what Ben Jonson called a "spir-
itual coupling of two souls."*

I could live with that. I vowed to convince myself that this
was possible.

The phone at the Salvation Army was busy. I hung up and no more than fifteen seconds later my phone rang.

"Sterling."

"I was just trying to call you," I said.

"And I was trying to call *you*." He laughed. "How about dinner tonight?"

"How about taking me to the airport at three thirty?"

I rattled through the morning's events so uncharacteristically briefly and with such urgency that I left Peter no choice but to agree. "And there's something we need to talk about on the way to the plane," I said just before hanging up, so he couldn't slip a word in edgewise.

The second thing I did was to call Ed Pavich as I threw a few things into my carry-on suitcase. We went over whether or not it would be necessary to have the pieces that we'd recovered from Jane Finn's house, plus the urn and pin, at the trial—or trials, as the case might be. And in his brusque cop way, Ed proceeded to tell me what to expect from the twelve men and women sitting in the jury box.

"Those folks won't know Sheraton from Sheridan, or Shaker from Shineola. Add in the fact that the victims were rich, and that's two runs for Sloggins's and Finn's defense. What will help us is that the victims were old and helpless. And, if we're lucky, the jury'll be impressed by the worth of the stuff that SOB was pilfering from them. But the things themselves? Forget it. Some good photographs will work just as well. What *will* help to build our case is your strong sympathetic presence to pull at their heart strings," he said.

We agreed that after documenting and photographing each piece, the items could be returned by the insurance company to the Hanesworth children, since there was no telling how long it would be before the case came to trial—or how long things would drag on after that. Clearly it was out of the question for me to take the pin and tureen and other pieces to New York with me. But it did make sense for me to bring the tea urn and Meissen pieces back from Layton's to Leemont for Jane Finn to identify as the ones she had taken from the Hanesworths' home. That would satisfy Babson and Michaels's offer to pay for my trip.

Only when I was positive I really would be in New York on Thursday did I call Sol. I hadn't wanted to get his hopes up.

That done, I called Howard Creighton. He had left a cordial message on my machine inquiring when I would be back to finish the appraisal. It would have been easy to ignore his call, but I felt a responsibility to the Creightons, maybe more than to anyone. I almost told Howard Creighton about Jane Finn and the important part that he and Mrs. Creighton had played in breaking the thieving ring but concluded that should wait till another time. Even so, with Howard Creighton's slow and deliberate way, our conversation seemed to go on forever.

No good deed goes unpunished, Mother reminded me.

TRUE TO HIS WORD, Peter was at my doorstep at three thirty, plenty of time to get me to the airport. It took about five seconds for him to jump to the heart of the matter. "Just what is it you need to talk to me about?"

"There's something that's been eating away at me ever since I talked to Sol last night and decided to get back to New York to see him as soon as possible."

"What's that?" Peter asked as I pulled a manila folder out of my oversized pocketbook.

"All my worldly goods."

He gave me a sideways glance. "All of them? Really? What about all those things on Bittersweet Trail?"

We both laughed.

"Seriously. That's what *this* is." I said. "A list—not an appraisal, mind you—a list of those things on Bittersweet Trail that I hold dear. The things I want Lily and Ketch to know about."

I opened it, took out the stapled pages, and held them so Peter could see them without taking his eyes off the road.

Instead, he looked at me. "But why tell *me?* Why now?"

"Oh, you just never know about life," I said.

Peter wasn't buying it.

"Okay," I tried again, "here I am dashing right back up to New York. We all act like world conditions are under control, but—"

Peter's eyes were focused on the traffic merging from the right, but his look grew askance.

"That doesn't sound like you, Sterling. What's up?"

That sick feeling I had had in the alley behind Joey's shop and later, when talking to Sol, started churning around in the pit of my stomach, then crept down into my legs.

"I've told you about Sol and Joey—"

"Yes," he interrupted me. "Which reminds me, we've been so consumed with everything that's been happening closer to home that I haven't spoken my mind about that situation. From what I do know, though, well, let's just say I don't like it."

"Oh, there's no reason to worry, honest, but—"

"Don't you know that nothing you say in a sentence before 'but' counts?" Peter interjected.

"Anyway," I said, trying to ignore his comment, "I've agreed to meet Sol and Joey when the man, whoever he is, comes back to get another figure. I don't expect anything to happen, but in case it should I want someone to know about these things that I love and that have historical as well as monetary value. That's all. Lily and Ketch have heard me talk about these things my whole life but with only half an ear." I remembered Matt telling how the Hanesworths' kids had purposely ignored their parents' attempts to tell them about the Paul Storr urn.

"And even less of a brain," I added. "They're just kids. You have to reach a certain place in your life to understand that things aren't just things. My kids aren't there yet."

"I understand," Peter said.

"So here's a copy for you," I continued, relieved that traffic was heavy enough that he was letting me talk. "I started the list a while back, but never finished it, and I didn't have much time to get this together, so this is pretty rudimentary. Anyway, this is what I've done. The pieces with an *S*, for Smith, came from my side of the family. The ones with a *G* came from the Glasses."

"That's clear enough."

"Then"—though he couldn't look, I pointed to a couple of items on the page—"I put an *L* or a *K* for whoever should have the piece, Lily or Ketch. Just in case."

I slipped the papers back into the envelope and tossed it onto the backseat, then settled back into my seat.

Peter took his right hand off the steering wheel and laid it on top of mine and left it there. "Sterling, if you're this worried, why are you getting involved? I know you're fond of Sol, but in truth you hardly know him."

"If you knew him, you'd understand. He's so, well, innocent. And deserving. And defenseless. I couldn't stand for any bad to come to him. And he reminds me of my grandfather. Look at it this way," I said. "I have to go to New York anyway to get things straight at Layton's."

"And you, my dear, are going to fend off this crook who is coming to get Sol's treasures? Sounds like some plot right out of a made-for-TV movie. What good could you do? To say nothing of putting yourself in danger. Think about it. You're showing me these things you want Lily and Ketch to know about? *You* should be telling your kids about them, not making up an impersonal list for me to be in charge of. Why, Lily and Ketch hardly know me." He smiled gently, spoke firmly. "Don't go. At least not out to Sol and Joey's. Let them handle it."

"I have to. I gave my word. You understand that."

I looked at his profile for some sign of approval. When I didn't see it, I smiled the biggest smile I could and tried another tack. "Anyway, there are those wonderful figurines. Somebody has to protect them."

"You?" he asked skeptically.

"Well, I can't trust Richie, the fellow at Layton's, to have Sol's best interest at heart," I said bluntly. "I don't know what else to do. I guess I'm just buying time until I can convince Sol of their value and advise him."

"Sterling, the figures may be beautiful. And valuable. But they're hardly worth putting yourself in harm's way for."

"Others have. Sol's grandparents and parents, and now Sol."

Peter's frown deepened. Then that irresistible smile of his spread across his face. He patted my hand gently.

"It's pretty obvious your mind's made up." Peter shook his head resolutely but kept smiling. "Tell me, has anyone ever changed your mind? Don't answer that. Just promise me one thing. You'll keep in touch with me every step of the way, and you'll come home safely."

And just when I was talking myself out of being in love with him. Men.

I should have known better, Mother said haughtily. *Remember, though,* she said, her smug tone melting into compassion, *friendship into love can turn, but love to friendship—never.*

THE INTERCONTINENTAL ON East Forty-eighth and Madison was a far cry from my Manhattan digs of the week before.

I was settling into my spacious room when there was a knock at the door.

"Yes?"

"A delivery for Ms. Glass."

I opened the door. A pretty young man, the type who speaks clearly and looks dramatic at all times, most likely an aspiring actor, stood before me holding an arrangement of orchids and roses.

"There must be some mistake," I said.

"Ms. Glass?"

"Yes."

He delivered his lines perfectly. "These are for you. May I?"

"Oh."

He strode across the room and set them on the coffee table in front of the sofa.

I came to my senses, rushed over to my pocketbook, pulled out two ones, quickly realized that I was in a different league now, and pulled out a five-dollar bill to add to them.

"Thank you." He bowed ever so slightly.

I opened the card hidden among the velvety petals. "For your diligence and trouble. Matt."

I sat down on the sofa, stared at the flowers, and pinched, yes, physically pinched, myself.

True, Hank Glass had had loads of money and we had stayed in tony hotels and lived well. But those days now seemed very long ago. In my determination to make it on my own after my divorce, I'd almost forgotten about my former life. And the long ordeal of Mother's illness had stripped away many of my physical and emotional comforts. Of late, I honestly had forgotten how luxurious life could be for the privileged few, even though I worked for the wealthy, went into their homes, and was invited to their dinner parties. I had many wealthy friends and beautiful antiques in my own home. But I couldn't spend freely. They could.

Are you trying to say what F. Scott Fitzgerald said best, Mother goaded me. *He said, "The rich are different from you and me." And you do remember Hemingway's rejoinder, don't you? "Yes, they have more money."*

Ignoring her, I read Matt's message on the card for a second time. Had Hank ever sent me flowers? Other than when the children had been born, not that I could remember—to say nothing of roses *and* orchids all in one bouquet.

I jumped up. The bathroom! The luxury hotels always had wonderful bathrooms. I wasn't disappointed. On the counter was an array of exquisite soaps, gels, and lotions. I glanced at my watch. I had a full twenty minutes before Matt called for me. How I longed to pause, have a glass of wine. Instead I splashed a little water on my face, slipped into the same black outfit I had worn just last week and fished my Mikimoto pearls out of the toe of my dress shoes, where I'd packed them for safe traveling.

Chapter 28

Dear Antiques Expert: What exactly is a "partners' bureau?"
I was reading an old book about English antiques and saw
this term describing something that just looked like a large
desk to me.

Your question requires a short lesson on the history of furniture. The chest of drawers was originally called a "bureau." As people began needing a place to conduct business, furniture makers designed a piece with drawers at the sides connected by a "writing board" top. This new form was also called a "bureau." (The term "desk" came along later.) The "partners' bureau" you saw is basically a "double desk." It has drawers at both the front and back and a top large enough for two businessmen (or partners) to sit across from one another and each have his own desktop space. Though these are handsome pieces, they do require a lot of room.

FIRST THING THURSDAY morning Matt and I met with Nigel Rhodes at Layton's to handle the legal work to get the Meissen pieces and tea urn released. Nigel was charming, as always, but he seemed a little rushed and bothered. With Matt along, I didn't mention Dana Henchloe.

Then Matt took me over to Babson and Michaels and I realized I'd been preparing for this my whole professional life. They knew insurance. I knew objects. The rest of the morning and early part of the afternoon I met with account executives. Thanks to what Matt had told me about his company, when I was asked questions about antiques or prices, either I had the answer or I could cite a good reference. Long ago, I had learned that *knowledge* is the tool of my trade. Mother had never tired of repeating the advice given by Samuel Johnson: *Knowledge is of two kinds. We know a subject ourselves, or we know where we can find information upon it.* I had taken those words to heart. They have held me in good stead.

Back in Matt's office, I took in the careful decor. Bookcases lined the wall opposite the floor-to-ceiling windows. The desk was a richly grained mahogany partners' desk, the sort that has become increasingly harder to find except in the highest high-end antiques shops. A blood red and black Bokara rug was laid on top of a nubby tweed wall-to-wall carpet. On the wall hung an impressive hand-colored eighteenth-century print of the ancient world, much more distinctive than those ubiquitous fox-hunting scenes in executives' offices. In the far corner of his office, a narrow console table held a cut crystal decanter, water pitcher, and four highball glasses perfectly arranged on a rectangular silver tray. Here the most sophisticated client would feel at home; take away the few neatly arranged files at one side of his desk and the room would have looked more like a gentleman's club's reading room than a workingman's workplace.

I pushed a mental snapshot of Peter's makeshift desk in the Salvation Army out of my mind and concentrated on the moment.

"How free are you to travel?" Matt asked me.

"Very."

"I can envision two ways we can use your services. Making appraisals for our wealthiest clients, just the way you do now for our Richmond office. But I think we can expand your territory, so to speak, *if* that's acceptable to you. Competent, truly expert appraisers can be difficult to find and we have many wealthy clients who choose to live in remote areas. You'd be surprised at the treasures that can be hidden away in some little town in the upcountry of South Carolina or out in some mountain lodge in Oregon." Matt corrected himself. "I take that back. You wouldn't be surprised, not considering your clientele.

"Babson and Michaels *and* our clients care much more about getting an accurate and proper appraisal made than saving money on transportation and expenses," he continued. "We even insure fine antiques in the outer reaches of Alaska. In fact, one of our most interesting clients has a museum-quality collection of antique furniture out there."

"Now that I *do* find hard to believe," I said.

"He has deep pockets and a deep, well . . . actually, come to think of it, he has more than a passion," Matt said, stretching his long legs out. "It's more like an obsession for eighteenth-century English furniture, primitive American paintings, and big-game hunting. The furniture and paintings I can understand." He rolled his eyes and laughed. "The big-game hunting? Go figure. Which, in a roundabout way, brings up the second way I see us working together."

I liked the sound of "us."

"Fire. Natural disasters. Those are our concerns for him. I'd hardly expect anyone to rob my friend up in Alaska," Matt said. "It would be too difficult to remove the items and then, how—and where—would you get rid of them? But we do have major thefts that occur in other places, unfortunately."

He smiled broadly and fixed his eyes on me the same way he had just last Friday. "We're not always so lucky to have a Sterling Glass as we did in this instance with the Hanesworths. I still can't get over the coincidence of your being in New York when I called you." Matt raised his eyebrows ever so slightly suggestively.

"Often we need an expert to represent our interest," he continued. "Our adjusters are bright and knowledgeable, but you can imagine that anyone who loves antiques—really loves them to the point of wanting to spend all day around them—isn't going to take a desk job for an insurance company. They get jobs in galleries or museums or, like you, become an appraiser."

"So you need . . . " I said, working hard to focus on the opportunity being placed before me.

"Someone who can give expert advice to the adjusters when they have questions. If we have one shortcoming, it's knowing the things themselves. We need someone who can actually be present as a Babson and Michaels representative to investigate, to talk to the owners, work with the police . . . do whatever is necessary on-site. Be a consulting appraiser-adjuster, I guess you'd call it. Interested?" He raised his eyebrows again.

"When do I start?"

AND SO I RETURNED to the InterContinental with a whole new career ahead, Matt on my mind, and Sol's problem eating away at my very soul.

On our way down to the street to hail a cab for me, I had told Matt that I had an older gentleman client in Brooklyn who genuinely needed my help, which was why I wanted to stay one more day in Manhattan. But I didn't go into specifics, other than to jokingly assure him that Babson and Michaels was not involved. When I told him that I would pay for my extra night's lodging, once again he dismissed the idea as absurd. "Who knows," he had said, "we may need to chat sometime tomorrow before you leave. Say I call you midmorning. Surely you won't be flying out until later tomorrow. And thank you again for a lovely evening last night."

I called Sol while quickly changing out of my fine clothes into a much warmer, more casual outfit. We agreed to meet at Joey's store. No sooner had I replaced the receiver than I was tempted to call Peter to tell him I was on my way out to Brooklyn. But why worry him? I would talk to him later tonight. Right now I felt a greater urgency to get out to Brooklyn.

I slipped a pair of cotton socks on over my tights, then put on the very sensible rubber-soled flats I'd been sure to remember to pack. I distinctly remembered how cold the dark streets and Sol's building had been on my earlier visits there. Just thinking about it made me chilly.

My real coldness was coming from my nerves. Who knew what lay ahead? Not I.

Chapter 29

Dear Antiques Expert: In an antiques shop a couple was talking about a coffee table that I thought was pretty nice. The legs were thick and turned in a series of ball-like circles and the top was inlaid. But the people were discussing how the legs and tops were different styles and then they said that coffee tables aren't that old, anyway. What were they talking about?

Serious antiquers know their periods and what distinguishes each style. For example, during the Jacobean period, 1558–1702, furniture was heavy and chunky, like that table's legs. During the Sheraton period, 1785–1815, furniture was delicate and often inlaid, like the table's top. They also know when furniture forms came into existence. For example, sideboards didn't exist during the Queen Anne period, and there is no such thing as an 18th-century coffee table—coffee tables are a 20th-century innovation. (The moral: a little study can keep you from buying a fake or reproduction or just a mislabeled piece.) The coffee table you saw probably dated from the 1920s or 1930s.

DUSK WAS SETTLING in by the time I got to Joey's. As I had done the whole ride out to Brooklyn, I was seriously questioning why on earth I was here.

You should have listened to Peter and let Sol and Joey figure out what to do, a tiny voice inside my head told me. Before me flashed my home and the things I loved back in Leemont. I had told my children only that I was going back to New York on business. Cool, they'd said. I translated that to mean, Aren't you lucky?

In my heart, I couldn't find any reason to bother them with the particulars. In my mind, though, I must have been worried about what might happen. Before I'd left Leemont I had even asked Ed Pavich about getting some sort of police protection for the showdown at Joey's. I hadn't spelled out the exact situation, but I spoke of the case, well, should we say, hypothetically. "What if an old man was being stalked for his very valuable antiques and his life and fortune hung in the balance. Could the NYPD do anything about it?" I had asked.

In his gruff way Ed sounded sympathetic, especially when I said some sketchy things about there already having been one break-in. "Now the helpless old man is afraid the thieves will come back," I said. But Ed said what I'd expected him to say—that I couldn't expect much, if any, help from the NYPD.

"Murder. Drugs. Terrorism. That would get their attention. Antiques? Don't expect the NYPD to put any tax dollars to work over some old antiques. A new threat, you say? But if the man wasn't hurt before, and there weren't any witnesses . . . Don't get your hopes up," Ed had said. "Look at it this way, Sterling. You aren't Dorothy and New York sure as hell ain't Kansas."

I should have listened to him, but there was nothing I could do about it now. I had made my decision. Resolutely, I pushed the buzzer.

Joey opened the door. The place didn't look any better in twilight than it had in pitch darkness. Used household items of every description cluttered the floor. There was no attempt to arrange things in any order. But what order would there be? Bad on one side, worse on the other? A puke brown Naugahyde sofa, its stuffing beginning to ooze out around the seams, was next to a once nice, probably custom-made, but now scarred and marred solid cherry end table. Teetering on the table were three tall stacks of assorted ashtrays—plastic, glass, bone-china ones all jumbled together. Some were plain white, at least two were decorated with tiny pink flowers, and you couldn't miss a very large avocado green one. Precariously perched on the top of one of the stacks was a shiny metal ashtray with the famous Mack truck bulldog emblem, his front feet poised in midair.

Mixed in with the group was a wonderful early nineteenth-century Mason's ironstone saucer. Its colors and design—deep Chinese red leaves on a cobalt blue branch—immediately gave it away. I wondered if the handleless cup that went with it might be somewhere else in the store. Maybe over there on the badly beat-up bookcase used to hold pots, pans, dime-store vases, chipped dishes, and paperback novels. If only I had the time to sort through it all, and some way to get the good stuff back to Leemont. If only.

"They said they'd be here early," Joey mumbled.

"What'd you say?"

Considering how scared I was, if I could still be thinking about things, that was at least reassuring.

"The men. They said they'd be here early."

"Men." I swallowed hard. "What's early?" I asked.

"The burly, short one. He said he usually goes to the gym on Thursdays, but since I wouldn't be here on Friday, they'd come straight here."

Reality was setting in. Over the phone the situation had seemed scary but still enticing and exciting—sort of like one of those Grace Kelly romps with adventure. But as zero hour rapidly approached, the tingle was slipping away. Terror was taking its place. If the short one was burly, what was the big WASP like?

"Maybe they'll get off work early if it's so important to them," I said, looking out through the grime collected on the front window.

Joey glanced at his watch as he wiped the sweat from his face. Other than a light bruise, his lip was back to normal, thank goodness.

"Sol's here, isn't he?"

"Over there." Joey led me toward the very same La-Z-Boy where I'd first seen him.

Sol stood up and reached into the paper bag he was clutching, pulled out a wad of towels, and peeled them aside. He took out a small female figure and held it up. I took her from Sol and began giving Joey careful instructions—instructions I'd agonized over for hours now.

"When they come in, pretend that I'm here shopping and have just seen the figure. Say you had it out on your desk waiting for them, Joey, and that I happened to see it."

She was clad in theatrical garb, her arms spread wide in a ballerina's pose. Only when I looked closely did I see that instead of having finely chiseled cheekbones and a sophisticated look—the way the Deco dancers were modeled—this figure's face was round, her look sweet. Her long, wavy hair fell to her shoulders. Yet it all fit well together—at first glance. Perfect.

"Clever, Sol. Very clever," I said, acknowledging his subtle combination of the two styles.

He beamed. "I had lots of those Deco torsos around, probably more than I can use. The face, though . . . it's so Nouveau. Don't know how it got mixed in with the Deco parts. But it did." He took the figure back and turned her once more in his hands.

"So I said to myself, a spare part. I'll try it. It fit perfectly. Art Nouveau Deco! A new style." His smile broadened, then faded. "But I still don't understand why you wanted me to make a bad one," he said.

"Shhhh," Joey signaled us. He saw the men first.

The tin bell rigged over Joey's front door jingled. In the dim light, I made out two figures, one short and thick, the other one tall and thin.

"Buzz them in, Joey," Sol said.

The heavyset one led the way.

Joey moved nervously away from us, toward them. I took the figure from Sol and acted as if I were studying it closely.

I heard a gruff, male voice. "So, you got a figure." It came from the shorter guy.

"I did get one in, but that's all," Joey said.

"Good. Let's see it."

"It's over at my desk. There's a lady looking at it now. She came in just a few minutes ago. She saw it on my desk. I didn't show it to her. She just saw it. I'd put it there and she saw it."

"TMI," I muttered to myself, hoping my telepathetic message telling Joey to *shut up* would register. "Too much information, Joey."

"Get it from her," the man ordered.

Sol started to say something. I nudged him.

"She just started looking at it. Just before you came in," Joey said.

"Get it from her," the tall person said.

My hands began to tremble and I had to steady the figurine as I put her back down on the desk. Summoning up every ounce of courage, I signaled for Sol to move away with me, as if we were shopping together. In a remarkably calm voice, I said, "I'll think about it. Let's see what else we can find."

I tugged Sol over to the bookcase that I'd noticed earlier. Lots of things to rummage through there. With my back to the men, I could eavesdrop on their conversation.

"So? How much did you tell her?" The shorter man sounded serious.

I heard the scraping of the figure's metal base on Joey's desktop as one of them picked it up.

"Careful." This time it wasn't the cocky-sounding man speaking, and it wasn't Joey, but the tall one. "Give it to me."

The short guy answered his own question. "You're not raising the price on me," he commanded. "I paid $350 last time. That's it—$350. And the next one—"

"But there aren't any more," Joey pleaded. "The man I got this from said it was his last one."

"Probably selling them one at a time," the man huffed.

I shot a glance in their direction. The tall one was holding the figure. That was all I could tell about him. I had a better shot at the shorter, stocky man. Was this the same figure I'd seen lurking in the alleyway at night? Would I ever know? I focused my eyes and tried to memorize what I could see of his face from across the dim room. His eyes were close set beneath heavy eyebrows. But it was the width of his shoulders that frightened me most. He could crush Joey with a hug. He took a step toward Joey, leaning with his massive upper body into that area we call our personal space.

"Look, I've got nothing against you. Just tell me where you're getting them," he said.

"I don't know. He doesn't tell me."

"You're gonna tell me what I want to know."

The man's taller companion sidled up to him.

"Come closer. Come closer," I mumbled under my breath. All I could really make out about the thickset man's companion was his towering profile.

"Where does he live?" the tall one said.

Picking up on the cue, the burly guy leaned closer. "Now you tell me where to find him and nothing will happen to you. You won't get hurt."

I held my breath. What to do next? Phone. Phone. Get your phone, Sterling.

As I reached into my pocketbook, my elbow collided with the handle of a pan piled up on the shelf. It fell to the floor.

The two men swung around. Joey shook from head to toe. I looked up.

The tall one wasn't a man at all. It seemed to be Anna, or someone like Anna, who was towering over Joey in her straight black coat, fedora, and high-heeled black boots. So that was what Sol had meant by big, when he'd described the short guy's partner. Tall. I couldn't tell if Anna recognized me or not. Surely she wouldn't expect to see me there. Or for me to be in New York, for that matter. I had that going for me.

"Sorry," I said. "Nothing broke."

Joey laughed uneasily.

"She's not interested in it," the big-shouldered man said, nodding in my direction, dismissing me as if I were just another piece of furniture. When he reached for the figure I saw his eyes. They were steely and black, the color of a loaded pistol. With all the commotion, now was my chance. I jabbed at the keypad: 911.

"What do you think?" he asked Anna, turning his attention back to the figure and ignoring us.

"That's him. The old man. I've seen him coming in here." Anna was peering straight at Sol.

I could see her clearly now. There was no doubt it was Anna. Why hadn't I caught that at the beginning?

Because you're always too busy either talking or else thinking, Mother managed to slip in.

Anna's hair was pulled up under her mannish hat, as it had been at the mall. Only today she wore no earrings.

Sol drew back in alarm. The thickset man moved forward. He grabbed Sol by his overcoat lapel. "You."

He jerked Sol around like a pup on a leash, knocking over a nightstand as he did so. Sol was pinned back against the bookcase. My hand went to my throat.

In that brief moment I wasn't in Brooklyn. I was back at Jane Finn's house, as helpless then as Joey and Sol were now. Only I hadn't been in any danger back there, and I'd had Peter and Ed to come to my defense. This time I had no one to depend on except myself. There was only one thing to do: go for the woman. This time, Anna.

I stepped forward, holding up my phone as I did so.

"Excuse me. Don't I know you, Anna?"

Joey looked from me to Anna to the man clutching dear Sol by the coat like a lion gripping a lamb. When he turned my way again, Joey's eyes were glazed with terror.

I don't think Anna immediately recognized me, but I had clearly given her pause.

"Yes. Yes, of course I do. Anna," I said strongly and clearly, despite the pounding of my heart.

I drew the moment out, giving Anna a moment to respond and myself a moment to summon up more courage. Anna glanced at the man holding Sol. I couldn't read her reaction. But I saw Sol pressing his chest out in silent confrontation to his assailant. If he could be that defiant in the face of such danger, so could I.

"Layton's," I persisted. "You work for Richie Daniel. Don't you remember me?"

Anna gave me a blank look. For a moment I didn't know if she was going to say No, she'd never seen me before, or bolt for the door. Cavalierly, I clicked my phone shut and put it into my bag, which I placed on the table. I stepped forward.

"Sterling Glass. Richie's good friend from Virginia. I don't believe I've met your friend. Does he work at Layton's, too?"

A glint of recognition flickered in Anna's eyes but not on her brow.

I had everyone's rapt attention. I chattered on. "Isn't she charming?" I said, motioning toward the figurine. "It's so interesting the way these pieces were so popular years ago and then went out of style. Now here they are. Back again. All hot and just the thing everyone *has* to have, at least according to Richie." I put special emphasis on his name. "What goes around, comes around."

"Yeah. Well, I'm buying this one," the short man announced, backing away from Sol and toward me.

"Anna, you know what?" I said, ignoring him. "I don't know your last name. I just realized that."

"Zurner," she said, too startled to do otherwise.

"Well. There you are. Anna Zurner. Tell me, Joey, how much are you asking for the little girl?"

"Four hundred," he whispered.

"I think she's worth more than that, don't you, Anna? *You*'re an expert in the field. You see these figures all the time at Layton's. What do *you* think it would bring there?"

Anna raised her chin haughtily, making her taller yet.

"Ralph found the figure," she said. "I'm just along to advise him. There's no reason why he should have to pay full value," she cast her eyes around the shop, "*here*." Anna gave me the most confident smile I've ever seen. Ever.

I bristled. The paralyzing fear that had gripped me earlier had melted away.

"What about the figure you sold at the antiques mall? You overpaid for that one. You had to scramble to get *any* money for *it*. How much did you lose on that deal? If I were you, I'd look at this figure more carefully," I said, reaching over and swooping the figure up out of her hand. "Don't want to get stiffed twice."

She looked stunned.

Out of the corner of my eye, I glimpsed Anna's cohort.

"Oh, didn't you know about that, Ralph?" I gave the man a sympathetic, pitiful look. I looked back at Anna.

"So, you thought if you could get this one cheap, maybe you could make up the difference? Think again."

I was gaining confidence as I went along. "You'd pay $350? Sweetie, you'd be hard put to get $200 for this figure from anyone who knows his stuff."

I shook the figure up in the air for effect. "It's as fake as a Queen Anne sideboard. As wrong as a string-inlaid Jacobean coffee table."

I was on a roll. Funny, New York seemed to bring out the best in me.

Anna's companion seemed to have lost interest in Sol. "What do you mean?"

"Come on, Ralph," Anna said. "She doesn't know what she's talking about."

"Oh *yes* I do. And *Richie* is going to be extremely interested when I start talking to him."

Richie was no longer my prime suspect, but on the other hand, never would I have suspected Anna.

"What's this about selling something at the mall?" Ralph said, grabbing Anna's arm. "Who's this Richie?"

Anna yanked back. He held his grip.

"I don't know what she's talking about," Anna said, tossing her head in my direction, then jerking her arm free of his grasp.

"Oh yes you *do*," I said. "It was last Saturday. You thought Anna was just out to buy some goods," I said, looking at Ralph. "She was doing some dealings on the side. You sold a figure dressed in a fringed skirt and Spanish shawl to Maribelle Mason, didn't you?"

I watched her carefully for any hint of response. She remained stone-faced.

"Don't remember Maribelle's name? Oh? Just her money? Her ten hundred-dollar bills? Don't worry, she'll remember you."

"That's the piece you said would bring between five and ten thousand dollars," Ralph said. "You damn liar." He raised his fist. Anna shrank back. Her shoulders instinctively caved in to protect herself. She turned toward me. Her face, up until now gorgeous, melted down into old and tired. Her eyes met mine.

"You aren't going to tell Richie," she said pleadingly. "I'll lose my job. I can't do that. I can't."

I flinched. "Why not?"

Then I remembered. Her child. Of course.

For a half second my heart went out to her, as it had to Jane Finn. But I'd learned from Peter and Ed that to get at the truth you have to keep chipping away, the way you do when you find a gold vein in a mine and you're looking for a nugget.

"What choice do I have?" I said.

Ralph came straight toward me, grabbing for the figure still in my hand. But as he did so, his shoulder caught the corner of a hutch filled with glass and china. It tipped, and the deafening noise of glass shattering was all around me.

I jumped back. The wall behind me seemed to be quaking.

I turned and saw it wasn't a wall, but a glass-front china cabinet that could easily crush me. I thrust the figure toward Ralph as I tried to angle out of the way. He snatched it away and held it close.

"Wait a minute. How do you know it's worthless? How do I know *you're* not lying?" Ralph's thick shoulders pressed against me, pinning me against the glass of the china cabinet.

This was more than I had bargained for. Thinking I might faint, I squeezed my eyes closed so hard that I saw red.

Red. Red lipstick. Red glasses. Red fingernails.

In a blinding flash I saw Maribelle, not exactly Anna's favorite person of the hour, all spunky and confident. You've got to have the eye and the touch, and the years, lots and lots of years, Maribelle had said.

Eyes wide open, I glared at him. "Who are you going to trust? Some young, good-looking babe like Anna here? Or me? One with years, lots and lots of years."

God! How my words stung.

"Anna? Ha!" I laughed at the black hulk swaying in front of me. "She's just a secretary at Layton's—works upstairs, like being in the back room."

Once you've hung around the New York auction scene, you learn pretty fast that most of the girls the international auction houses hire for the front desk come from loaded families, the kind with paid-for yachts and two summer homes. My bet was Anna hadn't—not with a child and hanging around on a Saturday afternoon with a guy like Ralph. Probably she'd been born with the right kind of looks and just enough smarts to know that rich people have a thing for antiques, especially rich old men. She'd likely gone to night school and aced her computer classes and put that down on her application. That's what had kicked her upstairs working at a desk, instead of down on the first floor, where she might have had the chance to meet a rich man.

That was how Judy Taubman had met her husband, Albert—working at the front desk of Sotheby's. Albert Taubman ended up buying the place, lock, stock, and barrel. Of course, he later ended up in jail for a price-fixing scandal, but she was still filthy rich.

Without the chance to snag a rich man, Anna had tried the next best thing—to make money the old-fashioned way, by outsmarting the competition. Sure, it could be done, but you had to know what you were doing, especially in the wilds of the antiques world where fakes and frauds—the human kind and the inanimate kind—lurked around every corner. Anna didn't. Knowledge of fine things could be learned. Taste could be cultivated. But true connoisseurship came only through experience and Anna was a babe in the woods.

Joey heard the sirens first. He bolted from his spot. In the confusion that followed, Anna darted after him toward the door, knocking him to one side along the way. Ralph turned and leapt over Joey in pursuit of her, dropping the figure as he did so. Joey, undaunted, yelled to us over the wailing sirens. "Fire. They're heading down your way, Sol."

Still fearing for my safety, I stood watching everyone scrambling into the street. Seeing a clear path should the china cabinet topple, I darted forward.

Sol was already down the street.

"Wait!" I called.

In the distance an ominous fiery bright orange stripe spread across the horizon. Golden halos encircled the deserted factories dotting the landscape. In the blackness of the night, yellow fire trucks whizzed past us toward Sol's block.

Forgetting my fear of moments before, I ran back inside and grabbed up my pocketbook, reached for the figure, then thought better of it. I tore down the street after Sol.

"Careful. It's still slippery in spots. Sol. Wait."

I got to his side and hooked my arm into his. When I did, fear struck my heart. The figures. I stopped dead in my tracks.

"Oh, your figures! Your molds." My heart pounded. Dear God, please. Please, I prayed.

Sol looked at me, his eyes filled with confusion.

"My molds? I thought you said the molds weren't worth anything," he said.

"Yes. But they are—the figures, the molds."

A sad smile crossed his face. "I'm not worried about the molds or the figures." His voice remained remarkably calm. "They're safe. It's all the things that others had stored there in my building. In the boxes. I don't know what they are. Who knows what they could be? Other treasures? I just don't want *anyone* to lose their property."

"Safe? Your figures are *safe?*" I jumped in. "How? The building. *Your* molds, *your* figures are in the *basement.*" Surely he didn't understand.

Sol looked at me and said nothing. Just looked. Then he spoke.

"Ah, I knew you were honest. Now I know how kind you are. Thinking of me."

His mouth twisted into a sad smile. He clasped my hands tightly. "My dear, you never lived like my family did back in Europe. Rumors of war came and we ran. We were always hiding. Running. Trying to keep safe. Trying to protect what was ours. When Joey told me about the . . . people—we can't call them men anymore, can we?" He stopped and chuckled, then continued, his brow furrowed. "The way they wanted the figures, and then, when they asked where more were, well, well . . ."

In the distance, the metal fire escape at the side of the burning building came careening down with a dull thud. The fire that was so close to Sol's building reignited and flared heavenward. Light and shadow danced on the dark street.

Across my mind's eye I saw the bombing of London, the destruction of Dresden, the burning of Atlanta. As has happened to so much art in those blazing infernos, Sol's life's work, too, now lay in the path of destruction. Since time immemorial, lives and art have been interwoven. Since time immemorial, lives and art have perished together.

Together we stood there, Sol, myself, and my mother. Mother spoke.

We cannot know how much we learn
From those who never will return,
Until a flash of unforeseen
Remembrance falls on what has been.

Edwin Arlington Robinson, I thought.

Sol's weak wheezing broke my trance.

"Some fire," he said. Again he chuckled, quietly at first. Then he laughed. His aged face glowed, not so much from the light of the fire, as from delight. His eyes were brighter, more youthful, than I had ever seen them, even more so than when he had shown me his figures for the first time.

"It's a good thing we did it," he said gleefully, excitedly tugging on my hands. "Yes. A good thing we did it."

"Did what?"

"Joey and me, we stayed up all night. You see, my dear, I learned something from you. Remember your story about the Triangle Shirtwaist fire?"

I nodded.

"Well, after Joey got so scared, I remembered the story

about that terrible fire and how your great-grandfather had passed it down in your family. I don't even know his name," he said. A puzzled look momentarily crossed his face. "And he didn't know the people who died in that fire, but their story touched him. *His* story, now *your* story, touched *me*, my dear." He clasped my hands even tighter. "It made me think about my family and how they struggled so hard to save their work. And so many times, Sterling. So many times. Now that I am the sole steward of my family's works, it was up to me."

"You."

"Yes," he said, suddenly calm and quiet. "I call it divine intervention." He smiled. "I think you would call it the grace of God. A nonbeliever would call it happenstance. What does it matter? We did it, Sterling, you and I. And Joey. *We* saved them. You told me the story. I took it to heart. So—"

He paused. I expected him to begin one of his coughing fits. Instead, he became more spirited.

"So. I started packing up my little darlings. All the pieces and parts I had unpacked, I repacked. I very carefully wrapped the ones I already had put together."

When I opened my mouth to speak, Sol smiled at me.

"Do not worry. I kept them separate from the ones I carved. As we boxed them, we labeled them, Joey and I." His face was beaming with unabashed pride at his painstaking work. "Joey called a friend who has a truck and a dolly. We moved them all away, far away where they would be safe. Away from this dark place. To a better home. But more about that later. You were so smart. You called the police. Why didn't they come?"

I fished around in my pocketbook for my phone. I'd been so frantic I'd never even turned it on.

Chapter 30

Dear Antiques Expert: I've found a really nice Empire chest of drawers that's a great buy, but some of the veneer is missing on the drawer fronts. Would it be hard to get it repaired?

Though a piece with richly figured veneer can be beautiful, unfortunately over time veneer does tend to warp and pop off if the piece is exposed to extreme temperature changes or excessive moisture. When that happens it can be just about impossible to match the color and graining of the veneer—plus it can be very expensive. In the long run, you would be wiser to pay more for a piece in fine condition than to think you're getting a deal on a damaged one.

"PETER, YOU AREN'T going to believe what happened today. You'll be so proud of me. Really, really, really proud. But do me a favor, please. Call me back. I forgot to pack my cell phone plug and my battery's low. I think I'm low on minutes, too. Babson and Michaels is paying my hotel bill, but I can't ask them to pay for this call and I can't afford these outrageous hotel phone rates. I'll pay you back. Promise. I'm at 212 . . . ."

Waiting for his call, I looked at the rose and orchid arrangement that Matt had sent me and felt guilty as hell. If Peter was my Ashley Wilkes, who was Matt? My Rhett Butler? I took a minibottle of Crown Royal and the smoked almonds out of the minibar. My indulgence was probably as expensive as a meal at the bistro around the corner, but I wasn't hungry for food.

I hadn't left Brooklyn until everyone was sure that the fire had been contained. Vagrants sleeping in a nearby building had started it. Sol's building wasn't damaged after all, but I was still concerned about him. I felt better when Joey said he'd take the dear man home with him. Sol and I parted with the promise to stay in close touch.

Now that all of Sol's figures were packed away—again— there wasn't anything I could do. Next time I was in New York, though, I would find the time to take pictures of his inheritance. I was looking forward to helping him disperse his treasures in the best possible way. He promised to keep putting more of the figures together—the parts correctly matched, of course. I was willing to make a special trip back to New York, if that was what it took.

A more immediate problem, though, was what to say to Richie about Anna. Or whether I should even tell him. I remembered Anna's panicked look and her plea that I *not* tell Richie. A sadness washed over me. I thought about her little daughter. Of one thing I felt sure. Undoubtedly she was beautiful, like her mother. But what would she do with all those good looks, I wondered.

Anna aside, I had to tell Richie about Sol's creation, the one he'd signed S. S., which was in Richie's office. I just hoped it would be possible for Sol to get the money from the sale of the figure. *If* Layton's would even put it in an auction after Richie heard the whole story, that is. Surely they wouldn't. To the true connoisseur, Sol's masterpiece was nothing more than a fake.

And I had to face up to the fact that I had been too quick to judge Richie, too quick and too harsh. I no longer thought he had any involvement with Anna's scheme. Still though, Richie was out for himself.

I thought then, too, of Dwayne Sloggins and Jane Finn and life's twists and ironies. For years Sol had sat on a treasure trove of art and money and paid it no heed, while Dwayne Sloggins—and Ralph, for that matter—never thought twice about tearing people's lives apart to get what they wanted. Was there any real difference between Sloggins and Ralph, other than their modus operandi of thieving while preying on the weak and helpless—one through deceit, one with force?

Some things will never change, Sterling. Mother's voice came from somewhere in the recesses of my mind. *The poets have railed about mankind's unquenchable thirst for wealth since time immemorial. In legend, just as in life, only the most humble are unaffected by greed and power, like Tolkein's Hobbits. Unfortunately, in life that rare breed is dying out.* I braced myself for what she would say next. *It's a shame people don't read Samuel Johnson these days.*

> *For gold his sword the hireling ruffian draws,*
> *For gold the hireling judge distorts the laws;*
> *Wealth heaped on wealth, nor truth nor safety buys,*
> *The dangers gather as the treasures rise.*

"The dangers for those who prey *and* their victims," I added, my thoughts bolting from Sol and Ralph and Dwayne back to

Jane Finn and those innocent souls she had scammed. I couldn't help wondering if she hadn't known Dwayne Sloggins whether she would have stolen all those things. Though not on so grand a scale, probably so. After all, Jane Finn's motivation was just like Dwayne's—and Ralph's. Greed. Pure blatant greed.

Thank goodness Jane Finn hadn't killed Sarah Rose Wilkins, at least not intentionally. Then again, I'd read or heard somewhere that if an intruder scared a person to death in his own home, it was homicide. Whether or not Jane Finn would be prosecuted and found guilty or innocent only time would tell. But her lack of remorse was still gnawing at me. On the other hand, Anna's situation begged for more sympathy than Jane Finn's.

Though I felt plagued with what to do about Anna, that didn't keep me from curling up in the lap of luxury while telling Peter about my day.

Maybe it was the Crown Royal combined with the day's events and the late hour that put the idea in my head. But at a little before 1 A.M., I impulsively hung the breakfast order form on my door handle. I never did things like that.

ANOTHER PRETTY YOUNG boy brought breakfast in on a rolling table. I watched as he spread a cloth and painstakingly arranged the breakfast tray, complete with a white porcelain bud vase with two deep purple cymbidium orchid sprays, on the coffee table. Imagine, all that effort for a croissant, some butter and jam, a little juice, and a pot of hot tea with extra lemon.

By 9:10 A.M., I was on the street flagging down a cab to take me back to Layton's.

I JUMPED THROUGH the hoops with the now familiar big-earringed young thing at Layton's front desk and found my own way to Richie's office per his instructions. Much to my relief, Anna was not at her usual perch. I instantly found out why. She was inside Richie's office and she didn't look much better than she had the last time I'd seen her. Maybe even worse. It was probably the first time in several hours she wasn't crying.

"Sterling."

Richie's demeanor and tone were dead-on serious. He closed the door behind me so firmly I had the feeling he would have locked it if he could have.

Anna nodded my way. I searched her face for any kind of response. I found none.

Richie pulled up a chair for me beside Anna. For a half second, I hesitated.

Don't be stupid, I told myself. She can't eat me.

"I think Anna's told me pretty much everything, Sterling. She came in about thirty seconds after you called. Layton's has been suspicious of Dana Henchloe for some time. Nothing concrete—up until now, that is. Just little things. Goods coming in, then being pulled just before auction time. Commissions being cut with no explanation. One time there was a query about an important piece of French porcelain being auctioned off before it was even offered to us. The next week, Dana showed up with it. Just an accumulation of strange things. Things starting to point in his direction."

"I think I'm missing something," I stammered, looking from Richie to Anna. "*Dana?* What about last night?"

Anna responded with a weak smile and tear-rimmed eyes.

"Last night, well, there was all the commotion. Everybody ran out before I could explain."

"Especially you," I retorted. "You almost stepped on Joey." She ignored my comment.

"I was trying to get away from Ralph."

"Did you?"

"Doesn't matter." Anna cleared her throat. "Here's what it is. I owed Ralph money. A lot of money. When he found out I worked at Layton's he wanted to know all about it." She looked away. "He didn't know I was just a secretary. I told him how dealers buy stuff cheap and sell it here for a quick turn-over. He thought that was a good idea and he came up with a scheme where he'd buy something and I'd bring it in."

"Why didn't he do it?" I asked.

She frowned. "You saw him. How'd he be getting antiques and good stuff unless he stole it or something? That's what the people working here would think. Anyway, what he didn't know was that I was getting money for bringing the things to Layton's."

"But is that right?" I asked. "You work here."

"I told them I was just bringing the things in for an old woman, a friend of the family's. I said she used to be an antiques dealer and was helping this man dispose of the better pieces he'd inherited. I told them that since she didn't get into the city anymore I was bringing them for her, but she needed the finder's fee."

"So," I said, "two checks were cut. One to Ralph for the proceeds from the sale of the pieces after Layton's took their commission. And one for the finder's fee. Who was that made out to?"

"My mother." Anna paused. "Look, I had to do it. Ralph's from my neighborhood. I'd borrowed money from him. He said he'd forget some of what I owed him if I worked this deal with him. He said he knew Joey's shop and others like it where he could get things cheap. Sometimes when he'd find something but it cost too much, Ralph would send me in to make the deal."

"Like on Saturday when I saw you in New York."

Anna nodded.

"Just the usual picker deal," Richie spoke up, "but in this case the picker is a thug and suddenly Anna was bringing in too many expensive things for this so-called antiques dealer. It just didn't feel right."

"Did Ralph know enough about antiques to be able to know what to buy?" I asked.

"Most of the time. He's got street smarts. Ralph learned to recognize good things real fast. He got taken a couple of times, but he'd unload those goods on some dealer who didn't know what he was buying," Anna said. "Ralph would tell him it was an antique and sell it for more than he had paid for it." She shrugged.

I hated to admit it, but I knew she was right—on both counts. Most thieves *knew* what to steal, and many dealers *didn't* know their wares. Little matter. They just pass the goods on to somebody else as ignorant as they were.

"But how does Dana fit into all this?" I asked, still miffed.

"Francie Golden. You've met her, haven't you? She handles consignments," Richie said.

"No. I've always worked directly with the department heads," I said.

"'Course. Well, Francie's the one who called Anna's excessive activity to my attention. We decided that since Anna worked for me, I needed to look into what was going on." Richie paused. "You know how coincidences are. Henchloe came up when Francie and I were talking. He got wind of the situation and got to Anna before I did. I was in the middle of cataloging a big sale and Anna wasn't going anywhere. I had put it on the back burner."

Richie rolled his eyes first in Anna's direction, then heavenward. "You can figure out the rest. When Dana confronted her, she confessed to the scheme. That's when he saw a way to do a little double-dipping himself. In exchange for not reporting her, he started slipping Anna's, or Ralph's rather, things in under his name."

"So that meant Dana got the finder's fee instead of your mother," I said. "That cut you out."

"What else was I going to do?" Anna sounded pathetic. Then dropping her eyes she said, "He paid me something so I wouldn't get behind with what I owed Ralph. We had a . . ." She shuddered. "An arrangement."

"Well," Richie broke in, obviously anxious to save Anna any additional embarrassment. "Now that we know Henchloe's role in all this, you can be sure he's out on his ear."

So. Little Richie Daniel still had a spark of humanity in him, I mused. A glimmer of compassion. I found that comforting. Almost sweet. But not sweet enough to wash away my memory that he had been willing to do some private dealings himself.

"Anna, that Art Deco figure you sold to Maribelle. You told her that Layton's was going to sell it, but then—"

Richie broke in again.

"My fault, Sterling." He laughed apologetically. "My fault. I had another figure too similar to that one already cataloged for the sale. Can't flood the market. Of course at that point I didn't know the new figure being offered for auction was one of Anna's." He gave Anna a contrite, regretful look. "The consignment sheet had Dana's name all over it. He took it back."

"And Dana gave it back to you. That left you holding the bag," I said to Anna.

I walked over and picked up the figure from the bookcase.

"What about this one? Where did it come from?"

"From some woman's estate. There weren't many good things, even though her family had once been well educated and wealthy back in the old country. Her daughter brought it in. The parents died only two or three weeks apart, over in Brooklyn. They were no longer wealthy people. Came here as immigrants from . . . Why can't I remember? You asked me the other day. It was either South America or Europe. I meant to look it up after you asked me before. It'll go into some sale. If not here, maybe one in Paris."

I ran my fingers over Sol's mark, S. S. Surely this was one of the figures Sol had carved and given to one of his old neighborhood friends. After all the love and care that had gone into making it, now here it was, just drifting from place to place, waiting for a new home.

I glanced over at Anna. She was sitting slumped down in the chair, her usually placid face fearful and pale. Richie didn't look much better himself. Now was not the time to spring the fact on him that the figure's ivory parts were newly carved.

I chewed on my bottom lip until I could reach deep enough

down into my gut to find the courage. "I think there's more to this story than you know," I said to Richie.

Anna's teary eyes darted up to greet mine.

"Not your story, Anna." I smiled at her, longing to tell her that she'd suffered enough for one day. "Dana Henchloe's story. Richie, you know that silver tea urn I brought up here to Nigel? Well, seems there's a Southern ring funneling things up to Layton's. Some of the items Dana's been sending to Nigel are from the leader, a Dwayne Sloggins. They both happened to be at an appraisal day in Montgomery . . ."

AFTER WE MET with the legal department, Nigel, Richie, and I pored over consignment papers relating to items Dana Henchloe had brought in to Layton's. Several of those pieces were not uncoincidentally ones listed as missing on the Hanesworths' appraisal. Henchloe, that pompous ass, was guilty as hell.

Most damning of all was the letter Layton's had received from Dana, just a day or so ago: it said he'd be sending up a fine Meissen tureen and Tiffany sterling vase, along with some other items that Jane Finn had been packing up when Ed, Peter, and I arrived on her doorstep.

When Ed Pavich tied Dana Henchloe in with Dwayne Sloggins, Dana's problems would be more far-reaching than some insider deals at Layton's. I wouldn't be surprised if once Ed started digging he found Henchloe had plenty of other schemes in the works. By the time it was all over with, I'd wager that Dana Henchloe would have some mighty steep lawyer bills mounting up. It couldn't happen to a more deserving guy.

BACK IN MY hotel room, I turned on the TV for no reason other than to remind myself that another world lay beyond the one of thieving and lying and blackmailing and double-crossing I had just left, a world centered around nothing but things. Right then I didn't care if I never saw another thing as long as I lived.

Yet how I was looking forward to getting home, home to the things that I loved, the things that held cherished memories of people, of places, of times of laughter and sadness.

What was that quote by Socrates that Mother was so fond of?

How many things I can do without, she answered.

How about making that, "How many *people* I can do without," I said aloud. For it wasn't the things, it was the people lusting after them. And too often people, like furniture, were little more than veneer—at least the ones I seemed to have been thrown in with lately.

Don't get me wrong. Veneered furniture had a long and noble heritage. When it was done properly, veneering was a real craft and made for a more impressive piece. Gorgeous veneer could turn a plain chair, chest, or table into an intricately inlaid, sophisticated object. But the flip side was that veneer was no more than a cover-up designed to conceal the inner structure, its real inner core. And chances were, over time, whether you were dealing with a person or a piece of furniture, that thin, outer layer would warp, crack, and fall away.

I pulled the hotel curtain back and stared down on Lexington Avenue at the cars and people rushing by on this gray, wintry day. Yes, I really had been in another world ever since yesterday. Well, actually, ever since I arrived on Wednesday. I didn't even know if the sun was shining or not. Not that it mattered now. Other than the dinner with Matt, what did I have to show for my trip to glamorous Manhattan? A case of frayed nerves and, thanks to no sleep, raccoon eyes.

Turning my back on the city, I made a firm resolution—never again to get involved in any sort of a mess like I'd lived through these past few days.

There was just enough time to make a pit stop and brush my teeth and still make the hotel's checkout time. I needed to leave early, anyway. Friday's 5 P.M. rush-hour traffic started at noon in the city. I stopped to double-check the closet to be sure that in my morning dash out the door, I hadn't overlooked anything. I'd lost a favorite scarf in a hotel a couple of years back when it slipped off the coat hanger onto the dark floor.

The phone rang.

"Sterling. You *are* there."

"Matt?"

I don't know who I thought would be calling me, except maybe the front desk. Or possibly Richie or Nigel.

"Yes, yes. For a minute I was afraid you might have had a change of plans and checked out. You're not going to believe this, but as luck would have it I already have a job for you. There's been a strange burglary in a house museum in Orange County that Babson and Michaels insures. Fingers are pointing at the curator, but she seems above reproach. Tell me, is there any chance that you might consider staying over tonight so we could discuss it at dinner? On our clock, of course. Overtime, if necessary. I know it's Friday and you surely have plans for the weekend in Virginia. I would say lunch, right now, but

I'm meeting with the attorney for one of our clients with multiple international properties and that's at twelve thirty. Who knows when that meeting will be over. Don't hesitate to say no, but . . . "

I looked out the window, then at my suitcase. Then I thought of Sol.

"I'll see what I can do," I said, settling back down on the hotel bed.

That's the thing about surprises, Sterling, Mother said. *They're so damn surprising.*

Acknowledgments

I THANK MY FORMER HUSBAND, Clauston Jenkins, for his great patience in listening to me drone on about the idea for this book twenty years ago. Jan Karon, thank you for encouraging me to stay the course. It was Claudio Pollio who suggested the title over dinner one night, and I freely borrowed my friend Sterling Boyd's name for Sterling Glass. (Though there the resemblance ends.) Thank you dear friends and fellow writers of Nectar. Without you, I'd probably be stuck somewhere in the middle of the story.

I received invaluable assistance and advice from Janella Smyth and Steve Minor; John Hays and Peggy Gilges at Christie's; Helene and Martin Schwalberg of the Meissen Shop, Palm Beach, Florida; Amanda Winstead at Neal Auction Company; Florent Heintz at Sotheby's; and Frederick Brandt at the Virginia Museum of Fine Arts. And I owe special thanks to Joslin Hultzapple, Charlotte Litzenberg, Cyndee Moore, Vickie Vaden, and Annique Dunning. I am privileged to be the beneficiary of three great publishing professionals' experience and wisdom: my tireless champ of an agent, Jeanne Fredericks, my incomparable and insightful editor, Kathy Pories, and that consummate bookseller, Nancy Olson.

I thank my fellow antiques lovers—amateurs, connoisseurs, and professionals—for sharing their stories with me over the years. We thrive on the thrill of the chase, the joy of the conquest, and the anguish of the loss in our ventures—those past, and the many yet to come.

My deepest love to my delightful husband, Bob Sexton, who sometimes doesn't know the cast of characters competing for his attention, but endures anyway, and to our family, Langdon and Amy, Joslin and Mike, Benjamin and Matthew, and Erika.